FINALLY FINDING HOME

Cindy M. Fay

ISBN 979-8-89043-919-2 (paperback)
ISBN 979-8-89043-920-8 (digital)

Christian Faith Publishing
832 Park Avenue
Meadville, PA 16335
www.christianfaithpublishing.com

Printed in the United States of America

"Good morning, Elizabeth. I trust you had a relaxing weekend?" Grace, the mid-forty-year-old receptionist, warmly greeted me from behind her desk. I pushed my sunglasses up into my hair while stepping inside the office of Hillside Academy, a kindergarten-through-eighth-grade Christian school, where I'd been working as a substitute teacher and classroom aide for the past seven months.

"As relaxing as possible with the twins, I suppose, but I can't complain. I'm alive and working, thank God! How was your weekend?" I answered, offering a warm and easy smile, as I placed my things in my locker in the front office of the school.

There was a refreshing feeling I've always found in Grace's motherly attributes that had me clinging to her since the first day we met. The heartfelt tenderness she offered me from the get-go brought forth feelings that I had found a long-lost family member or, at the very least, someone to depend on if I ever found myself in need. More than mere colleagues, whenever I was called in to work at my second job, Grace often watched my children. Even though there was a twenty-year age difference between us, we bonded instantly over our similar hardships and easily became friends.

Since moving from my hometown in Texas eight months earlier, Grace was the only friend I had made while living in North Carolina. After choosing to relocate my family, I kept my circle very tight (by choice), hoping to protect myself from the pain of rejection and loss that could come along if I let too many people in.

* * * * *

Originally discovering the small town of Spring View, when the father of my children and I were searching for places to raise our family, North Carolina was appealing to both of us since it wasn't too far off from the Southern Christian lifestyle we both grew up with and knew we wanted for our children, yet it was far enough away from our hometown that we looked forward to the opportunity of being able to get a fresh start together as a family. Being from a section of Texas that was pretty much hot, dry, and flat, we also looked forward to living in a place where there'd be breathtaking views and four distinctive seasons.

With my two children in tow, I made the decision to move three years after our original Internet search led us to find the town of Spring View. I willingly accepted a job offer that became available as a substitute teacher, knowing it was the perfect way to get my foot in the door, so to speak, and took comfort in the possibilities that could be offered by putting some distance between my hometown in Keybridge, Texas, where my parents (mostly my father) called all the shots, and myself would have to offer.

The people in Keybridge were, for the most part, good-hearted people, offering southern hospitality each chance they got. I used to joke around, saying, "They could be telling you that you just lost your job, had a terminal illness, and your house just burned to the ground, yet you'd somehow be standing there, still smiling." It was as if they took killing others with kindness to a whole new level. Unless, of course, you found yourself the center of the town's major gossip, and on the receiving end of that said "kindness," you hardly had the inkling to realize that it was all merely a facade. Truth be told, after all, kindness was for strangers, and let's not forget every church member that attended my family church. However, it surely hadn't been intended for me, the preacher's daughter, who made a mistake that I'd be paying for, for the rest of my life.

I may have stuck it out in my hometown had the gossip and judgmental jabs remained focused on me alone and hadn't trickled down to my innocent children. Over the years, I learned to ignore most of the town talk by praying for God to toughen my skin. In time, I found the harshness and judgmental comments didn't seem to cut as deep. When they did, I learned how to grin and bear it. Things altogether changed when my three-year-old son and daughter came home from church repeating some of the cruel things the older children had said about their father and me. At that moment, I knew it was time for us to go.

Not a day went by that they did not remind me I had become the poster child of what not to do. The narrow-minded townspeople would mumble warnings to their young daughters of how I was a single mother because "God doesn't take kind to those who engage in premarital sex," or I'd hear their judgmental opinions of how my "fatherless children needed extra prayer because of their momma's poor choices." Hearing regularly how much of a disappointment I was, not only to God but also to all the self-righteous people in my daddy's small church, helped make the decision to up and leave a little easier. Packing up the few material things we had, we got out of there before my children had to suffer the same fate I had the past three years and, truthfully, my entire life.

I wasn't always the trashy heathen the townsfolk painted me out to be. I grew up in a God-fearing home, with four generations of preachers—all men of course, because deep in the backward town I came from, a woman preacher was just blasphemous. Women were meant to get married, play piano, have children, and God willing, sing in the choir, or teach Sunday school if God hadn't blessed her with the gift of song. Until I came along, only males were born in the Strutton family (as far back as they had a record of, anyway), so no one really knew what life would be like if ever there was a girl.

Lo and behold, along I came. Not only did my gender cause a disappointment that my daddy struggled my whole life to hide, but having his unexpected daughter end up pregnant before getting married, well, that was the proverbial straw that broke my father's back. Sure, he had forgiven me publicly, but when the eyes of his parishioners weren't upon us, he treated me as if I were nothing more than a burden; and my children never found their way into what should have been a welcoming grandparent's heart. Instead, he burdened them with the weight of a sin that wasn't theirs to bear.

From very early on, I knew whom it was I was going to spend the rest of my life with; I actually knew Christopher my entire life. We lived next door to one another and grew up in the same church. Both sets of parents got along well with one another, and because the two of us were so close while growing up, Christopher and I spent nearly equal amounts of time between our two homes. But I remember clearly the day of my twelfth birthday, when I decided that that boy, the incredibly cute and loving boy who lived next door, was the one I wanted to spend the rest of my life with. Christopher, wanting to do something special for me, cut my favorite flowers from his momma's garden, knowing full well how angry she was going to be when she woke up the next morning to find her garden robbed of all its perfectly bloomed sunflowers.

Christopher was a year older than me and, as far as I could remember, wasn't all too secretive about his feelings. When we were younger, the two of us would play together, never really giving much thought to our gender differences. As we grew into the awkward stage of life where girls and boys become temporarily "yucky" to the opposite sex, we each respectively played our parts. I meant it a bit more than Christopher, though, thinking boys indeed truly had cooties. But Christopher would only give me a little grief now and then. Even though sometimes he would half-heartedly tease me, he never stopped looking out for me. He always said that he believed God created me just for him, and he loved everything about me, and he never took me for granted. Once the cootie phase fizzled out on my part, Christopher spread the sweetness on thick, making sure there was never a doubt in my mind that he adored me. We spent all of our time together, clicking in all ways, just as best friends should. As we grew older, we fell completely in love with one another, both of us realizing that our love was a beautiful gift from heaven. Together, we thanked God each day for gifting us with something so incredibly wonderful, knowing in our heart of hearts we had been blessed to have found true love at such a young age.

After I graduated high school, Christopher officially proposed, asking me to spend the rest of my life with him. We were young, of course, but there was no denying we would indeed be married one day, so he figured, why wait? The waiting part proved to be an issue between us anyway. We struggled with our sexual desires many times when we were alone, but thankfully, that wasn't all too often once we made it official that we were an actual couple. Nevertheless, our attraction and desire to be with one another proved almost too strong to deny, so together, we made the decision not to wait until I finished college before we would tie the knot. With the approval and blessing from both of our families, we agreed and set a date to be married two years after I graduated from high school. No one would have ever predicted that just a little over a year later, at nineteen, I'd be burying my fiancé and giving birth to twins three weeks after his death.

Right after our engagement, I followed Christopher from Texas to Florida for college, where he had already been attending school for a year. One issue we faced by choosing to go to a university so far away from home was sex. To the majority of students, physical intimacy was meaningless, and the idea of waiting for marriage was taboo to nearly all of them. With the ease at which sex was discussed and the frequency it was thrown around so disparagingly on campus, it wasn't long before we found ourselves dialing down the importance of what we were taught. No longer being near the people who helped hold us accountable to our promise to wait until we were married, our time alone quickly became all the time. More and more, we began making excuses to go further physically than we ever would have if we stayed closer to Keybridge under the careful watch of our loved ones. Nights together lasted longer, kisses began to linger, and before we knew it, we convinced ourselves we weren't doing anything wrong because we were, without a doubt, going to spend the rest of our lives together as a married couple.

After spending an entire day together, I fell asleep in Christopher's arms, both of us feeling as if life couldn't get any better. When we woke the next morning, lying face to face, our loving adoration, sexual attraction, and good morning kiss took us to a place of no return. It's true we were in love and precommitted to becoming one before God and before our family and friends, but we gave into our flesh before we had promised to. Fully, we offered ourselves to one another before actually making our marital vows. Neither of us felt any shame or guilt immediately about our decision, because we believed in our hearts that God knew and understood how we felt for one another, even without having an official wedding ceremony.

The pretend honeymoon period didn't last long, and the denial that we allowed ourselves to be blinded by began sinking in. We realized all we were doing was lying to ourselves. After being reprimanded by our family members, who were "let down" and "disappointed" by our choices, the two of us had a change of heart completely. Especially when they found out that I had become pregnant a full year before our previously set wedding date.

Being together and having one another to lean on made it easier for us to shake off the disapproval of our loved ones. Still sharing the same beliefs and desiring our original life plans we wanted before caving into the needs of our flesh, Chris and I rededicated our relationship to the Lord. Together, we asked for forgiveness and thanked God for the gift of life He had given us. We asked God each day to bless my pregnancy, wanting Him to keep my unborn children and me healthy throughout. Even though I was already pregnant with twins, we chose to abstain from intercourse once again until we were traditionally married. Clinging to one another, Christopher and I spent much of our time in prayer, believing we were forgiven yet still feeling the burden of contradiction caused by the snide, harsh comments that came from the ones we had hoped would love and support us regardless of our mistakes.

Both sets of our parents tried talking us into getting married before the children were born, but neither one of us could see any genuine point to it. Christopher often joked about our situation, saying it was as if our parents believed they figured out a way to fool God, if we'd only make our vows before giving birth. As if, somehow, the wedding itself would take away the sin altogether. What I couldn't understand was, all my life, they had taught me that Christ had already done that for me. The blood of Christ was what washed away my sins. And since no one knew my heart more than the One who created it and then sent His Son to die just to save it, why then was I being made to feel that His sacrifice wasn't enough for me and my sin?

Together, Christopher and I decided that once we were married, we'd move to a place where we could be a family and start over, to leave all the finger-pointing and whispers behind. Every week, we'd sit together searching the Internet for the place we'd one day call home. One night, our searching led to hope; that's when Christopher found the little town of Spring View in North Carolina.

Christopher's life on earth ended three weeks before I gave birth. His car was struck head-on by a drunk driver going the wrong way down a one-way road on his way home from work, killing him instantly.

There I was, just barely twenty years old, pregnant, in complete shock and denial. Not fully allowing my devastating loss to set in until my water broke at thirty-five weeks' gestation, I ended up giving birth completely alone in a hospital in the Florida Panhandle. After the horrific life-stealing accident, my family advised me to come home. Christopher's mother all but insisted on it after her son, the love of my life and the father of my children, had been laid to rest. Even though being a single mother to my twins was the hardest thing in the world for me at the time, I just couldn't bring myself to leave. I felt in my heart that if I just stayed where I was in Florida, where my life with Christopher still felt real, then somehow, he'd come back to me. My mother, Sara, and his mother, Julie, would call and check up on me, but most times, it was just too hard for me to talk to them. When I did, they'd unintentionally remind me I was desperately hanging onto a hope that wasn't real.

Despite making their debut in the world three weeks earlier than planned, my son and daughter were both healthy as could be. They needed only steroids and a nasal cannula to deliver oxygen to assist their slightly premature lungs.

I named my son after Christopher and gave my daughter his middle name, Riley, even though we had agreed on different names when Christopher was alive, deciding to use our agreed-upon names: Alexander and Alexis as middle names for my children instead.

I ended up going back to Texas shortly after the babies had been released from the hospital. I was able to transfer my credits to the community college in my hometown, where I finished the rest of my schooling partially online while taking a few classes at night to help balance out the demands of motherhood, along with my course load. Christopher's mother, one of the few people who didn't treat me like a social pariah, helped me with the twins whenever I needed her.

I was grateful for the help Christopher's family provided and knew that without it, I would've never been able to finish school and continue on to get my teaching degree. As grateful as I was, I still had a hard time living in my small-minded hometown, surrounded by all the people who caused me to miss Christopher even more; and without him there beside me, their whispers, at times, seemed deafening.

*****

"My weekend was busy, actually. We just got the final approval and the funds released so we can begin finishing up the childcare center at my church, the one that I was telling you about last weekend. Right now, it looks as if we're going to try a summer day-care program and see how that works. And who knows, maybe something full-time will come of it. It has the potential to be such a blessing for those who can't afford the dreadful expense of quality childcare, Lord permitting, of course," Grace answered with a smile, drawing from deep within her heart the passion she has for children.

Grace is an attractive woman who becomes drop-dead gorgeous whenever she speaks about things that matter to her. Her smile has the ability to brighten the darkest of days. Her love and compassion completely shines through every time she interacts with people.

"Oh, how lovely that would be. Between childcare and rent, it's a wonder the three of us can eat and still be clothed at times. This will be great for the people in need around here," I returned, hopeful the day care would help not only myself but others in finical need as well.

"I can hardly wait until fall when the twins can go to pre-K full-time. Thank God for the break this year by having them here for the part-time Head Start program. Every little bit helps. How far out will it be, you think?" I asked Grace while securing my things and checking the schedule for the day to see where I'd be needed.

"We plan to begin this summer. You should stop by and fill out an application so the twins get in. That way, you can catch an early break. I'm telling you, Elizabeth, they will love it! I know I've told you that before, and I'm not harping…I would just love to have you all with me at church. It's such a wonderful group of loving people. You'd all just fit right in."

Sighing quietly to myself, not wanting to reveal all of my angst at the thought of going back to church, I nodded at my friend, doing my best to force my mouth into a genuine smile. It wasn't as if I doubted

Grace's belief that her church would be a good fit for the three of us, and I certainly believed in God. However, I was leery, especially being an outsider, that the whispers would eventually start up again. I also didn't want to deal with any part of the heartache that came along with people's judgment when I had yet to fully heal from the pain that was caused by my old church. Saving money on childcare, however, was an entirely different story. Knowing that Grace's church planned on opening the center to all the townspeople, not just its members, I decided that if I had enough time on my lunch break, I would go and check it out.

The morning seemed to breeze right on by since I was assisting Mrs. Young with her first-grade class, helping the children at the sensory tables. One of my favorite things about the school I worked for is, being it's a private school, they aren't subjected to having to adhere to the Common Core teaching guidelines many public schools are forced to implement. The teachers, along with an elected group consisting of both staff and parents as well as the rest of the parents not on the council, have a say in the curriculum and can implement whichever teaching methods they agree are best for the students. One perk of being employed at Hillside Academy is that Chris and

Riley can attend the school's pre-K morning program free of charge, as long as they maintain good grades and aren't an issue with the disciplinary department. Thankfully, at three, so far neither of those requirements are an issue. Prayerfully in the future, my children won't become an issue either.

When lunchtime came around, I checked with Mrs. Young to make sure it would be okay for me to leave the campus for a while. I explained how I wanted to see about registering my children at Grace's church for their summer program. Abby (Mrs. Young) nodded her approval with a heartfelt smile, sharing that she, too, was sending her three-year-old daughter, Isabelle, there and then informed me exactly where to go and who to speak to when I arrived at the church.

"Don't worry if you run a little late. After lunch, I plan on showing a movie for quiet time. We'll be just fine," Abby assured with another nod. I returned the gesture with a smile before I stopped in the office to grab my things and head out the door.

The ride over was a breeze. I was familiar with the church's location, even though I rented a house on the other side of town. I drove past Faith Community Church on my way to pick up my kids from the aftercare center they were currently attending.

Faith Community Church itself was larger than my home church in Texas, but not so large that it caused it to lose its *homey* feel. They painted the outside a bright white, with large stained glassed windows. The landscape around the building and on the rest of the property was breathtaking. Wonderful touches and colors—pinks and lavender of spring from the flowers—accented the building's structure in all the right places. The steeple was massive and beautiful, especially when it was lit up at night; a true beacon, welcoming anyone out there who was lost or in need of a home.

I could easily appreciate the beauty of different churches and always assumed it was because I was the daughter of a preacher and grew up spending most of my time in a church. But after I parked my car in the lot at FCC and made my way up the church's walkway, something caused me to feel as if I was being pulled inside, more so than just the application for the summer childcare program.

*****

I hadn't gone in to an actual church building since I left Texas. I found a live online streaming link that served its purpose and enjoyed being fed a message from the comforts of my own home without all the distractions and messiness that belonging to a church could bring. In truth, I just wanted a break from people for a bit. My eight-month break hadn't fully weighed on my heart until I walked through the church's front door. As I stepped into the foyer, I instantly had a feeling I already belonged. Trying my best to shake off the immediate sense of ease and the desire I had to stay despite it feeling wonderful was a necessary defense mechanism I forced myself to implement in hopes of protecting myself from being hurt again. Continuing toward the sanctuary, I noticed a young woman inside the office off to the left of the foyer, sitting behind an L-shaped desk, busy on the phone. Not wanting to interrupt her, I walked further into the entryway and headed toward the stained glass doors to the right leading into the formal gathering place of worship. Both doors were propped open, allowing me to easily see into the large beautiful room. Red oak stained pews were arranged in three even-sized sections, forming two main aisles that funneled together toward the focal point in the back of the room, the actual *front* of the church. The rows of pews had burgundy-colored cushions that perfectly matched the highly trafficked areas of the floor that were carpeted. Hardwood aisles and the altar area were also stained, matching the wood of the actual pews themselves. They mounted a raised wooden cross on the back white wall, giving the impression it was floating in midair, or as if God Himself was holding it in place. It was lit from behind with a symbolic red light, reminding you of the blood of Christ.

With the room appearing to be empty, I stepped inside. Without any conscious thought, I found myself walking toward the front, where the preacher would stand as he led the congregation. Continuing forward, I stared at the cross, the backdrop that would dwarf any preacher in size while remaining the true focal point and meaning behind the building's existence. Before I realized it, I had slipped into the second pew on the left side of the church. My eyes were focused ahead on the beauty of the cross and the simplicity in which this particular church chose to represent its importance, and in that moment, I found myself giving thanks to God for His love. And as I sat there, I couldn't help but thank Him for sending me His Son, Jesus.

"Is there something I can help you with, miss?" A polite young woman's voice, with its heavy southern drawl and obvious uncertainty whether or not she interrupted a private moment of prayer, snapped my attention away from the cross.

"Yes, actually," I responded while getting back on my feet, trying to assure the young lady that everything was okay. "I was hoping to register my children for the summer program here. Grace Atkins, a coworker of mine, told me to come and fill out a registration form before all the slots were filled."

A beautiful smile lit up the young woman's face at the mention of Grace's name. "Oh, Grace. Don't you just love her? She's actually my aunt, so I am a bit biased, I suppose," she offered cheerfully as she turned and began walking slowly back toward the office, making sure I knew to follow.

"Let's head back to the office, and I'll get you an application. You can fill it out here if you'd like. How old are your children?" she asked, raising her brow, seeming to be genuinely interested in my answer.

"They'll be four in August." The two of us continued chatting while making our way back toward the office.

"Oh, how lovely! They're going to love it here! The volunteers are truly wonderful! Grace actually works with the infants, where she is affectionately known as 'the baby whisperer.' She has a gift for calming the crying ones, that's for sure," the young woman shared as she gathered the necessary paperwork before placing it in front of me to fill out. Offering me a pen, she nodded to the chairs placed at the front of her desk, letting me know I was welcome to have a seat as I filled out the imperative information.

"My name is Beth, by the way. I probably should have started there. My apologies…and you are?" she questioned, holding out her hand politely before taking her seat.

"Actually, my name is Elizabeth," I answered with a slight grin, noticing the placard on her desk and our shared name while returning the handshake. "But apart from my children's father, everyone actually calls *me* Elizabeth."

"Elizabeth it is then. So nice to meet you…I hope you'll come and check out more than just our childcare. It's not mandatory, of course, and if you have a home church, then my apologies…I don't want to step on anyone's toes, but we have so many groups and so much to offer here. I'm sure something will fit whatever it is you're looking for…if you are, in fact, looking at all," Beth rattled off so fast, almost as if all that she had spoken was in a single breath.

"I don't currently have a church, so maybe I *will* check out something. If not for any other reason, it'll be nice to know where I will be sending my children, right?" I countered, slightly caught up by the sheer enthusiasm that flowed effortlessly from Beth.

"Sure. Here's a flyer. Each of the different things we offer are listed—Bible studies, church service times, the number to the main office here, and also the email and direct numbers to each of the pastor's offices if you have any further questions." The phone on her desk began ringing once again. "You can also check out our website right here on the bottom." She pointed and excused herself before answering the phone.

Graciously, I took the flyer, placed it into my purse as I finished the application for my children. Once the forms were completed, I returned the pen back to its holder on the desk. I offered Beth a friendly smile and a quick wave as I mouthed a thank you for all of her help, then headed out to my car so I could get back to work.

Realizing I still had plenty of time and was hungry, I decided to open my windows and eat my lunch in the parking lot while enjoying the quiet, peaceful beauty of the property the church offered. Just before I took my last sip of water, I noticed a tall younger-looking man heading my way. For a split second, I thought about starting my car and heading off with a polite wave, but before I could fake not seeing him, the man was already within distance to notice, and I didn't want to appear rude.

"Hey there, I'm Luke. I noticed you've been sitting here for a little while and wanted to make sure you're okay. Can I help you with anything?" he asked while flashing a smile that had my heart beating nearly out of my chest from the unexpectedness of his sheer radiance.

"Oh, um…I'm sorry. I'm Elizabeth. I was just having lunch before having to get back to work. I stopped by to fill out an application for the summer program here, for my children," heart still pounding, I answered while meeting Luke's dark-blue eyes while working on the best I could muster up, around my out-of-control nerves, a genuine smile of my own.

"Well, hello, Elizabeth, welcome. I trust Beth was able to help you get the registration taken care of?" he replied while offering his outstretched hand.

Politely taking his hand to return the greeting, I let him know his assumption was correct and explained that I had to get back to work. I wasn't at all familiar with the feelings I was experiencing and wanted nothing more than to be on my way. Besides, I did actually have to get back to work.

"Absolutely," Luke said with understanding. "Please come again. I look forward to meeting your family." The smile that so easily appeared on his face did things inside of me I don't even know how to adequately describe.

Unsure of what more I could add and not trusting myself to speak, I offered a nod and another attempted smile before carefully driving off.

I felt something set ablaze inside as I approached Elizabeth's car. Her unrivaled natural beauty affected all of my senses. The way she smiled nervously up at me from her seated position, the hint I got of her faint perfume when she leaned out of her window, and the confident grip she had when shaking my hand appeared to be hiding something more timid within. As I made my way back to the church, I sensed a new pep in my step and decided to roll with it, hoping that somehow, I'd get a chance to see Elizabeth again and soon.

Funny how just before going to check on Elizabeth out in the parking lot, I just finished a conversation with my best friend about my decision to not pursue a relationship with anyone. I can, with

100 percent certainty, assure you that up until my eyes met Elizabeth's, I had never been so interested in wanting to get to know a female ever before in my life.

Taking the front steps of the church two at a time, I went inside and allowed a second for my eyes to adjust to the darker indoor lighting. Once my vision was clear, I rounded the corner into the main office, where my sister greeted me from behind her desk.

"You're in a good mood, Lucas. What's the deal?" Beth teased with an upturned brow, catching my lighthearted glide as I strolled into the room, whistling an unknown tune.

"It's beautiful outside," I answered nonchalantly before adding, "and it's also good to see so many inquiries about the summer program after only getting the final go-ahead Friday night."

"Guess Aunt Grace should be thanked for that. It was her persistence that got the approval from the board. And the eight families that have come so far all heard about it from her directly or from someone who knows her," Beth replied while entering what I assumed to be the information from Elizabeth's application into the church's computer.

"Yeah, accurate enough, but this is beyond just Aunt Grace, Beth. This is God's work for sure.

There's a need in our community, and thankfully we're able to help. I'm praying it will be easier to get everyone on board offering the full-year program once the board sees how much it's needed and how many people we can help," I said while fixing myself a cup of coffee before taking a seat in a chair in front of Beth's desk.

"Speaking of the program, you just missed Elizabeth. She has three-year-old twins—Chris, a boy, and Riley, a girl—who will be in Jamie's class this summer," Beth informed me as she finished typing in the last of Elizabeth's application. I couldn't help but notice my heart skip a beat at the mention of Elizabeth's name and was glad that her children were going to be placed in my youngest sister's class.

Jamie, as I just mentioned, is the youngest of us Walker children. I, at twenty-eight, am the oldest. Being single and deciding to dedicate myself to God, most women have found me to be a challenge. Especially when they learned that my choice to remain single was just that—a choice and not one that was required of me being one of the two lead pastors here at Faith Community Church.

Next is Brian, a twenty-six-year-old slightly smaller version of myself (I'm telling you, apart from the two inches I have on him, it's uncanny at times how much we look alike, and oftentimes, growing up, people would mistake us for twins), the music director at the church. My brother is married to Ashley, who also shares his passion for music, and the two have been married for a little over two years and are expecting their first child in a few weeks. Elizabeth (better known as Beth) is twenty-four and the pint-sized ultrafeminine yet fiercely competitive one of the bunch. Each of us towers over her five-foot-two-inch frame. No one's sure how it happened, but the joke is I stole two inches from her since I am the tallest. Anyway, Beth works as a full-time receptionist in the office and secretary for the pastors here at FCC, both Barry Wright and myself.

And last but not least is my baby sister, Jamie, the more average height at five feet, seven inches. Even though she's twenty-two and just got home from her honeymoon with her new husband, Mark, a few days earlier, she'll forever be known as the baby.

"I met her, actually. She was just finishing her lunch in the parking lot, and I think I may have scared her off." I half-heartedly chuckled before taking a long sip of my coffee.

"Let me guess, you high-beamed her with your killer smile, and she thought you were a serial killer?" Beth playfully teased, rolling her eyes, while we both made a snarky face at one another in typical sibling fashion. "She seemed really nice. I think she's the one from Texas Aunt Grace told me about the end of last summer. I didn't put two and two together when she was here, but when I noticed she didn't list any information about her children's father, and her previous residence is Texas, it clicked. I feel bad for not reaching out when Aunt Grace asked me to. Oh well, water under the bridge now, so to speak. I'm sure she is settled after being here for eight months, but I do hope she comes to one of the Bible studies or a service this Sunday. Are you preaching?" Beth pleaded with me, offering up a silent prayer to the ceiling it was true. It wasn't as if she didn't like Pastor Barry; she just felt as if I had more of a comforting presence when I preached, enabling me to better relate to people that were younger in age.

"Yes, actually I am, all but the traditional nine o'clock Sunday service, but hang on a minute…do you know how coldhearted that just came across?" Knowing that my sister oftentimes rambled on out loud while thinking things through when in the presence of people she felt comfortable with. I was trying to teach her to watch how she said things while she was at work in the hope of teaching her to show a little more consideration and professionalism.

"Tell me it wouldn't have been weird if I just called some girl I never met and said, 'Hey, let's be friends because Grace said so,' or do you mean about wanting you to preach? I love Pastor B, but I want her to hear you first…if she comes, that's all." Beth huffed, trying to offer a little remorse for blowing off Elizabeth completely when she first moved here and an honest peace offering in case Pastor Wright overheard her as well.

Sensing her sincerity, I took a small sip from my coffee mug and nodded. Wanting to assure her that I wasn't trying to be hard on her or pass any judgment, I offered, "I suppose it doesn't matter much now. You know it's never too late to offer friendship, though. Give her a call…invite her to tonight's group. Brian's leading, and Mom will be downstairs if she's in need of a sitter…" I suggested, hoping my sister would see my earlier intentions weren't meant to be harsh but merely teasing with a little side of brotherly advice.

While the two of us continued chatting, Beth decided to send an email to Elizabeth, inviting her to the young adult group scheduled for that night. Listening to my sister's fingers tap out their invitation, I swallowed the last of my coffee and got up to make another cup. Picking up the phone on her desk, Beth gave our Aunt Grace a call, hoping that she, too, would extend the invite to Elizabeth after work as well.

I headed into my office, turned on my computer, and placed my bag down on my desk before I went over and knocked on my colleague's closed door, wanting to touch base with him before starting my day. My office was located to the left of the common room that housed the reception desk. The room where Beth worked was lined with floor-to-ceiling bookshelves. It served as not only the main office but also a library of sorts, which housed any information a person may need. Barry's office was to the right of Beth's desk, and apart from our own personal touches and the different way we each chose to arrange our furniture, the rooms were identical.

Barry answered my knock, telling me to come in, and motioned for me to take a seat. We chatted about the day-to-day occurrences: phone calls, syncing schedules to fill in where we were each needed, and going over the prayer request. One of the deciding factors for me when making the decision to work at Faith Community Church was, like myself, Barry believed in the power of prayer. And we prayed together all the time. I took great comfort in knowing that neither of us only preach about the importance of prayer. We also practiced it every day, hoping to set an example for those around us. One thing I have learned is that when you're called to work for God, you've got to let Him lead in all things, or what you're doing won't matter. In order to fully allow Him to lead, you need to humble yourself before Him, and the best way to do that is to pray.

Jotting down some notes as Barry caught me up to speed with the things that transpired in my absence, I did my best to focus on the here and now. But my mind was scattered and kept replaying my all-too-short bump in with Elizabeth. Not being able to shake her from my thoughts, I decided to tell Barry about her, hoping that he could make some sort of sense of my distraction and sudden case of brain fog.

"Sounds to me like you owe it to yourself to see what's causing this spark of interest. She isn't married, so it's not like what you're feeling is immoral. Lucas, I've known you long enough to know that you don't just get caught up on a whim. I've never seen you get caught up in anyone, period! So pray about it, and see what and where it can go. Worst-case scenario, which isn't bad at all, is you make a new friend or maybe bring a new person into the church family. But until you find out and talk to her again, you'll never know. Now as for me and my humanity…I just have to say it's about time," he advised, letting out a boisterously deep belly laugh following his last admission.

Agreeing with the advice of my trusted colleague and friend, I went back to my office and began diving headfirst into my to-do list for the day, finding myself absently smiling each time I recalled the uneasy nervousness that was clear as day on Elizabeth's face. I knew full well that no matter what, I wanted to see her again.

Chapter 3

When the last bell rang, signaling the end of the school day, I let Grace know I had been able to stop by her church on my lunch break while collecting my things to leave for the day.

"I am so glad you could make it. My niece Beth called me earlier and wanted me to let you know she sent you an email inviting you to the young adults fellowship at the church tonight at six. My sister, also Beth's mother, Lynn, will be there in case you need a sitter. Of course, I can swing by your house and watch them there if you'd like so they can stick to their routine," Grace offered, as the two of us walked out of the building and headed toward our cars. Apart from the nudge to go to church, it wasn't too outlandish for her to offer her help since she often watched the children when I served at my second job at Benny's at night.

"Oh, Grace, that's so kind of you. I appreciate it. Beth was lovely, and I'd love to go, but mm. You know I have a bit of a chip on my shoulder still, and while I know it's not right to judge all churches…I'm finally starting to have a routine I'm comfortable with here, and I'm afraid if I go and it's not the place for me, things will become weird between us. You're the only real friend I have, and I don't want anything to come between us," I offered as a means of politely refusing her well-intended invitation.

"Don't be silly. Tonight's group is informal, more of a coffee hour where the twenty-something crowd goes to hang out and relax. One of my nephews, also one of Beth's brothers, Brian, is leading tonight's group. He's the music director at the church, and from what I hear, it's a great place to go and unwind. I promise if you don't want to go back, I will never bring it up again, and it will never come between us. You have my word," Grace countered, as she placed her hand over her heart to show her sincerity before opening the back door to her car and placing her things on the floor behind the driver's seat.

With a deep and long sigh, I breathed out, "Okay. I guess it won't kill me to give it a try...and I'm sure the kids won't mind getting out and switching things up a bit too. Thanks again, Grace. Have a great night!" I finally conceded with inward pleas that I wasn't making a mistake. After letting what I just agreed to sink in, I felt a mix of excitement and fear settle inside and couldn't wait for the distraction of motherhood to chase my uncertain feelings away.

Once home, after picking up Chris and Riley from aftercare, I started making dinner as usual. I then sat down at my laptop and began checking my email as I waited for the food to finish cooking. I opened the invite from Beth, just as Grace had told me earlier, and blew out another long breath, refusing to allow my nerves a chance to take over. Recalling how Beth and I seemed to be at ease with one another so effortlessly, I willed it to be enough to keep my nerves and fears at bay. And if I were to be honest with myself, I'd have to admit that I miss having friends my age. Life, since losing Christopher, had become lonely, in a sense. Once the twins were born, it was so simple to fall into a routine of having to care for them while financially supporting the three of us as well. Distracted enough by work and my parental duties, the loneliness I felt only crept in sporadically, and I thanked God that I barely had time to feel its pang.

Forcing more positive thoughts into my mind, I put on a smile as the kitchen timer alerted us that dinner was ready. I let my children know it was time for us to eat and began dishing out the food while they washed their hands. Once all our plates were filled, I placed the serving dishes, a basket of warm bread fresh from the oven, and a pitcher of water in the middle of the table.

"How was school today, you two?" I asked my children as they sat down at the table, waiting for me to fill their cups with some water.

"It was good, Momma," Riley answered before taking a sip from her cup, while Chris rolled his eyes and moaned, reaching for the warm buns.

In awe of how fast my children were growing, I loved how Riley looked so much like her father, with darker hair and eyes, whereas Chris resembled me, having lighter-brown hair and honey-speckled hazel-colored eyes.

"Hey, Crissy…you didn't thank God for that! And Ma-um, he's going to eat them all," Riley nagged while her brother sneered, quick to offer a retort of his own before grabbing his second bun from the basket.

"You don't know what I say to God, so na, na, and I'm hungry, so shush, and mind your own busy-ness, Ri'wey." It was hard for me to keep a straight face when my children tried using *grown-up* words but ended up mispronouncing them in the process.

"Hey, you two, please be kind to one another, and, Chris, I'm so glad you remembered to thank God, but if you don't mind, can we please thank Him together?" I gently scolded as the three of us joined hands, bowed our heads, and offered thanks for our food.

"We thank You, Lord, for milk and bread and other things so good. We thank You, Lord, for those who help to grow and cook our food. Amen."

The three of us took turns sharing the events from our day as we sat together, enjoying our meal. Both of my little ones agreed when I shared with them the plans I had for us to go to FCC after dinner and were genuinely looking forward to going. I think we were all open to the idea of switching things up a bit from our normal routine.

* * * * *

When we arrived at the church and stepped in the front door, a young man named Brian, who looked a lot like Luke from the parking lot earlier that day, greeted us. He led the three of us downstairs where I could sign the children in for childcare in what I assumed would be the location of the summer program. The large room was already set with plenty of toys and activities to entertain children of all ages. Brian introduced me to his mother, Lynn, who was going to be in charge of watching the children for the evening while the young adults met upstairs.

Riley and Chris, showing no signs of hesitation, happily split up and joined in with the other children who were already busy having a good time. Lynn got everything situated and explained to me how drop-off and pickup worked. Since we were now entered into the computer, she assured me that things would be smooth sailing from here on out. After everything was all squared away with the children, I followed my nose and the smell of coffee upstairs. After all, if you want to find a group of people, it was usually wise to find out where the coffee was, at least as far as church goes, anyway.

When I entered the main sanctuary, I saw a group of roughly thirty people, each close to my age. Initially, I was worried that it might be awkward being the new girl, but I did a quick scan of the room and found that many of the people were already smiling and introducing themselves. So the awkwardness never got the chance to set in. Brian waved, and Beth hurried beside me, thanking me for coming while offering a friendly hug. She made quick work of introducing me to a group of people who were already seated on couches and chairs facing what looked like a floor-level stage that held microphones and instruments.

The large room we were in was located in the back of the sanctuary, directly under the upstairs balcony behind the booth that controlled the sound for the services held in the larger chief gathering place. Two very large wooden doors separated the two rooms. Words such as *Hope* and *Faith*, along with encouraging Bible verses, were written on the whiteboards, while posters with more Scripture printed on scenic backgrounds were hung tastefully on the walls. The mismatched furniture pieces offered more of an inviting feeling than one might expect being in a church, allowing me to appreciate the overall feeling of belonging, which effectively set my mind at ease.

The group spent the first fifteen minutes chatting with one another; most of the conversation centered on me being the new girl. People were curious to find out where I was from, how long I'd been in Spring View, and how I liked it so far. A couple of the ladies were elated to find that I had children and offered to get together for playdates later on in the week. Although I secretly waited for signs of hushed judgment when I explained I wasn't married, it never came. In fact, everyone there seemed legitimately warmhearted and very accepting.

Things began to simmer down a little when Brian, who sat on the stool in front and center of the informal stage, picked up his Bible and placed it on the small wooden podium, set just a little to the right of his outstretched crossed legs. He began the group discussion by sharing the words found in Acts 10:39, which lately left me feeling as if they were a bit of a contradiction. If God truly accepted all who fear Him without any partiality, then why is it I felt so far away from Him lately? Why did it feel as if my works matter more than my belief and faith in Christ? Figures, out of all the scriptures in the Bible, tonight's group would lead with one that would have me looking like a nutjob if I shared how I was truly feeling. For tonight, I figured it'd be best to take on the role of observer, choosing not to share, at least this time around.

Apparently, my facial expressions told an entirely different story. While others shared their own sentiments and stories regarding God's mercy and unbiased love in their lives, Brian asked if I had anything I wanted to add. Politely refusing, I made a mental note to listen while withholding all judgment (especially from showing up on my face). After all, I didn't miss the irony of the whole situation. Judgment was what I feared most from people, effectively causing me to stay away from church for as long as I had. And now here I was, inwardly passing my judgment on the people I just met.

Once I forced my mind to focus on the stories being shared by the others, yanking myself out of my head and subjective thinking, I ended up having an overall positive experience with the group, learning the people were all refreshingly very pleasant. Once the discussion began to end, we closed in prayer, and two of the guys sitting at the higher bistro-like tables in the back of the room got up and joined Brian on the stage. The three men began to play some contemporary Christian music. The rest of the group refilled their cups and grabbed some snacks, while others shuffled around in their seats. Some chose to move closer, while others went further away so their quiet conversations wouldn't cause a distraction for the ones who wanted to share in the music. Ashley, the obviously pregnant wife of Brian, made it to the microphone beside her husband just in time to lead the group with a beautiful rendition of "I Will Follow" by Chris Tomlin.

After the praise and worship ended, I said my goodbyes and exchanged numbers with a couple of the girls I met that wanted to get together later on in the week for playdates. Beth and a couple of her friends thought it was time for me to get out and have fun, like a twenty-three-year-old should—without my kids for once.

The bellowing laughter coming from my children as they played with the others, while waiting for me to pick them up, warmed my heart, bringing forth a smile so big I ended up letting out a chuckle. I wasn't at all surprised when my little ones were disappointed it was time to go. And before we were even fully out of the room, the two were begging to come back so they could play with their new friends. Overall, the night was successful, prompting me to open my mind and heart to the possibility of going again and perhaps truly seeing all FCC had to offer Chris, Riley, and me.

* * * * *

The following day, I received a phone call from Beth inviting me to go dancing with a few of the girls she introduced me to at the meeting, while I was preparing dinner. Not taking no for an answer, Beth confessed that she already arranged for Grace to come over and watch Riley and Chris so the kids could go to bed on time. All I had to do was confirm, and we'd be good to go.

Because I became a mother at such an early age, I never really went out for a typical girls' night, and I was actually looking forward to it. Shortly after putting my children to bed, Grace arrived, giving me a nod of approval, agreeing with my choice of clothing, and sent me on my way, insisting I have a good time!

We arrived at the Stone Pony, where we found cowboy hats, boots, belt buckles, and tight blue jeans to be the standard choice of attire for nearly all the men and most of the ladies that were already inside. Luckily, being from Texas, I grew up living and breathing country, so I pretty much *fit in* without even having to try, as did the four other girls by my side.

Beth and April were the *cuties* of the bunch. Both had unbelievably gorgeous blonde hair. But April's eyes were a greenish hazel, whereas Beth's were a dark blue. The two were on the shorter side, five feet two inches at best, and both were rather thin yet still perfectly feminine. Being as tiny as they were, they easily maneuvered our group through the crowded room, securing us a table close to the dance floor. Deena, another girl I had met at the church the night before, was five feet and ten inches. Blessed with mile-long legs and curves that would inspire any artist to try to capture the essence of her beauty, she had an angelic face framed with wavy auburn hair that complemented her truly green-colored eyes and lightly freckled nose and cheeks.

Leighton, the only girl I hadn't met, was average height, around five feet and six inches like myself, and had light-brown hair with red undertones. Where my hair was long and thick, having lighter highlights strewn throughout, courtesies of the sun, Leighton's was poker straight and dyed a darker brown underneath. The style of her hair was cut into a blunt bob that landed just shy of her shoulders, showing off her long lean neck. The group of ladies I was with were each a sight to be admired on her own, but together, we seemed to have heads turning from all over the bar.

I was relieved when I wasn't the only one who refrained from ordering alcoholic beverages. It's not that I saw any harm in drinking when it was done in moderation—after all, Jesus Himself turned water into wine—but being raised by parents who believed that drinking was a sin, I really didn't drink all too often. And I never drank when I had to work the next day.

"So, Elizabeth, what's your type?" Leighton probed before taking a sip from her fruity beverage.

"Type of what?" I considered, unsure exactly what she meant.

"Guys…do you have a thing for blonds, or do you prefer dark and dangerous?" Leighton clarified.

Beth threw in, "Tall or short, athletic or nerdy?" Then all eyes were focused on me while they each sipped their drinks, waiting for me to answer.

"Actually, I don't really have a type. At least I don't think I do. I've only been with one guy, Chris and Riley's dad, and well, I knew him my whole life," I offered before pausing briefly to recall my late fiancé's appearance. "Christopher wasn't too tall, five feet ten inches, brown hair, light-brown eyes, athletic build. He was just an all-around good guy. I really didn't have much of a life without him. We were pretty much always together. Pretty lame, I know. When the kids were born, I really didn't have time to think about dating, so I guess I never really thought about it. Honestly." I listed off Chris's stats like he was some sort of athlete. Hoping I checked off all the boxes for the inquiring minds before me, I twisted my straw in my iced tea, stirring the ice in circles inside my glass.

"That's crazy. So sorry, honey... We'll work on fixing you up then," Deena offered.

"At least we can work on figuring out your type right here, right now. This place is packed tonight," April added as she scanned the crowed room, seemingly surprised by the large turnout for a Tuesday night. "And being married, I can look as long as it's for a friend, right?" She winked while nudging my shoulder playfully.

"I don't really have time for dating, but dancing...now that's an entirely different story. Let's say we hit the floor, ladies?" I suggested as I slid off my stool and glided onto the dance floor with my new group of friends, not wanting to deal with the thought of hunting for guys.

We ended up having a great time dancing together to three songs before the tempo changed, from the standard country line song into the slower pace of a two-step, offering the girls a chance to break for another drink. Before we made it back to the table, Beth and Leighton were both asked to dance by what looked to be brothers.

Most of the night, we spent talking, laughing, and getting to know one another, setting in motion feelings of belonging that had me truly grateful that I had accepted Beth's offer to go out with all of them.

* * * * *

The rest of my week seemed to whiz right on by, between the two separate playdates for the children after work and checking out all the different groups and services FCC offered on the website, where I realized that Beth hadn't been exaggerating at all. There *was* something for just about everyone.

With the way things seemed to be falling into place almost effortlessly, I found myself seriously contemplating the idea of attending a Sunday service and looked into a few of the other activities the church had to offer for my children. With that thought in mind, I decided to send an email requesting to meet with one of the pastors to see if he agreed, for the most part, with the same core religious beliefs that I held true in my heart. I don't consider myself to be completely set in my ways, and I know there is no such thing as the perfect church, but since I was going to be entrusting my children's religious teachings to the people at FCC, I wanted to make sure they weren't going to be teaching them things I completely disagreed with.

Grace agreed to come over to watch Riley and Chris after dinner Friday night so I could meet with Pastor Walker in hopes of discussing the church's teachings. Arriving twenty minutes before my scheduled time, I sat and listened to music in my car, while jotting down a short list of things I hoped to discuss so I wouldn't forget. Five minutes before my appointment, I turned off the engine of my Hyundai Sonata, gathered my things, and headed into the church where I bumped into Luke, the guy I met on Monday while on my lunch. Once again, I felt my nerves unsettle, shaking up my normally mild demeanor.

"Hello…Luke, right?" I uttered while offering my hand in greeting, hoping he didn't see through the facade of my mustered-up bravado. "Can you tell me where I can find Pastor Walker?"

With a strikingly brilliant smile, revealing the slightest hint of a blush, Luke shook my hand while informing, "That'd be me." Total disbelief must have appeared on my face, because he quickly began again.

"Were you hoping to speak with Pastor Wright? I got the email request you sent, and since I was already scheduled to be in the office this evening, I was the one who accepted. If you'd rather speak with him, I can arrange that for you," he said apologetically as he headed into the office before slightly turning toward me, waiting for me to follow. "Let's step over here, look at the schedule, and see what Barry has open," he continued, sliding in behind Beth's desk, moving the mouse with quick jerky movements to wake the computer.

Sensing a bit of awkwardness caused by my confusion, and not wanting to hurt his feelings, I did my best to assure him it was okay. "No, no, really, it's fine. You just caught me off guard. I had no clue you were a pastor…I wouldn't know Pastor Wright from Adam. Obviously, I don't know much," I pleaded, noticing that Luke really looked to be a bit shaken by my mistake.

Hoping to relay how terrible I felt, I insisted, "I'm really sorry. I just didn't think you were a pastor that's all. I didn't mean any disrespect. Forgive me."

Glancing up from the computer screen, I believe Luke was searching my eyes for sincerity, but during his evaluation, my breath caught in my throat once I looked fully into his face. He truly was gorgeous. And for the first time in forever, I felt like a giddy schoolgirl. I was a complete nervous wreck.

Catching a slight smirk on his face and appreciating his reclaimed assurance my explanation offered, Lucas continued, "Not necessary. I probably should have mentioned that on Monday when I introduced myself to you in the parking lot. If you're okay with me, then we can step into my office, right over there to the left."

There were wooden doors on each side of Beth's desk. The one on the left, just as Lucas had mentioned, was his, and the placard on the door clearly read Pastor Lucas Walker. The one on the right read Pastor Barry Wright. I have no clue how I missed that on Monday, but I figure it was because I didn't give it much thought. The question that was weighing on my mind then was why it even matters, and why in the world was I so nervous?

Taking a seat behind my desk, I motioned for Elizabeth to make herself comfortable in whichever chair she preferred. Choosing the love seat directly across from me, up against the back wall, she took a seat, crossed her legs at the ankles, and placed her purse on the cushion beside her. Politely, I offered her a drink to which she graciously declined. I pardoned myself while I made a cup of coffee in the Keurig beside me.

"So how can I help you? Are there any particular questions you have about Faith Community?" I began, noticing how tightly she clenched her fist by her side. I found myself wanting to set her at ease, help her loosen up so she wasn't so rigid.

I added creamer and a little sugar to my cup of coffee before turning my full attention to Elizabeth and was once again pleasantly reminded of just how beautiful she was. Taking a hesitant sip from my cup, not wanting to burn myself, I waited patiently for her to begin. Seeming as if she was forcing herself to make eye contact with me, she began in an almost childlike shaky voice.

"Well, I guess I am just looking to find out what it is you believe here, what you'll be teaching my children if they come to Sunday school, or join the kid's clubs you offer. I grew up in a church, come from a long line of preachers, and my previous church family is um, how should I put it? I guess rather set in their ways, so to speak, and I just want to know if this is the right fit for us," she began, giving off the impression that she clearly hoped that what she started with was enough to get the dialogue moving and the spotlight off of her for a bit. Wanting to offer her some sort of clarity while figuring out if this was indeed the right place for her and her little ones, I tried my best to show her a genuine smile before offering my response.

"Okay, fair enough. I hope I can help set your mind at ease. Here at FCC, we believe that all Scripture is God-breathed. We believe that Jesus is

God's one and only Son sent to be sacrificed for the sins of all mankind. We believe that Jesus actually died on the cross, was sent to hell, where He stayed for three days before rising from the dead, conquering all sin—past, present, and future—so that we may be given salvation and forgiveness for those very sins. We believe and teach that this forgiveness is for anyone who believes in his/her heart and professes with his/her mouth that Jesus is Lord. As for teaching in Sunday school, it's pretty much age appropriate. Lots of singing and the familiar Bible stories are shared, Noah, Jonah, Adam and Eve, and, of course, we teach the children about Jesus. As for the church itself and our mission, we hope to be the hands and feet of Christ, showing love in practical ways to our community and people in need."

Even though I have given that same speech more times than I can count, the passion and truth behind my proclamation of faith is something that I try my best not to regurgitate in hopes of gathering a new follower but by sharing something that actually matters to me. I believe what I preach, and sometimes I am guilty of getting caught up in those beliefs. So much so that I can come across as *over the top* to some people. Not wanting to further scare the clearly frightened Elizabeth, I tried my best to rein it in some when I answered her. Without being untrue to my heavenly Father and myself, I did my best to speak from my heart without going over the top. Using this approach, I learned that sometimes it gave the impression that my words are nothing more than a memorized passage all pastors learned before meeting with new people interested in their church. Unfortunately, my desire to offer comfort to Elizabeth without being overbearing unintentionally caused my response to do just that. With hopes of rectifying the situation, I deliberately willed myself to calm down.

Being able to sense the wheels of uncertainty cranking inside Elizabeth's mind, thanks to my generic answer, I took a deep breath in through my nose, trusting God to lead me through the rest of this meeting, and listened intently as she began to speak.

"I guess any gospel-preaching churchgoer would be content with that answer. Thank you for that," she snapped, causing me to become slightly off guard by the sudden edge the tone in her voice offered, putting forth a completely contradictory emotion than the words she had actually spoken. I understood why she might have felt that way, but I couldn't understand why I was having such a difficult time doing the thing I am usually very confident doing. I'm a preacher, and preaching and meeting with new people is what I do!

Not wanting to make the situation any worse, I cautiously decided to pull back and regroup. From here on, I was going to allow Elizabeth to set the mood and the pace she felt comfortable with.

"Why don't you tell me what it is *you* believe or what *you* are looking for in a home church, Elizabeth?" I questioned respectfully, leaning back in my chair and sipping my coffee before holding it in my lap with both of my hands. I willed my body to offer a feeling of calmness while I met her gaze, doing my best to assure her that no matter what she shared, I wasn't going to judge.

"I don't know. I haven't been to a church since I left my hometown. I watch sermons on the Internet, read my Bible, and do devotions with my kids. Let me ask this…Do you truly believe all sin is really forgiven?" Elizabeth asked, once again seeming as if she wasn't completely prepared for the focus to be back on her but rolling with it.

Not at all bothered by her obvious need for me to do most of the talking, and now having a little more insight as to what she was looking for, I wanted to make sure she knew what salvation means. I began again, this time aiming for a more gentle approach.

"If you confess your sin and believe in Christ, yes, absolutely." I stopped just long enough to finish the last of my coffee.

Just before I was ready to continue, Elizabeth released her lower lip from between her teeth and blurted out, "I do too. I just feel like I have this weight on me, though. All my life I was told that my sins were forgiven, and then I do something everyone can actually see, and it's like I'm no longer good enough to be forgiven."

As she finished her revealing confession, two things took place simultaneously that were at complete odds with themselves. First, I noticed what seemed like relief washing over her. It was apparent that for whatever reason, she had been holding this inside, and the magnitude of finally letting it go was unmistakable. The other thing was, that doubt seemed to take the place of the nanosecond of relief I had just witnessed, and she appeared to be second-guessing her unplanned outburst. Noticing a tear begin to fall from the corner of her right eye, I opened my desk drawer, pulled out a box of tissues, and handed them to her, wishing I could take away her obvious pain.

As I thought of words to help comfort her, she began again in a voice just above a whisper, "I guess

I'm afraid. I don't want to like it here. I don't want to feel as if I belong and then have the rug pulled out from under me again. I don't think I could handle that a second time. I've been living in this town for a little over eight months now, and I've been doing okay... Then I come here and realize I don't want to be alone anymore, especially since everyone's been so welcoming." She paused, shook her head, and slowly blew out a long steady breath before adding, "Okay...I think I got a little carried away. I didn't mean to throw all that at you at once. I'm sorry!" Pressing both of her hands into her eyes and bowing her head in her lap, I watched as she seemed to try her best to tread water of her own making. I knew just how much strength it took to be real with not only herself but to then share that truth with others, and I wanted to make sure she knew how grateful I was that she trusted me thus far.

"You don't need to apologize at all. I'm glad you opened up to me. I think that it's a good start in finally getting some of that steam out. If you don't mind me asking...what sin do you think you can't be forgiven of?" I pressed in hopes of preventing her from shutting down, wanting to put in place a means to which she could release the burden she's been needlessly carrying.

Elizabeth explained how she conceived Riley and Chris out of wedlock. She admitted to the guilt she was forced to carry by those who not only claimed to love her but who also claimed to love the Lord. A part of her had hoped that she was right in believing that she wasn't damned to hell for her mistakes. The relief I could see with my own eyes came over her as I explained salvation through Christ and what it meant to be washed by the blood of the Lamb—had me thanking God for the way He works and for allowing me to be a part of it.

Feeling honored that Elizabeth shared some of the heaviness she had carried around with me, in a silent prayer, I asked God to lead me through the rest of our conversation, ensuring that I wouldn't add to the already-harmful misguided teachings she had already been brought up believing.

"I think—and I may be out of line here—but… it seems as if you're carrying around a lot of anger. Are you angry, Elizabeth?" I challenged, knowing fully I was right but not wanting her to feel trapped or as if I was passing judgment on her.

"I don't think I ever really thought about it. I guess I am a little." She paused while tossing the idea around in her mind for a bit, more likely than not, trying to find if there was any truth in my assessment before clearly coming to the realization that she wasn't fully committed to delve any deeper into it yet, or maybe not ever.

Sensing she was erecting a wall around her and not wanting to scare her from opening up in the future, I smiled reassuringly before I continued.

"Well, it's okay if you are. You know…God already knows your heart. He also knows when we're mad, and He knows exactly why…and when you're ready, He'll be there waiting to heal you from whatever pent-up anger you have inside. You just have to give it to Him, and when you do…it'll be like nothing you've ever experienced before," I promised and knew that she, if nothing else, wanted to trust in the truth of my words.

* * * * *

As much as I would have enjoyed talking with her longer, I sensed that she was emotionally spent. Dealing with raw emotions really is rather draining, and a glance at the clock on the wall behind her showed that we had already passed our scheduled time by a full hour. Not wanting to push her out of the door, I made sure to go over some of the things we offered here that I thought might be of interest to her. Before I knew it, when I walked her out to her car, I got her to agree to come back and check out one of the sermons. We exchanged our final niceties, Elizabeth thanked me for my time, I thanked her for coming, and we bid one another farewell before she got in her car and drove off.

Looking up at the countless number of stars in the night sky, I prayed with all my heart that whatever Elizabeth was going through, she'd find her answers soon so she no longer had to be bogged down by the weight she carried. I didn't even care if it wasn't me that would be able to help her with her healing; I just wanted her to heal. Before I got in my truck, I sent Barry a text asking him to keep Elizabeth in his prayers, knowing I needed no other details and trusting that he would do as I asked without pressing the issue.

Chapter 5

I drove home in silence. Didn't even have it in me to bother myself with the distraction of turning on music. Thankful that as I pulled into my driveway, my meeting with Luke had run later than I had planned. Not completely in control of my feelings but knowing that I was nowhere near ready to have a heart to heart with Grace, relief washed over me when she chose to not hang around after I had gotten home.

Lost deep in thought, I found myself on autopilot, replaying over and over all the things Lucas and I talked about, as I washed up and changed into my pajamas before settling in for the night. After going over our conversation for the umpteenth time, I focused on everything that transpired during our meeting and found myself absently smiling as I recalled just how good-looking Luke was. My heart sped up, and I trembled a bit as I recalled my body's similar reaction each time I was around him. My pulse raced, and my cheeks flushed whenever he flashed me one of his dimpled grins. Anyone with working eyes could appreciate Lucas was an incredibly handsome man; but until tonight, I never paid any mind to men because for my entire life, I had Christopher. Thinking about it now left me feeling lost and so very alone. Rocking myself in my bed, I gripped my pillow tightly as tears poured from my eyes. In between my heart-wrenching cries, I begged God for His peace and pleaded with Him to take away my pain so I could just go on. Before I knew it, I had fallen asleep.

* * * * *

The next morning, I was startled awake by the sound of cabinets opening and closing in the kitchen. Springing to my feet, I went to see what was going on.

"Momma, go back to bed. Ri-wey and me are gonna make you breakfast, 'kay?" Chris ordered while he lovingly tried to shove me back toward my bedroom.

"Hmm, that sounds lovely, but what on earth are you going to make me when you can't use the stove yet?" I asked, worried that *three* was a bit too young to be fixing breakfast alone but not wanting to discourage their independence.

"Why don't I lie here on the couch. That way if you need help, I'm right here at your service," I suggested as I bent down and pulled my son into a big momma bear hug.

"I guess…but we don't need help. Don't peek okay, Momma?" my stubborn child demanded as he returned to the kitchen to help his sister.

After a few whispered words, papers crinkling, and the fridge door being slammed closed, Riley and Chris headed out to the living room with their hands full and presented me with a thoughtful selection of treats for breakfast. My momma heart melted, surveying the orange, Pop-Tarts, paper bowl filled with Cheerio's (no milk since they couldn't reach it yet, let alone pour it), along with an entire box of doughnuts and a juice box they had brought over to me. I thanked them both, wearing a proud mommy smile that I knew was brought forth from gratitude I felt from deep within.

"I don't think I can eat all of this yummy food by myself...would you two like to share with me?" I asked as my little ones nodded their approval of not only my willingness to share but in response to my gratitude and praise I had offered them. The three of us snuggled up together on the couch, enjoying our breakfast as we watched their favorite episode of *Veggie Tales.*

Chris was in the middle of a deep belly laugh when the phone rang, interrupting Larry the cucumber singing about *loving his lips*. I went into the kitchen, grabbed the phone from its base on the counter, moved further into the room so I wouldn't disturb the kids. Deena, one of my new friends, was calling to invite the kids and me to a family get-together at the church later on that evening. She further explained that every other Saturday, a bunch of the church members would get together for a potluck dinner. After dinner, the kids usually played on the playground and/or in the bounce house that a member who attended FCC owned and would allow the church to use whenever they planned a function where there would be children, when it was available. Wrapping up the night, they would usually sit by a fire roasting marshmallows, talking, and singing before everyone headed home. Thinking that it would be nice to get together with some people I already met, and wanting the kids to have fun, I accepted my friend's offer and thanked Deena for thinking of us before letting her know we'd see her later.

After *Veggie Tales* had come to an end and sitting still for too long had reached its limit, I took the kids to their room so we could get dressed before heading to the grocery store. We needed to pick up the ingredients for a pasta salad we'd be bringing to the family night later at the church.

Riley and Chris loved helping me in the kitchen, and since I knew they'd one day grow up and be *over it*, I tried to include them as often as I could, finding age-appropriate things for each of my children to do. This time, Riley helped wash the broccoli, cauliflower, and carrots, while Chris was in charge of adding the black olives to the already-cooked and cooled tricolor pasta in the bowl. When all the vegetables were drained and added to the cooling macaroni, Chris poured the Italian dressing over it. The two took turns stirring and mixing everything in the bowl. Once the dish was finished, I sealed the lid and placed the salad in the fridge to keep it cold until it was time to go.

A little after one, the kids, being tuckered out from all their hard work earlier, went to their room and fell asleep without a fight.

Taking full advantage of the break the nap offered me, I poured myself a cup of coffee while I checked my email. Giving a little thanks to God for the extra time the nap provided, I could actually take my time getting ready before we had to leave. Instead of having to choose between doing my hair or makeup as usual, I was able to do them both. Being as it was time to go, both Chris and Riley were relieved when they woke up, and their excitement helped bypass the crabbiness that sometimes came when they took a longer nap than usual.

* * * * *

After pulling my car into the back of the church parking lot, I was surprised by the amount of cars that were already there. I looked forward to the night ahead and the chance to spend more time with everyone we'd met so far. Each of the people I had already met helped make the three of us feel welcomed immediately, as if we all truly belonged.

Taking the salad from my car, I brought it over to the food table where I met with Deena and April, easily slipping right into their discussion on which is harder to potty train—boys or girls? The ladies worked together, getting all the side dishes set up and ready to be served, while a group of guys kept busy manning the grill. Once the first round of burgers and dogs were ready, the kids were gathered from the play area by whomever was free, and everyone helped one another get situated like one enormous family.

My attention was torn away from helping my son make up his plate, when I heard my daughter's cries coming from the play area. After quickly scanning the grounds and locating Riley on the playground mulch by the slide, I hurried over just in time to see Luke kneeling down, making sure that my crying little girl was okay. "Uh-oh, I think we need to clean that up and get a Band-Aid. What do you think?"

I heard Lucas ask as he picked up my teary-eyed daughter. The three of us headed inside the church while Lucas explained to me that Riley tripped and skinned her knee on the walkway near the playground. Once inside, Luke sat Riley on the counter next to the sink in the kitchen, turned the water on, and began to first rinse off Riley's hands. Once they were cleaned, he repositioned her so the water could reach her scraped knee.

"*Nooo*, it's gonna hurt!" she screamed and grabbed onto Luke's neck for dear life.

"I won't let it hurt you. Here, watch. You can do it yourself when you're ready." Reaching around her, Luke grabbed a paper towel, ran it under the cold water, and placed it in her tiny hand, saying, "Here, you do it. That way, if you think it's going to hurt—which it won't, because it can't hurt if you're in charge—you can stop, got it?" he asked in a matter-of-fact tone, and her little arms loosened their grip from his neck as she trustingly took the paper towel he offered.

"It tickles." She giggled, looking my way, adding, "It's really cold, Momma," before shivering from the chill of the cold water and bursting into laughter as if nothing had happened. Riley gave Luke a big hug around his neck after he put a pink-heart Band-Aid on her knee and set her back on the ground where, together, they walked outside hand in hand. Just before they got to the door, Luke turned his head and winked at me. He effectively melted my heart when he pleaded for Riley (his new friend) to slow down so they could wait for her momma to catch up.

"Momma, can you get me food while I sit with Pastor Wookas and Chris, pwease?" Riley asked, searching for her brother and tugging Luke's hand when she found Chris already sitting at a table.

"Sure thing," I answered, offering a sympathetic look toward Luke, hoping he knew he didn't have to sit with the kids if he didn't want to.

Being thankful for his help and knowing that he was now at the mercy of my little ones, I made up a plate with a little of everything to give to Luke, while I put Riley's favorites on another plate for her. I placed the plate of food for Luke in front of him when I got to the table and smiled at the man who now appeared to be both of my children's new *best friend.*

"I wasn't sure what you liked, so I got you a bit of everything. After all, you were coerced into sitting with my children! It's the least I can do."

Taking inventory of all the food, Lucas grinned. "I don't mind at all as long as you'll share with me. That's a lot of food. Thank you." Inwardly chuckling at the amount of food I piled on the plate, I nodded my agreement. Picking up a carrot stick, I popped it into my mouth. The two of us shared food with one another, while Chris, Riley, and a few of the other children at the table all excitedly shared stories with Pastor Luke.

The rest of the evening left me feeling impressed by the simple comfort Lucas exhibited while interacting with all the children, and on more than one occasion, I felt myself staring at him and smiling. There was something about him that drew me in, and each time I looked at him, I felt my heart skip a beat.

"He is great with little ones, isn't he?" April asked, grinning as she caught me once again staring at Pastor Lucas.

Nodding my head and blushing, I nonchalantly agreed before returning to clean up with the others. With expectations of distracting myself, I kept busy throwing away the garbage and wrapping up the leftovers from dinner.

"You know he's single, right?" Deena teased, bumping into my shoulder while she ogled her eyes in a knowing manner. "The ring he's wearing is a purity ring, not a wedding band," she informed me, as if she had read my private thoughts. So private that until she had pointed it out, I hadn't consciously realized I *had* been wondering about Lucas in the first place.

"Good to know, but I'm not really looking… who has time to date, anyway?" I quickly dismissed, hoping to end the awkward conversation that was now causing my stomach to flip-flop nervously.

"Ha...you've *been looking* all night, and who can blame you? Lucas is dreamy—I mean, not as much as my husband here, of course." April snickered before patting her husband's back when he lifted his brow at her outright confession of Luke.

Knowing I had been caught but convinced the teasing was all in good fun, I excused myself from my group of friends and went to collect my children before heading inside to the restroom for a potty break. Riley and Chris were both having so much fun they hurried as fast as they could, making sure they wouldn't miss too much. Once we were all finished in the bathroom, the two were off again ready to rejoin the other children outside.

The rest of family night was spent around the fire. All the families sat together, some on blankets, some on chairs they brought from home, each contently talking with one another while roasting marshmallows. After the side conversations came to a lull, Pastor Barry led the group on his guitar, and we sang a few well-known children's songs by the light of the fire and the moon. Chris and Riley both fell asleep on my legs, completely spent from their night of fun. Listening to the crickets chirping, the frogs croaking, and the fire crackling, while the people around me sang out praises to the Lord was magnificent. It was nice to just sit and be.

As the last song came to an end, forcing my mind to quickly snap back to the situation I was in—pinned under my sleeping children on the ground. Before I had time to figure out how I was going to get up, Lucas was there, picking up Chris and offering me his hand so I could stand up with Riley in my arms. Grateful for his help, I took his hand, and once I was up on my feet and steady with Riley, we each carried a sleeping child to my car. I quietly thanked Luke as he helped me put Chris into his car seat, while I secured Riley in hers.

"Looks like they had fun," he whispered before closing the car door and walking over to where I was standing. "I'm glad you came out tonight. It was really great seeing you again, Elizabeth," Luke said, looking deep into my eyes, causing my heart to once again pound erratically.

"It was fun. Thanks again for helping out earlier with Riley too," I returned unwillingly, revealing a hint of nervousness that seemed to seep into my voice whenever he looked at me. With an air of confidence and with utter smoothness, Lucas winked, and the smile he flashed directly at me wreaked havoc on my already-disquieted nerves.

"Oh, it was nothing. I'm glad I was there to help. Drive safe, alright? See you either tomorrow night or Sunday, since you said you'd at least give me one shot, right?" He comfortably teased as he opened my door, allowing me to get in. Keeping up with my end of the bargain, I agreed, feeling a smile grow wide across my face as I got into my car, and put on my seat belt. Simultaneously, we said goodbye as Lucas closed the door, and I headed on my way.

* * * * *

Taking turns, I carried each of my children into the house and placed them into their beds before taking off their shoes and tucking them under their covers. Realizing the time and feeling the exhaustion from the day's activities wash over me, I decided it was too late to worry about changing them into PJs. I whispered my *good nights* and *love yous* to Riley first, followed by Chris, before kissing them each on their forehead, switching on their night-light and pulling their door slightly closed, making sure not to latch it entirely. Once I was in the hallway outside their room, I heard Riley, half asleep and smitten with her new friend, beg, "Momma, can you ask Pastor

Wookas if he can watch us next time you have to work at night?"

"We'll see, baby girl...We'll see," I whispered, blowing her a kiss while willing my smile to encourage her to fall back asleep.

It appears each time that I spend time with Elizabeth, no matter how limited our interaction may be, I can't help but feel an almost magnetic-like pull toward her. Nothing significant has happened in the grand scheme of things. Nevertheless, I can't help myself from figuring out ways to spend time with her. Since I first laid eyes on her, it's almost as if I, all of a sudden, hit my puberty stage, and I'm seriously crushing on the new girl in school. She's like a song to the melody I have been singing in my head all my life, that up until we met, I wasn't even aware that the song had an official tune. I'm a pretty confident person. I am more than content with who I am and who it is God has called me to be, so this newness and the unfamiliar feelings I was experiencing were somewhat of a concern for me. Not anything that spells out trouble necessarily, just something that I'm actively bringing before God. Wanting to make sure whatever it is that I am feeling is indeed His will for me and not some misguided, unknown desire that, up until now, I never felt the eagerness of its message.

* * * * *

Growing up, I was obsessed with sports. When other boys my age started to balance their love of the game with the time they spent dating, I took advantage of their distractions and upped my game even more. I lived and breathed baseball. I wanted to play professional ball more than I wanted anything else. With all my hard work, dedication, and stubbornness, life was lining up all my little ducks nicely in a row. All signs were pointing to my dreams becoming a reality. My senior year of high school, I had offers from my top college picks for a full ride to play for their schools. I also had offers from professional teams interested in signing me on if I was willing to forgo college, making my dream a reality even sooner than I had hoped.

Shortly after learning of my options, I found out that life had other plans for me. Instead of playing ball, I was going to be fighting for just a chance to live the rest of my life. Baseball and my dreams of fame and glory finally took their proper place in my life. Baseball is something I still enjoy but with new meaning. I thank God each time I get the chance to play now for the simple fact that He has allowed me a chance to simply just go on. To live!

One of the side effects of beating the ever-living heck out of cancer—twice—is that I ended up becoming sterile by the treatments. Where I come from, right here in good ole western North Carolina, family means the world to everyone. Of course, not being able to have any children of my own didn't make me any less of a family man. It did, however, make taking a vow of celibacy an almost-too-simple decision. Of course, doing so wasn't something I took lightly, and I spent years praying on it and fasting over it before I took my stance and declared that it was what I desired and what God was asking of me at that time in my life.

I tried the dating thing twice. The first time, I was in college. I dated a girl from up north; she was a city girl through and through. Even though she didn't see kids in her future, I knew there was no way I'd be happy living a city life, and I knew even more she'd be miserable if she had to live in the South for longer than the time she took to get her degree. And who's to say she wouldn't have changed her mind about having children later on in life? Point is, we didn't last very long.

The second girl I was involved with was a local girl I grew up with in school. We had always been friendly with one another throughout the years, and when we both returned home for summer break from college after our first year, it seemed almost natural that we gave things a shot, seeing as we had a lot in common. She loved sports, as did I. After seeing each other for close to two years, serious talks about the future and where we were headed started to change things between us. She loved children and always dreamed of having a large family of her own one day, and because of the cards I had been dealt previously, before the two of us had gotten together, she tried her best to downplay her desire of becoming a mother, which wasn't fair to either of us. Not wanting to stifle her dreams and having enough respect and concern for her ultimate happiness, we ended things amicably and still remain friends to this day. She is happily married and the mother of three little ones, and still counting, Lord willing.

As I was saying, after giving it the good ole college try, I realized I was content with being alone. I've never been the guy who needed an accomplice or felt some sort of void because I lacked a female counter-part. I know who I am and what makes me happy, and I found that true happiness comes when I am serving God. I have lots of friends with whom I am very close to and consider my family. Being single has enabled me the opportunity to be available whenever a crisis arrives within our church, giving Barry the means to which he could balance his family life with his church family and the duties that go along with being a pastor. Singleness is definitely a gift. As long as deep within your heart, you are okay with being alone. Until I met Elizabeth, I thought nothing of it. In fact, oftentimes I offered genuine thanks to God for not having that distraction in my life. I'm not saying that being in a relationship is a negative thing per se, but I do know that putting God first in your life is hard enough without an actual living distraction needing and wanting your attention.

So now here I am. I just met Elizabeth, not much more than a half a second ago, yet I find myself not only thinking about her but trying to figure out ways to spend time with her, all while trying not to scare the living daylights out of her by coming on too strong. I'm trying to find a balance while trying not to overthink the shy nervousness she throws off whenever I'm around. I'd be more at ease (especially since I've never been that guy) if she was inherently shy around everyone else, but she's not. She appears to be at ease when she interacts with others. She has a sureness about her that catches one's eye at the way she just slips right in, as if she has always been there, while remaining the furthest from being arrogant as one could get. I can almost sense, in the slightest of ways, that she's trying to build up walls. But it seems to go completely against her innermost self that's longing to find her place in this world.

Shaking my head, I fondly recalled the shaky tone of her voice as we parted ways at the church. Closing my eyes, I smiled from ear to ear as I went before the throne of my heavenly Father, seeking counsel, not only for my sermon on Sunday but what His plans were for bringing Elizabeth and her children into not only my life but the lives of my church family as well.

* * * * *

When I woke Sunday morning, I took a little extra care when getting ready. Normally, I'd dress without giving much thought to what anyone in the pews would be thinking. Don't get me wrong, my momma raised a gentleman, and I'd never leave the house looking disheveled or anything, but I had hopes that Elizabeth would keep true to her promise to attend one of the services that weekend. With that in my mind, I even used a little hair gel and spritzed myself with a bit of my cologne, brushed my teeth, not once but twice, and threw some mints in my pocket, seeing as avoiding coffee wasn't going to happen, and coffee breath—not so hot, if you get my drift.

Chapter 7

My alarm on Sunday morning sounded, giving me more than enough time to shower and get dressed before having to wake the kids to get them ready for church. Chris and Riley, although still a little sleepy, were looking forward to seeing all their new friends and going to Sunday school. The three of us ate a small breakfast. Then we headed over to the church, just as I had promised Lucas during our meeting Friday night and again before leaving last night's family dinner. If I was being truthful with myself, I wasn't only looking forward to hearing the message Lucas would be sharing, completely drawn to the passion he had for Christ and his charismatic personality, but I also found myself wanting what he had and hoped that he could somehow show me the way. What I wasn't looking forward to was the way just looking at him caused my stomach to feel as if it dropped right out of my body, leaving me uncontrollably flustered.

*****

After signing my children in downstairs and making sure they went to the right class, I spotted an empty seat toward the back of the church and sat down. The worship music was a pleasant mix of traditional and modern songs, with Brian and Ashley as lead vocals. The rest of the band appeared to be the others from the Monday night group as well, with a few I hadn't seen before.

It didn't take me long at all to spot Lucas, who was seated off to the side in the front the church, singing along with the congregation. Assured that the surrounding people wouldn't notice, I allowed myself a chance to fully take him in while the music filled the church around me. He had longer purposely tousled waves of dark-blond hair and a faint shadow of a beard on his strikingly handsome face. His eyes—not that I could actually see from where I was sitting, but from what I remembered with no trouble at all—were a blue that certainly gave the skies and the ocean in the Caribbean a run for their money. He was tall—six feet four—with a large, muscular build, one you'd unquestionably find on a person that enjoyed working out and keeping active. His shoulders were broad, and his torso tapered down into a *V* at his waist. To finish him off, he had long strong legs. Again, not that I could see beneath his current black dress pants, but I have no problem at all recalling him perfectly in my mind, wearing shorts as he had the night before. As comfortable as he seemed in front of the church, he looked as if he could easily be on the cover of *GQ* magazine.

Thoroughly self-assured, Lucas made his way to the podium and addressed the congregation, completely in his element. My heart jumped into my throat when Luke's eyes found mine through the sea of people, and he smiled. Keeping my gaze for a moment before turning his attention to his Bible, Pastor Lucas asked us all to join him by turning to John 15 in our Bibles. My heart pounded, thankful when his mention of Scripture caused a natural break of our eye contact. Flipping my Bible open to the book of John helped snap me out of my inappropriate, unexpected assessment and admiration of Luke, shifting me into a more fitting mindset as I anxiously waited for what it was he was going to say.

"Today, I'd liked to share with you what it means to have a personal relationship with Christ."

As Lucas spoke, I couldn't help but feel as if it was my first time ever hearing about Jesus. The relationship he had with Christ was one that left me hanging on anticipating his every word, desperately wanting what he had with his Savior for myself. I grew up listening to and singing all the Sunday school songs, knew all the right words and each hymn. But it seemed that, up until now, I was just going through the motions. Since as long as I could remember, I have known about the Son of God, but I didn't know Jesus in the intimate way the man at the podium did; I was certain of that. Sure, I loved Jesus, but, I wasn't in love with Him like Lucas was. He was on fire. One that was burning deep from within his soul, igniting my own need to know Jesus in an intimate way. No longer would God's Son be enough for me on Sundays in church or within the pages of my Bible. I wanted to know Him personally. It's what I had been longing for my whole life but figured maybe it wasn't meant for everyone, because no matter what I tried, I just couldn't feel it for myself.

I could have listened to Lucas all day. The way he shared what it meant for him to walk his walk with our Savior, to the way he quoted Scripture from memory (not because it was forced but because this was his life, and it meant everything to him) had me soaking in every word like a sponge absorbing water. Without a doubt in my mind, I was delighted that I had agreed to come and was already looking forward to returning.

After the sermon was finished, and the last song ended, I was greeted by Grace, who was overjoyed I had finally made it to a service. Lovingly, we embraced one another in greeting and began talking in the back of the church, where I had been sitting during Luke's sermon. The two of us continued talking as Grace showed me the back way leading to the children's church area. Together we went to pick up Chris and Riley from the nursery.

Chris squealed when he saw Auntie Ga'wace (as my children affectionately addressed my friend) and asked if she could come home with us to play. Grace refused, joyfully insisting we come to her house for family dinner instead. I agreed, caving to the pleas and leg-hugging demands of my children, and let Grace know we'd see her soon.

After we finished at the church and were back home, the three of us changed out of our church clothes into something more comfortable for dinner. I fed the twins small snacks and played a quick game of hide-and-seek before it was time for us to head over to Grace's.

* * * * *

As the kids and I pulled into the driveway of my friend's house, I wasn't exactly sure why I was surprised to see Luke there (since it was, after all, a family dinner, and he was, in fact, Grace's nephew), but I quickly checked my reflection in the rearview mirror and felt my pulse quicken at the thought of seeing him again. After I closed my car door and began getting Riley and Chris out of the back seat, I spotted Luke heading our way and immediately felt what had to be thousands of butterflies frantically fluttering around inside my stomach. I've never been more thankful for the distraction that came with having energy-filled three-year-old twins!

"Momma, we want to go see the chickens now, okay?" Chris asked as Riley added the sweetest, *pwease*. Both of them mustered up every ounce of their strength to stand in place, waiting for me to give the *go-ahead* instead of running around back to play with the chickens.

"Hold on a second. You know it isn't polite to not say hello first. Get on inside, say hello, then you can go see the chickens," I scolded, noticing Luke had now almost reached us. He was right by my side just as I reached the porch, following behind the twins. Our natural movements and a slight breeze caused a perfect mixture of manly musk and warm spices to reach my nose, causing me to close my eyes slightly and breathe the smell of Lucas in as he held the door open. His scent was far from overpowering, more welcoming and truly inviting.

"Glad to see you survived your first, and hopefully not last, church service today. Thanks for giving it a shot," he said while motioning for me to go on ahead as he held the door open.

"It was great, actually. I am glad I went. You have that preaching thing down, or so it seems," I managed to get the words out while breathing the closeness of him in, frustrated by how nervous he made me and how tiny I felt as I stood next to him—completely at odds with my normal self.

Once Chris and Riley were inside, they hugged Grace and offered a hello to everyone else before seeking my approval to play with the chickens in the barn, like I promised when we arrived. Offering my approval with a nod, I followed my ecstatic children through the kitchen, out the back door, and down the familiar path that led to the barn that housed the chickens. Greeting everyone politely, before taking off after my kids, I let Grace know apologetically I'd be back soon, intending to help in any way needed just before the back screen door closed shut.

About fifteen minutes into playing with the chickens, I let the children know that it was time to go inside so I could help Grace with dinner. Between the whoas and but Mommas, I heard Luke's distinctive voice from the barn door offer to stay with them, explaining he had come out to clean up the coop and feed the chickens for Grace anyway and wouldn't mind the help. Both children, overjoyed, agreed to help and promised to be on their best behavior. I thanked him with a smile, not at all surprised when my heart switched into overdrive this time. I found myself lingering for a few moments, making sure he was truly okay with watching the children before I headed back into the house.

Easily, I made conversation with everyone while helping out in the kitchen and noticed just how seamlessly we all worked together. There wasn't any forced chitchat or uncomfortable moments of awkwardness; we all just seemed to mesh well with one another, so much so I found myself feeling as if I belonged. Not only with Grace at dinner but with all the other people I was surrounded by as well. Once all the food was set on the table, and before people began taking their seats, I made my way to the barn to collect the twins and let Luke know it was time to eat.

I was captivated by the intoxicating laughter coming from not only my children but Lucas too, as they sang a silly song they made up about feeding the chickens and cleaning the "coop poop." I hung back by the barn entrance for a moment, allowing myself a chance to take it all in. Lucas smiled when he caught me standing there; he knew, without me having to say anything, dinner was ready.

"Alrighty there, my stinky little helpers, it's time to let the chickens eat, and wash up so we can feed your bellies some yummy food. Let's go…Forward march," he commanded. Even though they followed right behind him and washed their hands at the sink right outside the barn, Riley made sure that her buddy Woo-cas was going to be eating dinner with them too.

The table was already set, the twins being placed one on each side of me. But Lucas, being the new favorite, ended up switching places with me so he could sit between Chris and Riley, just like they wanted. We all sat together around the table surround by a feast of roasted chicken, potatoes, fresh bread, vegetables, and salad. The twins stole the show when it was time to bless the food. Immediately, they each grabbed one of Lucas's hands, closed their eyes while bowing their heads, and recited the offering they were used to saying together as a family.

"Look at that, Lucas, you finally got a break," Andrew, Lucas's father, lovingly joked his approval as he grabbed the salad bowl in front of him, officially beginning the feast.

"Amen to that. Thanks, you two. That was an outstanding prayer. You think you can teach it to me one day?" Lucas asked. The two happily nodded, offering their promise to one day teach their friend their prayer, as everyone was busy filling their plates and passing the food around the table.

* * * * *

After the filling and delicious meal, Luke and Brian took the children out back to play a game of capture the flag, each claiming a child and one of their sisters as their teammates, while Grace, Lynn, Ashley, and I cleaned up the table and dishes from dinner, and Andrew went out and took a seat on the back porch to relax and watch the game.

"I'm so glad you're here, Elizabeth. It's been great getting to know you. And your little ones are such a hoot. They fit in great with the other children over at the church, and they are so well behaved," Lynn said, placing her arm around my shoulders and giving a squeeze.

Propping myself against the wall, I admired the beauty of the early evening sky. Brian then came running, holding Riley over his head, chanting, "We are the champions—again!" as his tiny teammate squealed, waving both the orange and green flag over her head.

"Cheaters," Lucas fired back as my pouty faced son followed close behind to join everyone on the porch for dessert.

"Ashley, do you have to actually hide the flag someplace, or can you hide it on someone when you're playing capture the flag?" Brian asked his wife, trying to defend his plan of having Riley hold onto the flag as they searched for their opponents, causing them to win the game for the second time.

"I don't think you can keep your flag, Brian. Sounds to me like y'all cheated," she informed, agreeing with Lucas, Beth, and Chris.

"Fine, you traitor…" He teased his pregnant wife. "We still won fair and square the first time around," Brian said as he gave his teammates, Riley and Jamie, both high fives.

Carefully watching from my spot against the wall, I observed once again how each of the surrounding people interacted with one another. They playfully teased and lovingly appreciated being in each other's company. I couldn't help it as my feelings of longing began to creep in, causing me to miss the one person I ever remotely came close to having that sort of relationship with—Christopher.

Lucas must have noticed something I wasn't aware I was revealing, because as he walked over, his concern-drenched eyes locked on to mine, clearly searching for answers I didn't have in me. Claiming the space against the wall to the right of where I stood, he waited for me to make eye contact before he asked if everything was okay. Doing my best to be convincing, I insisted I was fine, brushing off my sudden withdrawn temperament as being tired from the long day. Lucas must have sensed there was something more to it. But thankfully, he didn't pry. Because whatever it was that he was feeling, I couldn't handle, so I forced myself to look away from him, successfully halting any possible further connection. I pretended I hadn't noticed the frown on his face when he nodded, deciding to hold in whatever else he may have wanted to say. Thank God!

I couldn't handle the feeling of being trapped, standing so close to Lucas under the weight of his piercing stare. I was torn between shutting him out and sharing my thoughts with him like I had so easily done at the church when we first talked to one another. I couldn't understand what it was about him that caused me to react so intensely when he was near. I decided it would be best for the kids and me to head home, wanting desperately to get away from the unfamiliar feelings I didn't want to face.

One by one, I thanked everyone, explaining it was getting late, and I wanted to get home so I could put the kids to bed. With a bit of whining and nagging, Riley and Chris reluctantly obeyed but begged their best buddies, Bwian and Woo-cas, to race them to the car. Being the good sports that they were, the two ran after the children, allowing Chris to take the lead. Once at the car, they both helped my two little ones into their car seats and buckled them in. Brian headed back to the house after waving a quick goodbye. And Luke, in all his complete and intimidating glory, stood beside the driver's side door he had already opened, and he waited for me to get in.

"I'm sorry I made you uncomfortable," he hoarsely offered, just barely louder than a whisper. "I'm glad you were here tonight, though, and I enjoyed spending time with your little ones. Thanks for allowing me to." He nodded to the back of the car with a smile on his face, revealing the honesty of his spoken words. Focusing his attention on the back seat, Lucas squished his face up, distorting his handsome features with his fingers, making a silly face, effectively bringing out a chuckle from the two it was intended for, even a little laugh from me as well, lightening the mood a bit.

"It's fine, really, and it wasn't you. They had a great time with you and your family today. Much better than if we had just stayed home, that's for sure," I ended the lie with a complete truth while forcing myself to look away from Luke. My heart once again betrayed me, returning to its rapid beat, as it had each time I was in his presence. Just as I was about to turn to get into my car, Luke grabbed my hand that held my phone, boldly snatching it from my grip. He then swiped what was obviously his number into the keypad and called himself before handing it back to me with a flirty grin. Before I could think of anything in response, he turned away, waved to my children in the back of the car, and jogged off while yelling out for me to drive safe.

On the short ride home, I basked in the excitement of my children's voices but never fully processed what they were saying because my mind was lost, thinking only about Lucas.

I could not, for the life of me, figure out what caused the smile on Elizabeth's face to suddenly fall away when we were all on the porch. It was as if she was wrestling with ghosts that wouldn't allow her the happiness she was so obviously feeling the moment before her mood abruptly switched. I wanted to fix it. I wanted nothing more than to see her face light up with her breathtaking smile, but I knew that she had effectively shut herself down. If I pushed her any more, I would stand the chance of pushing her away for good. So I reluctantly let her go, but not before I got her number. If I had to wait and see, taking things slow with her, that was fine, but waiting just to talk to her when I wanted to do just that wasn't going to work. We're both adults, and there's nothing wrong with reaching out to the person you want to spend time with instead of waiting for accidental bump-ins.

Once I was sure that she was home safely, I sent her a text, saying:

> *Hope you made it home okay. Sleep well. Good night.* 🙂 😴

As a smile began to work its way widely across my face, I allowed my mind to recall perfectly Elizabeth's beauty as she stood on the back porch of my Aunt Grace's, proudly watching her children as they laughed while having fun. My mind painted a perfect picture that I was thoroughly appreciating when she sent me a returned text back:

> *Who is this?* 🤔 😜

I laughed out loud, deciding to play along.

> *It's Luke…Sorry. I didn't realize so many unknown numbers reached out to you. Silly me. I can't say I blame them. Please forgive me.* 😞

I kicked up my feet and waited for her to respond.

We continued to message one another for a while, going from silly chitchat and gradually slipping into things a bit more serious. Not wanting anything to get lost in translation via text, I chose to call her immediately after she asked about my sermon from earlier that day.

She answered on the second ring, and the quietness of her voice almost gave the impression that she was trying to hide from me.

"Sorry I called. But I don't want to misinterpret what you are asking. As much as I enjoyed texting, things can get lost by the lack of tone," I explained, then continued by asking her what it was she wanted me to clarify.

"You seem so sure of yourself. I don't know. You have something inside you. It's almost too good to be true."

Sensing the nervousness saturating her voice that was so innocent, and maybe even a little cute, too, I shared my testimony with her. I explained how I'd grown up in a "Christian" home, the average one that went to church on Sundays but, other than that, pretty much lived in the world. I confessed until I was diagnosed with leukemia, at the age of seventeen (just before graduating high school), that I never picked up a Bible on my own to read.

"Some say that it takes the darkness to make you want to search for the light, and for me, it was true. It took being isolated from the world, at least as I knew it, to so-called *find* Jesus."

"Why did you say *so-called*? I mean, you obviously found Him," Elizabeth asked, losing some of her nervousness as I continued to share.

I went on to further explain that Jesus was never the one that was lost; I was. "Spending time alone and in Scripture, I learned the truth about God's Son, Savior to the world, Who chose to leave paradise to take on the flesh of man so He could not only live but also feel the same things we feel. He taught those He met how they should live, His life being the ultimate example. All the while explaining, He Himself was going to be the very bridge between mankind and their heavenly Father. Most importantly, Jesus loved! Period. He not only loved the ones who loved Him, though. He loved everyone regardless of what he or she had done in the past or what he or she would do in the future. Jesus loves each one of us—you, Elizabeth, and me—enough to offer His life in place of ours. In place of *mine*! For the sins that I committed just so I could be forgiven. Once I read the Scriptures for myself, I realized the Bible was written for me as my very own love story, history lesson, prophecy of what's coming, as well as the instructional manual for my life…I knew I wanted nothing more than to live my life for Christ and share His love with others," I finished and faintly heard what sounded like a muffled sniffle on the other line.

"I want that… Help me," Elizabeth was barely whispering her plea between her soft sobs. Her brokenness hit me with full force. No longer was she able to keep it hidden, no matter how hard she tried.

"Oh, Liz…You've got it right there, I promise. You know God, and you know His Son. Reach for Him. He's been standing beside you all along," I pointed out, my desperately aching heart wanting to help her find what has been right there all along. Not wanting to continue on my own and needing God's guidance, I began praying.

"Lord, thank You so much for not only sending us Your Son but for bringing Your beautiful daughter Elizabeth into my life. Speak to her heart and hold her close as You reveal to her the Truth that You have been with her all along. Help her see that she already has the means to become closer to You. She just has to ask. Help her search in her heart of hearts and see You for Who You really are—her Savior, her

Redeemer, her Friend, her All in All. Praise You, Lord, for You are mighty to save, and Liz is here now, ready to be saved."

Once her sobs settled, and she seemed to be in a better place, Elizabeth thanked me for opening up and sharing so freely with her. In her silence, I sensed something was off again. Much like when I witnessed her shutting down both times before, once at the church and again after dinner on the back porch that evening. More likely, I felt as if Elizabeth was doing everything in her power to build a wall, trying her best to keep me out. With deep regret, I agreed to allow our conversation to come to an unnatural end. In that moment, I wanted nothing more than to cling to the fragile girl on the other line, but knowing that if I did, I'd potentially push her away for good.

For the second time that night, I gave all I had over to the Lord. All my confusion, my feelings, my concerns, and my desire to, above all else, minister to Elizabeth. And if that was all God was calling me to do, I asked for His strength to do His will over and beyond the will of my own.

Chapter 9

For the second time in the past week, I found myself confused by a barrage of feelings I wasn't at all familiar with. A part of me wanted nothing more than to continue talking with Luke, while the other part wanted me to shut him out so I wouldn't set myself up for the pain that losing him would cause if I allowed myself to fall for him. As I once again cried myself to sleep, I drifted off, remembering the passion in Luke's voice when he called me Liz. Such a raw intimacy, drenched in just three letters, caused me to feel as if I was hanging on for dear life to something that could never be mine, no matter how much I may have wanted it—if I'd even admit that to myself in the first place.

*****

Monday morning found me rushed and tired, barely making it into work on time after dropping my children off at their Head Start program. I was never so thankful that the morning program my twins attended was in the same building I worked in that as I now had after my conversation with Luke. It saved me enough time that I ended up making it to the office right on time. After I put my things away and was ready to start my day, Grace let it be known that I was needed in the office rather than as a sub or classroom aide. Relieved for the change of pace, I waited for the caffeine to kick in before taking my place behind the empty desk in the school's main office. Continuing to sip from my mug, I waited for my friend to explain what she needed for me to do. Grace handed me a stack of papers and showed me which program they needed to be entered in to. Once I was familiar with my job requirements for the day, Grace and I began chatting as we worked together.

"Thanks again for last night, Grace. I had a wonderful time with your family. The kids were in their glory too. They were begging to go again all morning."

"Oh, honey, anytime, you know that. I'm just glad you finally came. I hope you don't mind me asking, but did something happen between you and Lucas that made you hurry off?" Grace asked, sensing there was more to my sudden departure than I claimed the night before.

"It was a lot to take in, I suppose. I went from it being just the three of us with a part-time—you thrown in for a good measure, of course—to being surrounded by, well…" I trailed off. Not at all ready for or expecting the tears that threatened to make an appearance when I recognized their unexpected sting before adding, "You know, things were so different for me in Texas. I never really had what you guys have, as far as how easy and fun things are between you and your family. Being there reminded me of the life I thought I was going to have with Christopher and…"

"You closed up because it felt good, and you felt like you were betraying him, didn't you?" Knowing the truth that her words held and declaring them with sincere compassion, Grace filled in the gaps when I couldn't find the words for myself.

"I think that's it. I never realized how much I wanted what I was feeling, and before I knew it, it all snuck up on me. You know, I never thought of anyone but Christopher my entire life? Lucas has been so nice to me the past few times we've seen one another. I know it's part of his job duty and all, but seeing him with Chris and Riley…I don't know. I just got spooked, I guess. I don't even get it myself, really," I confessed, wanting my friend, Lucas's aunt, to somehow ease my mind.

"I think there's a little more to Luke's kindness than just the pastor thing where you're concerned. Don't get me wrong, Lucas is a great guy, but I'm definitely *not* blind. I see the way he looks at you. You're beautiful, and I don't think you realize it because apart from Christopher and the life you were robbed of, you don't think you deserve to be happy." But as her words turned themselves into cognitive thoughts, I found myself taking in a deep breath, seemingly overwhelmed with where things in my life might be headed. I forced the near panic attack to lose it's footing as she continued on.

"I know what it's like to lose the man you love and planned on spending the rest of your life with. It's one of the things that caused us to click so easily—birds of a feather and all—but you have your entire life ahead of you. I don't want you to pass up a chance at finding happiness again. Even me, twenty years older than you and perfectly content with living the rest of my life single, if that's what happens. I still surround myself with love so I won't feel so alone. I'm not saying it will be Lucas who will fill the void in your heart that losing Christopher caused, as much as I would love that and hope selfishly it will be...But I saw a hint of something there between you two, and I think you owe it to yourself to at least give friendship a try. Allow yourself permission to let go of the guilt that you were never intended to carry in the first place," Grace offered, fully broadcasting how much she hoped that at least some of her words would seep in.

Letting the events from the past week and the advice from my friend toss around a bit in my mind, I worked in silence for a little while. I wasn't at all sure what was going to happen, and at that moment, it didn't matter. All I knew was that I appreciated Grace, valued her opinion, and wanted to continue sharing with my friend.

After quietly working for a half an hour, I decided to open up to Grace a little more, sharing with her the details of the only relationship I ever had. I explained my life with Christopher and found it was sometimes difficult for me to articulate because, until I left my hometown, I never had to. Everyone there just knew.

"The closest thing I can compare us to is an arranged marriage, though it wasn't at all. Christopher and I always knew one another, and from as early as I can remember, we just planned on being together, forever. We didn't date the way most couples do. Didn't have to do anything special to even try to woo one another. We just always were. He and I had a great time together, and it was never awkward between us. We just made sense.

"I don't honestly think I'd know what to do if I ever decided I would try again. Heaven knows I am a complete mess when I am around Lucas, and we're not even trying to date," I confessed to my friend, slightly embarrassed as I finished up the last of my work pile, surprised at how fast the workday was moving along.

"Try not to think about it. Allow yourself to talk to Lucas, to spend time with him if you'd like, but only if it's what you want. Don't let it be fear being what stops you, though. And you need to let go of the guilt that's weighing you down. That load is not meant to be yours and it's much too heavy for you to keep carrying. If you're happy spending time with Lucas, then praise the Lord. If you aren't, then let it go, and go back to whatever it is that makes it so. You'll see he's a really great guy, and if for no other reason at all, trust that God put you into one another's lives for a reason. You owe it to yourselves to find out what it is," Grace offered encouragement, and I could tell that her declaration of "You *go*, girl" wasn't meant just for me but maybe, just maybe, a silent prayer that she, too, would be open to the possibility if one should ever present itself in her future.

On autopilot the rest of the day, my body continued to function while my mind silently processed all the new and unfamiliar emotions that had been stirring inside since meeting the people at FCC and before meeting Luke.

* * * * *

Once my day of work was through, still on autopilot, I went to pick up my children from aftercare. As we drove past the church, my mind snapped back into focus, realizing it was Monday. Since I had been in and out of it mentally with all I was trying to process most of the day, I had completely forgotten that I had agreed to go to the young adult meeting again. Going allowed the twins and me the opportunity to continue developing our new friendships. So I looked forward to it.

After picking up Riley and Chris, we happily decided on having pizza for dinner. Finally, since pulling myself out of my thoughts, I could be in the moment with my children. Fully feeling the enjoyment from the conversation taking place with my son and daughter as we ate together in the pizza place, each of us took turns relaying the events from our day. Once we finished, and it was time to head over to the church, Riley and Chris simultaneously asked if they'd be seeing Pastor Woo-cas and were a little bummed when I let them know I didn't think so.

We were each pleasantly surprised when we got to the church and saw that Pastor Luke was indeed in charge of the childcare that evening. Even though my heart, once again, nervously began pounding against my chest the moment he smiled at me, I found that I couldn't help myself and smiled back. I was even familiar with the feeling of butterflies that threatened to consume me whenever I was around Luke. Going upstairs after dropping off my children, I realized I was much more comfortable this time with all the people I had met last week.

Being among this wonderful group of people caused me to feel as if maybe there was more to life than I ever imagined. Even though it scared me, I wanted nothing more than to believe that it was true. Something shifted somewhere between last week and this week's meeting; I admitted to myself that I had stepped beyond a point where there'd be no turning back. The people I had met at Faith Community Church all meant something to me now. Just like losing Christopher changed my life forever, meeting these people and experiencing life in an entirely new way, I realized I could no longer picture my life without any of them.

"Hey there, Elizabeth. Do you want to get together again for another playdate? I figured we could invite April and Mikey and all head over to the park if you're free one day this week?" Deena asked in between the lesson for the evening and the worshipping-through-music part at the end of the group.

"That'd make my two very happy, that's for sure. Wednesday works for me again, if it's good for you?" I suggested, pleased with the realization that the life I so desperately wanted for my children was finally becoming a reality.

* * * * *

As the last song finished, signaling the end of our group session, Deena and I caught up with April, and the three of us walked together to collect our children from childcare.

"Fair warning. When Pastor Lucas is in charge, Mikey is always hyper as ever, but he sleeps soundlessly through the night," April warned before poking fun at Luke.

"You know it isn't fair that you won't sell your services, Lucas. I could really use you every night to get him to sleep the way he does after he spends time with you."

Lucas laughed as he *flew* Mikey over to his mother, helicopter sounds and all, proving April's point and flashing a gorgeous Lucas smile.

"Well, what can I say? This church has the best kids in the entire world..." He winked while encouraging cheers from the children with his playful boasting. "Really, April, I love it. You know my number if you need a sitter. *Call it!* Go on a date night with Big Mike or something," Lucas added sincerely, assuring that he wasn't just making the offer to be polite.

"I'm going to take you up on that, Lucas. You'll see, and then you'll start charging and regretting you offered your services in the first place," April teased.

Lucas supplied another one of his stop-my-heart-from-beating smiles and simply shook his head, adding, "Never!"

Once I officially signed my children out of the system, ready to collect them, Luke leaned in and whispered playfully in my ear, loud enough so that Riley and Chris could still hear, "I hate to break it to you, but I seemed to have lost your children," Lucas teased. Winking and motioning with his eyes and a slight tilt of his head, my two little ones were hiding in the clubhouse in the back corner of the play area.

Going along with the game in a pretend-panicked voice, I cried out, "Oh no! What will I ever do? Guess I'll have to go get ice cream alone to drown my sorrows." Lucas laughed as Chris and Riley both hurried out, smiling ear to ear, thrilled with their trickery but clearly hoping the ice cream part wasn't just a trick of mine as well.

"Momma, can we pwease go for ice cream?" Riley begged sweetly before flashing her eyes at Pastor Lucas and asking him to come too.

"I don't know if Pastor Lucas wants to go for ice cream. And begging him isn't polite, Ms. Riley. No matter how many times you flutter your lashes…" I scolded, feeling my cheeks warm with slight embarrassment before turning my attention to Luke. "My word, I'm going to be in trouble with her. You don't have to come. It's okay," I offered as an apology and a way out.

"Are you kidding? Who doesn't love ice cream? And I am, sort of, the one responsible for the hiding thing in the first place," Luke agreed, picking up a happier-than-ever Riley and making wide silly eyes at Chris because they were going to have ice cream!

* * * * *

The twins were momentarily devastated when they found out Luke was going to be driving in his own truck instead of coming with us in our car; however, he offered to let them drive over with him. I had no chance of refusing when all three simultaneously hit me with their relentless *pleases* and pouty mouth-begging faces. Luke helped me put the car seats into the back row of his pickup truck before we each strapped a seat belt over a child. Taking the lead, I found myself grinning each time I glanced at the man following behind me in his gun-metal gray Dodge pickup, with both of my children inside. Trying my hardest not to overthink what was happening, I chose instead to cherish how happy Lucas made my children.

Once we arrived at the ice cream shop, Riley and Chris chose their usual kid cones, soft serve twist with rainbow sprinkles, and went to sit at one of the empty tables as they waited for their treat. Lucas ordered the same, only large, and even though I tried to decline (not trusting my stomach), Lucas insisted and ordered me one to match the group. There was a peaceful silence as my children worked on eating their cones before the ice cream began to melt, and I found myself finally beginning to relax and enjoy what was happening around me in the here and now.

"Your momma is entirely too clean. Do you think she is a professional ice cream eater?" Lucas observed while engaging the children so naturally, like he had known them all their life.

"No, Pastor Woo-cas. Momma is always clean," Chris explained, fighting against me as I wiped his face with a napkin before I starting cleaning his hands.

Riley happily swung her feet as she sat between her brother and Luke and nearly fell from the bench, laughing heartily as Lucas touched his cone to the tip of my nose. I couldn't believe what he had actually done, and it took me a moment to even process that it was real and had, in fact, happened. I'm sure the shock on my face made its way into my eyes as I sat there, momentarily dumbfounded. Regardless of my initial reaction, the look on Lucas's face as he waited to see whatever consequences his actions may have set in place was captivating. I offered a smile as Chris laughed out a warning.

"Ut-oh…you better run, Pastor Woo-cas," he warned as he waited to see just what I was going to do next.

Before I had come up with any logical plan on how to react, I began wiping my face with a napkin. Without thinking it through, I lunged toward Luke, trying my best to return his face painting with my cone, hoping to meet his face. With much quicker reflexes than I had anticipated, Lucas grabbed my forward-moving hand while playfully laughing and maneuvered me into his broad chest, lessening the blow from my would-be cone face painting attempt, causing me to miss his face completely. I could barely catch my breath between the laughter and the feel of his arms around me.

We were so close.

Fighting through the nearly paralyzing nervous beats of my heart, I glanced up at Lucas, effectively taking in the daring threat hidden beyond his laughter, where I happily fell victim to the hysterics surrounding me. Settling back into my seat at the table,

I was relieved when Luke apologized to the children for being such a klutz. He explained that even though he was just playing around, it definitely wouldn't be a good idea to paint people's faces with ice cream in the future.

Once the four of us had finished our treats, and both of the car seats were back in my car, we were all ready to go. Lucas thanked me for letting him tag along and half-heartedly offered an apology for putting ice cream on my face. Without thinking, he reached and grabbed hold of a strand of my hair that had fallen in front of my eye and gently tucked it behind my ear. Without thought, I closed my eyes and smiled, relishing the feel of his fingers and his ever-so-gentle caress.

"I'm not sorry for the smile it put on your face, though. You really should do that more often," Lucas said confidently. I found myself absently chewing my lower lip while I sighed, coming to the full realization that as long as Luke was around, I knew I could no longer resist whatever was building between us.

Chapter 10

Over and over, I thought about the events of the night. Having ice cream with Liz and her children was just what I needed to try to make sense of my feelings for her. Just seeing the shock in her beautiful hazel eyes and witnessing the most magnificent carefree smile, perfectly placed upon her face, was worth whatever backlash she briefly thought about hashing out on me but seemingly sparing me at the last minute.

Everything seems so natural to me when I'm with her, but because she seems to catch herself each time she smiles, I know it mustn't be the same with her. It's almost as if she's afraid of who might be watching. She always stops herself whenever she begins to open up and share, pretty much shuts down completely, as if she's purposely trying to end whatever it is between us before it even gets a chance to start. The only thing I know for certain is, since the day I laid eyes on her in the parking lot, I haven't been able to get her out of my mind. As much as I don't want to push her or give her any reason to be scared, I know I don't want to miss any moments with her either. I want to spend as much time as possible with her. So I'll continue to let God lead, trying my best to go with the flow. If I felt her starting to pull away again, I'd make a conscious effort to take a step back, but I refuse to miss any chance I may have to spend time with her. For the first time since deciding that relationships weren't for me, I have completely changed my mind. Now I wanted nothing more than to spend my time with Elizabeth, Riley, and Chris.

* * * * *

Once I was pretty sure she had made it home and more than likely had gotten the kids into bed, I sent her a text message, thanking her for the night. I didn't realize how badly I wanted her to reply until my phone alerted me to her response, wishing me a good night with a smiley face.

How in the world has she gotten under my skin so fast when exactly a week ago, I was perfectly content with my life?

Clueless but hopeful, I shared how I was feeling with Christ, just as I have for the past seven days, thanking Him for bringing the three of them into my life. I asked for His guidance each step of the way, not just as a pastor and mentor but also as a man that was very quickly and effortlessly falling for the ready-made family I never knew I wanted, never for a split second imagined I needed, and now I couldn't picture my future without.

*****

The sound of birds chirping and the smell of coffee brewing in the kitchen from the automatic coffee maker had me up with little to no complaints. Ready to start my day, I thanked God for the gift of the new day as I read Acts 17:27, "*God did this so that men would seek Him and perhaps reach out for him. Though He is not far from each one of us.*" I pondered the idea of what this scripture really meant to me before I bowed my head, and I prayed, "Lord, I can't help but think of how blessed I am to know You are right here beside me. My heart breaks for Elizabeth and those who struggle with legalism that You have already freed us from. Please lead me! Show me how to be there for her so she will let me in…so she will let *You* in. Bestow unto me the words that will help her find You. I'm ready to jump, Lord—I'm all in—and trust You will either catch me or teach me to fly, and for that, I give You thanks. Amen."

Once all of my normal morning tasks were finished, I sent Liz a good-morning text and wished her a wonderful day before heading over to my office at church. I began working on the piles of paperwork that had been collecting on my desk, since my mind and all coherent thoughts had turned to mush after meeting *her* a week ago yesterday.

I spent the better part of the morning managing to catch up with all of my work and finished filing everything away just in time for lunch. Ready for the break, when my sister Beth showed up with our youngest sister, Jamie, carrying sandwiches from Richie's Subs.

"Aren't you an answer to my famished stomach's prayers?" I hungrily poked fun, as Beth placed the bags on my desk. I began unwrapping a roast beef, ham, turkey, and Swiss sandwich fixed just the way I liked it—the works, plus mayo—with a bag of kettle-cooked salt-and-vinegar chips that was handed to me.

"What is it with men and their food? It's so easy to make y'all happy," Jamie supplied while gathering three cups and pouring us each a drink before taking a seat in the chair in front of my desk. My sisters nodded at one another in agreement, as Beth sat in the chair that was off to the side.

"You caught up, I see…that's good. You still mushy-brained over Elizabeth?" Beth teased before taking a bite of her sandwich.

"I'm so confused. I hardly know her, but she is all I can think about. Up until last week, I planned on spending my life as Pastor Lucas, a man who lives his life for Christ alone," I confessed to my sisters in my best narrative voice in between bites of my food.

"Well, I, for one, think it's great. And just because you may have found someone doesn't mean you won't be living your life for Christ, Luke. I was never okay with your decision to be alone. I tried to be happy for you, and a part of me even envied your devotion, but I just felt like I wanted you to have what I have with Mark, what Brian has with Ashley, what Mom has with Dad, and what Beth here is also looking for," Jamie openly offered, throwing one of her *hot fries* at Beth, teasing our sister a bit.

"I'm fine, and I know I'll find a man, but I agree, Luke. I really like her, and it's sort of cool that she has kids already, seeing as that was the whole point of your forever-bachelor status thing. It's like you four were all meant to be, God's handpicked perfect little family," Beth added before stealing one of the chips out of the bag she brought me. "It's got the makings of a Hallmark movie," she chided, before popping the stolen chip into her mouth, fluttering her eyes and flashing a cheesy grin.

"Yeah, yeah, I suppose, but let's not get ahead of ourselves. As it stands right now, I've got about as much game as a desperate freak. I know she is suffering inside. That part is obvious. But I'm not even sure she is open to the idea of pursuing anything, period! Each time I think there's some sort of spark, she shuts down instantly," I shared my feelings easily with my sisters, baffled by the way Elizabeth was getting to me and affecting my life so completely in such a short period of time.

Overhearing our conversation from his office, Pastor Barry offered his opinion.

"I knew Mary was the woman I was going to marry the first day I met her. We didn't actually speak officially for three weeks after we met either."

"Hold up, you're kidding, right? Come in here. I-I need to hear this," Beth pleaded and offered him one of the three different half sandwiches, still wrapped up from our lunch. Nodding his refusal at the food, he took a seat on the couch on the back wall of my office.

"How come I didn't know this?" I asked, like it was something I should have known with both of us leading the church and walking our faith walk together and all.

Explaining with simple resolve, he said it *just never came up* and then shared how he and his wife began their lives together.

"When God puts someone in your life that you're meant to be with, you just know. It was like that for me, at least. At the time, I guess I just felt like I imagine you do now, borderline obsessed. Every thought I had was of her, but the more time we spent together, the more I knew she was the one. We got married and started our family less than a year after our first date. We've been together twenty years now, and the rest, they say, is history, as you know." He paused, taking a sip from the water bottle he brought with him when he came in the room and added, "If it's God's will, you'll know, Luke. There's no stopping it. I agree with Beth, though. From sitting on the outside looking in, you two just fit, or should I say, you four. I agree she is struggling, and it's going to take lots of prayer. I've been praying for you and will continue to do so. You know I am always here if you need advice. Sometimes the hardest thing we are called to do is offer counsel to those we care for when they're the ones who are hurting," Barry offered. The four of us then joined hands and prayed for whatever it was God was calling each of us to do by bringing Elizabeth, Riley, and Chris into our lives and our church family.

* * * * *

Once I had finally finished up working for the day, I decided to give Elizabeth a call to try out my decision of *letting the chips fall where they may* between us. I called from my office, hoping to catch her before she picked up the kids. When there was no answer, I left her a voice mail. Collecting my things, I got ready to head out for the night. I shut down the computer, turned off my office lights, and said goodbye to Barry and Beth before heading out to my truck. Just as I clicked my seat belt into place, my phone rang. I answered through the Bluetooth in my truck when I excitedly saw Elizabeth's name flash on my screen.

"Hello," I greeted, wondering if she could tell I had on a big ole dorky grin just because she called me back.

"Hey, Luke, I just listened to your message and figured I'd give ya a quick call on my way to get Riley and Chris. You think of some other things you'd like to smash in my face?" she teased. But I wasn't completely convinced there wasn't a little animosity hidden in there from the night before.

"Whoa…hey now, I didn't smash but more like gently dabbed a small, the tiniest amount actually, of ice cream on your—from what Chris had so kindly agreed was a—*too-clean face*. I'm sorry. You can't be mad. And if you are, then you at least have to let me make it up to you. Let me bring you dinner—the three of you—tonight," I offered, hoping she'd realize I was just playing around and didn't mean any harm the night before.

"You don't have to do that, really. Besides, I just agreed to cover the rest of a shift over at *Benny's* tonight. I was planning on picking up some takeout and giving Grace a call to see if she could watch the little ones for me, but thanks anyway," she declined, and before she could say another word, I offered my services, hoping that I'd get to spend a little time with her after her shift.

"I don't know what I am going to do with you. You are trouble, Lucas. I just know it, and the three of you together, I don't have a snowball's chance in Hades. But I do need a sitter, and well, thank you," she gave in, her frustration mixed with relief all wrapped tightly with a bit of fear coming through clearly in her tone. She rattled off her address, and I once again insisted on bringing dinner, letting her know I was already pulling up to Sonny's drive-through. I'd be there faster if she'd just tell me what they wanted instead of refusing.

I pulled up in the driveway, grabbed the food, and was just about to knock on the door when it was yanked open, revealing the craziness of a single mother trying to get ready for work, quickly as possible, while her three-year-old twin children ran around like tiny little pint-sized lunatics. As I stepped in, Chris, who flopped on the floor and clung to my leg, filled with excitement, attacked me. I easily maneuvered my way toward the table with Chris in tow and placed the bags on the counter before I leaned down, lifted him up, and asked him and his sister to help me with the food. Elizabeth followed us into the kitchen and began pulling out plates and dinnerware before I nodded my refusal, assuring her we'd be fine.

"Go get ready. I have superhelpers. You, I'm afraid, will just be in our way," I teased, which brought forth happy giggles of approval from her children. They began gathering the things they could reach while pointing to the things that were too high for them. Noticing a slight look of concern on Elizabeth's face, I offered a smile and suggested the kids hug their momma and tell her how pretty she was, effectively wiping away whatever doubts were stirring in her pretty little head.

The three said their goodbyes as I witnessed from the corner of my eye the tangible love being shared between a mother and her children, touching my already-conquered heart.

"Thanks again, Luke. I really appreciate this," she said, trying to smile as she forced herself out the door. She was clearly torn between helping out her landlord, her boss at Benny's, while making a few extra bucks and spending time with her kids after already having to spend all day apart.

* * * * *

After dinner, the kids helped me clean up. We then decided to go for a bike ride. More like the twins decided and begged until I caved. Since I didn't have a bike and figured they'd be a bit slower, I walked behind them. Boy, was I ever wrong! Bike-riding, they had down pat and, a few times, even found myself having to run just to catch up with them.

Who would've thought training wheels could go so fast?

Halfway through our trip, Riley informed me that their momma usually told them where to stop and wait. Once I started doing things her way, the rest of our journey was a breeze.

Observing the way the twins interacted on our journey, I was amazed at the sheer love and care they showed one another, which was a direct demonstration of how Elizabeth not only raised them but treated them as well. Chris was all boy, taking joy in the fast and dangerous, all the while making sure he looked out for his sister. Riley loved the attention of her brother. Even though it was clear to see she was a faster and stronger bike rider than Chris, she happily let him take the lead. Pretending she was trying to keep up just to make him feel good about himself.

Once our trip around the neighborhood was complete, and we ended up back where we began,

I helped the two put their bikes back in the garage, and the three of us headed inside. I asked them what they would be doing normally if their momma were home and was pleasantly surprised when they said, "Bible time." They brought me their Bible storybook. Figuring that was right up my alley, I joined them on the couch, where Riley opened the book, handed it to me, and they both waited patiently for me to begin.

We shared the story of Zacchaeus and even sang a song from Sunday school when Chris, mid- song, blurted out, "Can you come here every night, Pastor Woo-cas?"

Being caught off guard and lost in the moment, I froze as Chris and Riley looked up at me, waiting for my answer. "I think you'd get tired of me. And besides, I can't imagine your momma would want another person to clean up after or taking up all the room on her couch." I demonstrated by kicking my feet up and lounging playfully across the two of them.

"I'm rather large, you know." This scored me a hearty round of giggles and successfully changed the topic. The idea of seeing the two of them and their mother every night caused my heart to beat in hopeful joy.

I heard the key in the front door just after eleven o'clock. Chris had fallen asleep on the love seat next to me, and Riley had her head propped up against my side, sound asleep as well.

"How long have you been sitting like that, watching *Veggie Tales*?" Elizabeth asked, looking as if she was exhausted and more than happy to be home.

"Forty minutes or so. I think I am even starting to love Larry's lips myself," I joked.

"I just didn't have it in me to wake them if I moved," I admitted truthfully.

"How were they?" she asked as she picked up her daughter to put her in her bed, barely able to hide the tiredness in her voice.

Once Riley was in Elizabeth's arms, I stood up and grabbed Chris, following her into their room and placing him in his bed, saving her a second trip.

"They were great," I answered. "I know I told you this before, but you have wonderful children. How was your night?" I added as I picked up the toys from the floor in the living room and began placing them into the toy bin.

"*Long*, and you don't have to clean, you know. Stop that!" she said, playfully swatting my arm in warning. "You already have done more than enough. I'm sure there are a million other things you could have been doing tonight besides watching *Veggie Tales* with three-year-olds." She flopped down on the couch, kicking her feet up onto the table in front of her.

"Actually, I wanted to spend time with you and the kids, remember? I missed out on having you here, but Riley and Chris made up for it. I had a good time, even brushed up on my Bible verses," I assured her, wanting so badly to stay but knowing she was tired.

I grabbed my keys from the counter and began walking toward the door and was shocked, frozen in my tracks, when she said, "What's your deal, Lucas? Is this just part of your whole nice-guy-pastor thing or am I some sort'a bad bet?" She never turned her head to look at me, instead, staring coldly ahead toward her kitchen.

"Wow. I'm not sure how to answer that. I am sorry if I've done something wrong or something to upset you, and just to be clear, I'm not a gambling man, way too risky. I like you, Liz, and I enjoy spending time with your children. I thought there might be a chance that you like me as well. I know I make you nervous, and I assumed it was because you felt something between us. Am I wrong?" I asked, waiting for her to answer one way or the other but not sure if I was ready for what she had to say.

"I don't know how to do this…" She waved her hand back and forth between the two of us before looking me in the eye and continuing, "I can't stop thinking about you, and I'm not sure I like it. I'm used to it being me and my kids. I accepted that it was going to be just us. And then I met you. Now I can't help but think about the possibilities of there being something else out there, and it scares the living daylights out of me," she confessed, throwing her head back against the couch to stare at the ceiling. "Luke, I'm a mess, and I don't know if I can ever figure out how not to be." Before she finished, I sat down in the love seat and grabbed her hands in mine, willing her to look at me.

"Liz, I'm right there with you, really. Before I met you in the parking lot last Monday, I was content being alone. Even believed it was God's plan for me. I get that you're afraid. Me too. I'm afraid that I am going to push you too far, too fast, and blow it. I really want to get to know you and spend time with you, Chris, and Riley," I explained, trying my best to plead my case as I stroked my thumbs across the top of her knuckles.

“I’m not just afraid, Luke…I’m petrified. I really don’t think I have it in me to do this. I can’t.” She yanked her hands away from mine.

Afraid I lost her before she was even truly mine, I pressed on, “Can I ask why? What are you so afraid of?” Not ready to let her go, I watched her closely, waiting for her to say something. I witnessed in her eyes that her mind was bringing her someplace that was obviously very painful for her. As the seconds ticked by, I prayed that God would take control of the situation and help me, help her, even if it turned out we weren’t meant to be.

“I’ve never been with anyone other than Riley and Chris’s father, and I was with him my whole life. I spent close to twenty years thinking we’d be together forever, and that wasn’t in the cards for me.” Listening patiently, my heart broke as I watched her try her best to be strong but then tensing up as a tear slipped from her eye. “I’m going to sound like a complete jerk right now, but it’s the truth, okay?” she said, staring me down, daring me to stop her, but I encouraged her to continue instead. “You shared with me that you had cancer when you were younger, and well, I don’t want to let you in and end up losing you too. I barely know you, and I’m already a mess. There is no way I will be able to survive you, Luke.

Besides, for some reason, God wants me to be alone, so be it," she confessed.

I knew, in that very moment, I was falling in love with this broken girl who sat stubbornly before me, trying her best to do everything in her power to push me away.

Grabbing her face between my two hands and stroking the few tears that escaped her eyes with my thumbs as they steadily made their way down her cheeks, I smiled, whispering, "If God wanted you alone, then why did He bring you to me? And why am I sitting here on your couch, falling for your silly stubborn self?" I tried my best to let her see in my eyes I meant every word I spoke.

"Liz, please don't push me away. Give me a chance, that's all I ask. I will try my best not to spook you, but I'm warning you, you already have managed to get your way into here," I pleaded, allowing my hand to drop from her face. I grabbed hold of one of her hands, brought it to my chest, and positioned it over my pounding heart.

"Why don't you get some sleep and try not to worry about it. Let's take it one day at a time, okay? I'm not going anywhere," I promised and placed a gentle kiss on her knuckles.

"Don't make promises you can't keep, Luke. My life has been one big broken promise so far," she snapped, but I simply smiled deeper, pushing her once again.

"Do you like spending time with me?" I shifted my face in front of hers, forcing her to look me in the eye as she nodded her response.

"Then live right here, right now, and don't think about anything other than the moment before us, okay? We will figure this out together, I promise—and yes, I said it again. I trust God's got this, Liz. You'll see," I finished, pulled her close, and placed my lips on the top of her head, where I just breathed her in for a minute. Realizing I just verbally committed to the long haul, knowing full well the road ahead for us was sure to be rocky, I was prepared to give it my best. Before she could figure out any more reasons why we couldn't be, I said good night, stood up, turned, and walked out the door.

* * * * *

Not expecting to hear from her again until the next day, I was shocked when my phone rang as I pulled up to the light halfway between our two homes.

"Hey there, you alright?" I cautiously answered, trying my best to be patient, willing her to feel calm when inside, I felt a storm was headed my way.

In the faintest of a whisper, she desperately pleaded, "Lucas, what if I can't?"

My heart sank. And the panic I felt in that very moment had me pulling over to the side of the road, praying for whatever words I needed to set her mind at ease.

"What if you can't what?" I prodded, hoping that the playfulness in my voice was holding back all my fear and would somehow lessen the doubts that were stirring in her mind.

"What if I can't *not* think?" she added with the tiniest hint of a hope that I'd have the perfect answer, somehow making it all better.

"Oh, that…Well, perhaps I shouldn't have said that. I want you to think. In fact, thinking is *real* good. What I meant was let's not think too much. Don't overthink, okay? Let's just spend time together, enough time that being around me doesn't scare you so much. Let's get to know one another and have fun," I tried my best to assure her of my intentions without scaring her away.

"I *am* afraid of you..." She laughed, and in that moment, I thanked the Lord. There was hope. "It'd be nice to not be afraid of you."

"Well, then, Ms. Strutton, I'm positive the only way to fix this is for you to fully see how completely *unscary* I am is to spend more time with me. Let's do something, the four of us, when you're free, of course. I figure Riley and Chris can help set your mind at ease. You can be all up in your momma bear role you've mastered so well, and hopefully it will distract you enough that you won't have time to overthink but rather go with the flow. What do you say?" I suggested, successfully getting her to agree to think but not *overthink* about it. Before hanging up, she promised she'd text me soon with a day that worked for her.

Before I got ready for bed, I shot Liz a text, saying:

> *I hope you sleep well, Liz. Thanks again for tonight.* 😉

To which she replied:

> *Thank you, Luke. Sleep well yourself. Good night.* 😴

Chapter 11

My heart raced in my chest as I hugged my pillow tightly and rocked back and forth, replaying Lucas's words over and over in my mind. The calmness and certainty he seemed to possess in all things I wanted for myself, more than anything.

How could this have happened?

I wasn't prepared to meet anyone who would have my heart and head colliding into what, more than likely, would turn out messy. I wasn't ready to deal with all the things I happily put aside and locked away, to never think about again. When I thought of how Luke made me feel each time I was with him, I thought of Christopher and how he left me here, completely alone. I never wanted to give someone the power to hurt me like that again. I've spent over three years learning to live without the promise of love, three years of raising the twins alone. As I continued to rock myself, I was convinced that I was nowhere near ready to let someone in, no matter how good it may have felt.

* * * * *

The next morning was pretty much the same as it was every morning, Monday through Friday. I went in to wake up my little munchkins so they could get ready for school, picked out their outfits, and placed them on their beds so they could get dressed. As I waited for them to finish getting ready, I headed into the kitchen to start breakfast and make our lunches before I had a chance to sip on my much-needed cup of coffee. Chris was in a particularly good mood when he joined me in the kitchen, sitting down in his chair and digging into his bowl of fruit.

"Momma, are we going to play with Mikey and Marybeth today after school?" he asked, overflowing with excitement, causing Marybeth's name to sound more like Murbeth.

"That's the plan, Stan," I joked, as Riley quietly joined her brother at the table and smiled. I didn't pay too much attention to how quiet she was; just chalked it up to being tired from having so much fun with Luke the night before.

* * * * *

Thankfully, I wasn't needed as a substitute in a class today because the office phone rang a little after ten, informing me that Riley wasn't feeling well and needed to go home. Lucky for me, my children spent their mornings at Hillside, so I didn't have to go across town to pick her up. After I hung up the phone, I let Grace know I was going to have to leave for the rest of the day, and she kindly offered to bring Chris home for me after work.

"Oh, Grace, that'd be fantastic. Thanks so much," I agreed, grateful I had someone to help in my time of need.

Once Riley and I got home, I sent a text to Deena and April, letting them know that that night's playdate was going to have to be postponed, and went to retrieve Bluey (Riley's blanket) and Mr. Sicky (her bunny that she only snuggled when she wasn't feeling well). Since she was burning up from a fever, I gave her some Children's Tylenol and sat down next to her on the couch after turning on a Disney movie for the two of us to watch.

I didn't realize I had drifted off to sleep until a knock on the door startled me awake. I told, whom I thought was Grace, to come in, figuring she decided to bring Chris home after Head Start instead of picking him up from aftercare. I was surprised when it was Lucas instead.

"I've come bearing gifts. Lunch for the momma, who looks as if she has forgotten to eat," he said in a hushed tone as to not wake up the sick-and-sleeping Riley. "I bumped into my Aunt Grace when I was online at the deli, and she told me that Riley wasn't feeling well. Hope you don't mind." He went into the kitchen to get me a paper plate and asked what I wanted to drink.

"You're crazy, you know? Why in the world would you come here and subject yourself to whatever it is she has, like this?" I asked, completely dumbfounded by the actions of the incredibly thoughtful man before me.

"A simple thanks, Luke, would have been fine," he teased, flashing one of his dazzling signature smiles.

To which I, of course, obliged, "Thanks, Luke."

"I got some chicken noodle soup for Riley, in case she was hungry too. I didn't know what you liked, so I played it safe with turkey and cheese." He unwrapped the sandwich he got for me, placed it on the plate, and sat down on the love seat next to me on my right, where he sat the night before when he held my hands.

"It's perfect…thanks, really," I said before cautiously taking my first bite, unsure if my nerves were on the fritz because of Luke or if I was coming down with something myself.

"Pastor Woo-cas," Riley managed to grunt out before sitting up and vomiting all over the floor.

"Well, there goes my appetite. Sorry, Luke. You can run now. I won't blame you. Barf is way beyond the territory of new beginnings. Let me go and get her in a bath, clean up this mess, and I'll try to give you a call you later, okay?" I said as I carried Riley into the bathroom, sat her on the toilet lid, and started the water to fill up the tub. I explained to Riley I'd be right back to put her in her bath once I finished cleaning up the living room. "If you need Momma, give a holler, okay, lovebug?"

"Kay, Momma," she answered. I began making my way into the living room, hating the thought of keeping her waiting when she wasn't feeling well. I planned on being quick and doing a more thorough job after she was asleep in her bed, thinking I had my share of surprises for the day, only to find how very wrong I was. When I reached the living room, I found Lucas on his hands and knees just as he was finishing cleaning up Riley's *mess*.

I couldn't believe this man. I, her mother, felt ill just thinking about barf duty, yet here he had cleaned it up while I was busy taking care of my sick child.

"Go, give her a bath. I'm almost done," Luke ordered, shaking his head at my glare and insisting, "It's no big deal, really." He winked at me, causing my heart to do backflips. How could he make cleaning throw up look so good?

Once Riley was all cleaned up and tucked into her own bed, I went out to join Luke. He was sitting on the love seat again, flipping through the pages of the kids' devotional, smiling. He turned his head to face me once he realized I was standing there.

"Anything good, Pastor Woo-cas?" I teased, mispronouncing his name the way my children would at the sight of him holding and reading their children's Bible.

"Actually, I may have to borrow this from you. The lessons are clear enough that even a child could figure them out." He pulled gently on my hand, letting me know he wanted me to sit beside him.

Reluctantly, I caved, still afraid of being close to him, and played back. "Imagine that, kids getting something out of a kid's book, the absurdity of it all!" And we both laughed, side by side, in my living room.

"I can feel it, you know. The minute you put up your wall. I'm sorry that I make you uncomfortable," he said as he stared patiently at me, willing me to relax.

"It's not you…well, maybe it is. You make me nervous, Luke," I managed to get out, unable to look him in the eye. Nervously, I pulled my lips inward and ran my tongue over them, dismayed by the thought of being so close to him. I was angry with myself for wanting him to be there and scared by the thought that he wanted to be there too. A part of me realized that somehow, not only did I enjoy spending time with him, but I was beginning to feel as if I was starting to need him too.

"You're afraid I'm going to hurt you. You're afraid that you like me, and…" he said as he turned his body to face mine, "you're afraid I'm going to kiss you." And with that, his eyes focused on my lips, as he leaned toward me in a steady-but-slow-paced movement, gently taking my chin between his fingers. Shifting and locking his eyes onto mine, he searched to see if I was going to stop him.

I was frozen.

I stared into his beautiful blue eyes. And in that moment, I wanted him to close the distance, but another part of me wanted to run. Run as fast as I could to the airport, jump on a plane back to Texas, never to look back. I closed my eyes just as his lips met mine, barely touching yet scorching me all the same. He pulled away and whispered, "Don't be afraid." He gently pressed his incredibly soft lips to mine once again. And I tried, in that moment, with all I had in me, to trust this man and let him in.

"Now that that's out of the way, we can address the thousand-pound elephant in the room…Will you tell me about their dad?" Luke uttered in such a way that made me feel as if I was safe. And I found myself wanting to open up to him.

"Where to begin…" I started as he put his left arm around me. Taking my right hand into his, he began stroking my knuckles lightly as a means to encourage me to continue.

"I never knew anything, anyone, other than… Christopher. He lived next door and was always a part of my life. It was as if we were always meant to be since birth—we just always clicked. He looked out for me all the time. Sometimes I can almost see him in the way that Chris looks out for Riley. I never figured out how to go on without him," I said, as I blinked back the tears beginning to form in my eyes. "You know, his death, living without him brought me to the conclusion that he was my entire life. I never figured out who I was apart from being his, and when he was there, when he was alive, it didn't matter. Once he was gone, I realized I was empty inside. Just a shell."

There was something about Lucas that made me want to open up to him. I wanted to share things about myself when he asked. Not understanding the pull he had over me, I usually forced myself to stop and shut down because I didn't know if I was ready emotionally to let him in. However, once I shared my heart with him, I knew there'd be no turning back.

"I'm sorry, Liz. I can't imagine losing someone so close…Wow," he offered his condolences while blowing out a long steady breath before continuing, "You know, I don't want you to think I'm trying to replace him. I never want you to forget him. I just want a chance to know the *you* that's here right now. One day, hopefully, you'll allow me to shoulder some of the hurt so we can, together, lighten your load," he said. The look in his eyes caused my heart to, once again, begin pounding.

"Well, what if I want you to? What if I just want to forget him already? He left me alone, and now, because of you, I don't think I know how to be alone anymore. I don't want to be lonely, Luke," I confessed, and he pulled me into his arms as I wept. I released not only the heartbreak of losing Christopher but the emotions I suppressed by never allowing myself the much-needed time to process my loss.

"Oh, Liz…You know that isn't true. You aren't mad at him for dying. But you are angry, and believe me, I understand. Until you face that anger, you're always going to push people away," Lucas informed me as I continued to cry in his arms.

* * * * *

Lucas held me in his arms as I sobbed for what seemed like hours, but really, it was only ten minutes. I pushed away from him, ran into the bathroom, bent over the toilet, and threw up. I heard Luke's footsteps start up the hall and panicked, not wanting him to see me like this, especially after I just emotionally vomited all over him a minute ago. Just before he reached the bathroom door, the doorbell rang, as the front door opened. Chris squealed when he found Woo-cas at our house.

Not well enough yet to face Grace, I yelled a thank you and was relieved when I heard Lucas explaining that I more than likely caught whatever Riley had.

"Tell her not to worry about work tomorrow, and let her know I'm here if she needs me," Grace said before kissing her nephew and my son goodbye. "You want me to have Chris come sleep at my place so he doesn't catch it?" Grace offered, assuring me she could also take him to school in the morning.

"What do think, Chris? You want to go spend the night with Auntie Grace or help me take care of the sickies?" Luke asked, leaving the decision up to Chris, assuming in my condition, I'd be okay with it too.

"I want to take care of Momma and Ri-wey with you, Pastor Woo-cas," he answered. And at that, Grace was on her way.

After I washed my face and rinsed my mouth, I poked my head into the kids' bedroom when I noticed that Riley had awakened. I asked her if she was okay, to which she nodded, got out of her bed, and hugged me when she got to the door.

"You're burning up again. Let's go get some more medicine," I said, and we headed to the kitchen, hand in hand.

Lucas and Chris were talking about what they were going to have for dinner, and just the thought of food had my stomach revolting. Luke must have seen it on my face when he hurried to Riley's side, picked her up, and placed her in her seat at the table before coming back to me. He touched the inside of his arm to my forehead and asked if I was feeling okay.

"Us men, we've got this. You, go lie down and get some rest," Luke ordered, making sure it was okay to give Riley medicine and then handing each of my children an ice pop.

"You can have one, too, after your nap," Luke uttered, slipping into caregiver mode as easily as flipping a switch.

My mind wanted to protest, but my body refused, so I headed back down the hallway, went into the bathroom that was attached to my bedroom, took some Tylenol for my fever, and climbed into bed, falling asleep almost immediately. The last thought I remember having was, *How nice it was to have help when I was sick.*

When I finally woke and headed into the kitchen for something to drink, I found Lucas asleep on the couch, holding a sleeping Riley on his chest, and Chris curled up on the love seat. My heart clenched at the sight, as I stood there in silence for a few seconds, taking it all in, grateful that twice now, he was here to help when I needed him the most.

I quietly filled a cup with water and tried to sneak back to my room but noticed Lucas's eyes open and focus on me.

"How are you feeling?" he asked in a hushed tone, trying his best not to wake the kids. He effortlessly sat up somehow, doing his best to place Riley on the couch without waking her as he stood. Once he was close enough, he felt my head again and seemed pleased that my fever had broken.

"I feel like a mess. First, I barf up my emotions, and then I just barf. Lucky you. You're a glutton for punishment," I joked and headed out onto the front porch for some fresh air. Lucas followed, assuring me not to worry so much, saying it is what it is.

"And as far as your emotional barf goes, thanks for letting me in. I know it wasn't easy for you."

I wanted so badly to beg him to show me how to fix everything, but I also knew that I wasn't quite ready to fully jump right into anything. Not just because I was sick either. We sat together for a little while on my porch in silence. I fell asleep against his arm and briefly remember him picking me up and tucking me into bed.

With a hushed voice, Luke managed, "Feel better, beautiful." Then he lightly kissed the top of my head before adding, "Sweet dreams."

Chapter 12

After I put Liz in her bed, I went back into the living room. Not wanting to wake either child by bringing them into their room, I grabbed a pillow off Chris's bed and stretched out on the floor in front of the living room's television. As I lay there in silence (television glowing in the background for light but muted so I could hear if Riley or Chris woke up), I began sharing my thoughts with God like I do each night before falling asleep. I knew that so much had happened in such a minimal amount of time, and I wanted to make sure that I asked God to lead me each step of the way so I wouldn't get caught up in my feelings for Liz or the children if it wasn't meant to be. The three of them so easily worked their way into my heart without any effort, and lying there on the floor, I found myself begging God not to take them from me. I knew it was selfish, but I couldn't imagine going through a loss like Elizabeth had, and I'd just met her. I didn't think I would survive if I loved her as long as she loved Christopher and ended up losing her as she had lost him. So I prayed with all I had in me for God to heal her from the hurt of that loss so she would let me in and allow me to love her. And one day, maybe she could learn to love me too.

* * * * *

I woke as the sunlight hit my eyes through the open blinds of the living room window. It was early still, and from the silence and after a quick peek, I noticed the twins were still asleep. After pushing myself up off the floor, I knocked softly on Elizabeth's door to see if she was awake. When she didn't answer, I headed into the kitchen, thinking I'd make tea for her to ease her stomach. I filled the teapot with water and placed it on the stove before making myself a cup of coffee.

"Can we make Momma and Ri-wey breakfast?" Chris asked in a cracking voice, giving away that he had just awakened.

"Let's wait on that, okay, bud? We don't want to have them getting sick again if they aren't ready to eat. We can cook something for you and me, though. Whatcha want to have?" I asked, and easy enough for me, he decided on cereal.

Once I poured the milk in the bowl and Chris began to eat, I headed to the bathroom to Lysol everything again in hopes of keeping Chris from catching their bug. After I finished, I saw what I hoped was a no-longer-sick Riley heading down the hall. Before I could catch her, she pushed open the door to her mother's room and climbed into bed with Elizabeth, who looked guilty as ever while she was pounding away on her laptop.

"I'm just sending an email… Sorry! I was going to come out in a second…"

Holding up my hands from the doorway, I assured her she had nothing to apologize for, and I was glad she appeared to be feeling better.

"Would you like some tea?" I asked, and she nodded, letting me know how she took it, and she let it be known to me she'd be joining me in the kitchen in just a moment. After closing her door, I went to fix her a cup of tea. Just as I finished, Riley and Elizabeth were there beside me, warming my heart that they both appeared to be feeling much better.

Elizabeth handed Riley a cup of ice water, and the little girl went to join her brother on the couch to watch cartoons.

"Thank you for everything," she said, and I could see on her face that she not only meant it but also was having one of her moments of doubt again. She twisted her fingers together nervously and tried her best to avoid eye contact with me as much as she could before I finally stepped right in front of her; grabbed her chin, forcing her to look into my eyes; and simply shook my head. "No. You don't get to weird out on me now. I know things were crazy last night, but stop… Don't overthink this, Liz, please. If it will make you feel better, as long as you are, in fact, feeling better, I'll leave. But I'm not walking away from you, understand?" I pleaded, hoping to stop her from being lost inside her mind any longer. I kissed her forehead before pulling her into my chest. I held her in my arms for a bit.

I loved the way she tucked in so perfectly under my chin, how tiny she felt in my arms, and how our bodies, even with me being close to a foot taller than she, still seemed to fit together as if we were made for each other. With her in my arms, I felt as if all was right in the world, and I never wanted to let her go.

Reluctantly, I let her slip out of my embrace as I reached behind her for the cup and offered her, her tea. She smiled up at me, and the look in her honey-colored eyes melted my heart completely. I was lost—head over heels—completely, and it's only day ten.

I finished the last of my coffee and washed the empty cup in the sink before gathering my keys off the counter. I then let Elizabeth know I was just a phone call away.

"Please use it," I said, holding up her phone to emphasize I was serious.

* * * * *

When I got home, I took a quick shower and then hopped onto my computer, checking to make sure I wasn't needed anywhere for the day or hadn't missed anything from yesterday. A smile warmed my face when I noticed there was a message from Elizabeth. When I noticed the time stamp, I realized she must have sent it from her bedroom (when she was looking guilty) earlier that morning.

An unsettling feeling threatened to set in, but I blew it off and decided to see what she had to say before jumping to any conclusions. I could almost hear her voice as I read the words she typed.

Dear Lucas,

What can I say? I am a big chicken. I punked out and decided to email you so I wouldn't have to say any of this to your face. I'm sorry I am such a mess. I wish I could get my stuff together and be as cool as you, but sadly, that isn't the case. I know that you're correct in thinking I have to work on my issues, and so I guess what I am trying to say is...maybe it's best if we just take things slower or maybe forget about pushing things any further between us. I don't want to hurt you, but if I am being honest with myself, I really don't want to be hurt. Since you somehow figured out how to get inside my head and mess with my heart already, I just can't imagine what will become of me if we keep this up.

Thank you so much for all you have done for my children and, well...me. I know that even though things won't be going any further between us, you already mean the world to Riley and Chris. It's been sort of wild seeing them with you. We've all been blessed just by meeting you. You are an amazing man, and any girl would be lucky to have you.

God bless,
"Liz"

PS—I'll be praying that while you were stepping up and helping me out, we didn't get you sick, especially since you kissed me.

PPS—I still can't stop thinking about it either. Thanks for that!

I knew things were going to be hard with her, but once I finished reading the words she wrote, I took a few deep breaths, asked God for wisdom, as I typed my response to her.

Dear Elizabeth,

Please note that I didn't address you as Liz, as you quoted, because I am a bit agitated by your letter. I'm trying my best to give you the benefit of the doubt, and I have even reasoned that you sent this while your mind was still loopy from sleep after being deliriously sick. I also noted that you sent this before our pep talk in the kitchen, where I sensed something was off and insisted that you NOT freak out on me. Seeing as I left your home in a good place, I am going to take the time and address your letter, hoping to clear up a few things for you.

First, you state that I am "cool," suggesting that you are less than or not at all. Well, I can assure you I am anything but cool. In fact, my emotions are running amok, and if it weren't for me giving this over to God and having sisters to confide in, I'd be far from the illusion of "cool" you are perceiving. You somehow managed to sneak into my heart, and I can't think about anything other than you and your freakishly adorable children.

Second, I'd like to address that while I did say that you needed to work on things, I didn't mean to suggest that this is a "you alone" problem. We all need to work on things. No one is perfect. I am far from it, in fact! Thankfully, I serve a more-than-capable God that has enough "perfect" for the two of us plus an entire congregation times the entire world (past, present, and future). Have a little faith, would ya?

Third, I'm not interested in stopping what we have between us, but if you need to take things "slower," then I'm willing to hear you out and see what this entails. I don't want to push you away, so help me help you here. I can't agree, however, not to spend time with you because as it is right now, I want to spend whatever time you will allow me to have with you. I enjoy each moment, be it in person, on the phone, or texting (and I guess now emailing too). You can tell me that you don't like when I am around, but I know you are just fooling yourself. I see it in your eyes. I feel it when you tense up around me, and I know that you love that Riley and Chris enjoy having me around too because you get a break. And I love that I can not only help you but that also, you have trusted me enough so far to allow it.

Now, if you meant physically, I can promise you that I will never take us to a place beyond kissing you, holding your hand, and you in my arms no matter how much I may want to regardless of how strong the temptation may be. I made a promise to God to wait, and until you and I have exchanged vows, I can promise you with all I am that

IT WILL NEVER HAPPEN. You can trust me with this!

Fourth, you said you don't want to hurt me. Pushing me away is doing exactly what you claim you're trying to avoid. So stop. I think you were more accurate when you admitted you were worried I'd hurt you. Only time will prove to you that I will never intentionally do anything to hurt you. Reread the above justification in the third section, which offers proof as to why we shouldn't be apart, to reassure yourself that spending your time with me is, in fact, a very good thing.

Fifth, don't imagine what will happen if we don't work. Just be thankful and enjoy what we have. I must admit, though, that I enjoyed reading that I, too, have gotten under your skin a bit.

Now, for points six and seven, I love and cherish every second I spend with your children (even the sick and ouchy moments). Thank you for thinking any girl would be "lucky to have me," but I've gone nearly thirty years of my life never wanting anyone other than you. Wouldn't that, then, make you the "lucky" one, if we were using your words, that is?

I trust this helped make things a bit more clear for you, and I hope that after voiding yourself of all the necessary food needed to keep your mind as sharp as a tack, my letter along with some food and fluids will get you back on track and bright as ever real fast.

All my heart,

"Luke" (notice I didn't use Lucas like you do when you get scared or when you're trying to be serious, even though I am as serious as ever, "Liz")

PS—IF I get sick, so be it. I'd do it all over again just to kiss your lips. But I am humbled and thankful that you will be praying me through. That's the faith I'm talking about. (Tap into that.) Thanks for having my back!

PPS—I can't stop thinking about it either, and that's because it was meant to be. XOXO

I sent my response and decided to take a walk over to the main house to visit with my parents in hopes of keeping me from going back to Liz's and kissing her repeatedly until she finally stopped fighting her feelings for me.

Once I stepped inside and hugged my mother, I confessed without a doubt, "I met the woman I am going to spend the rest of my life with, if that's even possible. I think I love her, and I've only known her for ten days. Now, what'd ya have for lunch?"

The shock on my mother's face said all that needed to be said. I lost my composure when she jumped up and down like a schoolgirl that just found out the juiciest of secrets, as she took turns squeezing me and kissing my face.

I thought she was checking to see if I was being serious.

"Oh, Lucas... I am so happy to hear this. It's Elizabeth, isn't it? I see the way you look at her. Did you tell her? Are you two a thing? Wait, sit down and tell me everything," she pleaded.

After we sat down at the table, I shared with my mother all I could about the girl who stole my heart.

"Lucas, my heart is overjoyed! I am so happy for you! I love her, by the way. She is just wonderful. And those kids of hers? They are just the cutest. It's not going to be easy, but you've got this. Just don't let her go no matter how hard she pushes you away, okay, baby?" And just as I had done to Elizabeth, she kissed the top of my head.

I couldn't help but laugh out loud when I read the text from Elizabeth that came after I finished having lunch with my parents.

> *I read your response, and I will get back to you when my sick mind is once again "as sharp as a tack." Please be advised that my children are one 'Woo-cas" away from being shipped to your house. Hope you are still feeling well. ~Liz*

Lucas replied to my text in record time, simply stating, he was on his way.

I let Chris answer when Luke got to the door, and I have to admit, seeing them all together really plucks at my momma heartstrings, and hearing Woo-cas, knowing he was now there, was much better than having to answer a million times why he wasn't.

"How's everyone feeling? I know your momma was a bit loopy there for a while. Is she any better, bud?" he teased, picking up Chris and putting him on his shoulders, then heading to the couch to collect Riley.

"How are you feeling, Princess Riley? Good enough for food, or do we have to stock up on ice pops?"

"Loopy, huh?" I asked, lifting my brow while smirking.

"What else could it have been? You tried to Dear John me before even giving me a chance. That's loopy for sure," he scolded and winked while flashing me his perfect Lucas grin.

"Who's John? You're Woo-cas," Riley's three-year-old self giggled, thinking I messed up Luke's name.

"See, I told you, your momma was loopy for a minute. Thank heavens you two took such good care of her while I was gone," he answered while carrying them into their rooms so the three of them could play. They ended up building a zoo with blocks, while I reread Luke's email response for the fifth time since receiving it. I tried my best to poke holes in his logic but came up empty each time. The only thing I ended up finding was confirmation that Luke was great. I loved his thoroughly witty response. I enjoyed having him around, even though just being near him made me so nervous. The butterflies in my stomach became so active, I swore I was close to taking flight. And for the first time since I met him, I admitted to myself that I was falling for him. But none of that changed the fact that I was still afraid.

Lucas took care of dinner, deciding to pick up some more soup from the deli. He made Riley's and Chris's day by taking them with him in his truck while I stayed behind to set the table and make some iced tea. When the three of them returned, I couldn't help but think how normal everything felt. After we sat down at the table, Luke reminded the twins that he wanted to learn their dinner prayer. They happily recited it for him twice before the four of us held hands, bowed our heads, and together, gave thanks to the Lord for our food.

I caught myself staring at Luke while he was eating, not realizing it until his eyes met mine, and he smiled. It was nice having him there with us, and before I allowed myself any time to overanalyze how I was feeling, I forced myself to just *be*.

Once everything was cleaned up after dinner, and bath time was over, Riley and Chris begged Woo-cas to stay and do devotions with us. Before agreeing, Luke looked at me for approval and then took a seat in the center of the couch after I nodded my head. My two children each sat beside him as they would normally do with me, one on each side. I gladly took a seat on the floor on the other side of the coffee table, facing the three of them. I was perfectly content when Luke agreed to read that night's lesson. Because I not only loved listening to his voice, I also found the enthusiasm and passion he possessed when he spoke about Christ left me with a hunger that had me praying, I, too, would feel that one day.

Lucas and I each carried a child into their room after they brushed their teeth. I had Chris, and Lucas had Riley (better yet, Riley had Lucas wrapped around her finger), and we each brought them toward their beds. Lucas had Riley giggling away when he put her down on Chris's Batman bed, pretending he didn't know the difference.

"I am not sweeping in a princess bed, Momma," Chris protested, wiggling out of my arms and climbing into his own bed.

"Silly me. I guess I caught the loopies," Luke joked as he brought Riley to her bed, gently laying her down so she could slip under her covers. Once she was all tucked in, he gave them both a kiss on their foreheads and wished them sweet dreams. I repeated the same but added I love yous before turning out the lights and shutting their door, leaving it cracked just a bit, as always.

* * * * *

Lucas took my hand into his, led me down the hall into the living room, where he guided me to the sofa and encouraged me to have a seat while he went into the kitchen and turned the kettle on to make me some more tea. He sat down beside me as he waited for the water to boil.

"Apart from getting a baffling email earlier, I had a pretty exceptional day today. Thanks," he chided, while nudging me with his shoulder.

"You're relentless. You are never going to let me live that one down, are you?" I rebuked, shoving him back in the same teasing manner.

"Not until you take it back and promise to never send me a Dear John again. If you get spooked, talk to me. That's all I ask," he pleaded while turning my face to look at him.

I silently agreed with a nod while taking my bottom lip between my teeth and sighed. This man was truly magnificent, and he looked at me as if I was his everything. Luke brushed his thumb slowly over my lips before he lowered his head toward mine and kissed me. This time, it wasn't slow and gentle as it was the first time. Instead, he kissed me as if I was his life preserver, and without me, he'd be drowning at sea. Once I was lost and left feeling as if I, too, was gasping for air, he pulled away, pecked me gently, and then tucked me under his arm, where he held me close and stroked my hair. Forcing myself to regain some composure, I told him how much I admired his love for, and relationship with, Christ.

"I'm sure you heard the saying 'I can't brag about my love of Jesus because I fail Him every day, but I can brag about His love for me because *it* never fails.' Well, it's true. When I was growing up, I loved playing baseball. My entire life was built around me becoming a professional baseball player, and as far as plans went, I was on my way. At the end of my senior year of high school, I started feeling off, and I just didn't have my usual drive. My mom, being the worrywart she is, took me to the doctor, and a week later, I received four phone calls—three from my top-choice colleges, offering me a full ride, completely free and clear to play ball for their schools, and the fourth saying I had leukemia, and I needed to be aggressive with my treatment, or I wouldn't make it. I went in to the hospital thinking, 'Hey, I'll beat this thing and be back in the game in no time.' And I actually did, in a sense. I responded well to the chemo at first, got to ring the remission bell after six months of treatment, but three months later, it was back and much worse than the first time around. That's when I got angry with God.

"I screamed at the top of my lungs from the roof of the hospital, asking God why He had forsaken me. And then I cried until I could no longer stand because I didn't want to die. I wasn't ready. At that moment, at my weakest point, I begged God to save me. The next year, I spent in His Word pretty much all the time. And in His Word, I realized He had been right beside me all along…and He had saved me. Even if I lost my battle to cancer, I knew I was saved. Once I received a bone marrow transplant and was told I was going to make it, I gave all aspects of my life over to Him completely and knew I wanted nothing more than to share my love of Christ with whomever God put in my life." As Luke relived the events that led to his ultimate redemption (stroking my hair and kissing my head in between thoughts), I realized that he, too, lost a future he had planned his whole life around. But instead of holding onto his anger and shutting down, he allowed it to grow him into the man he was now.

"You think there's hope for me?" I asked, keeping my head down, afraid to look him in the eyes.

"In what sense?" he pushed, kissing my temple once again.

"You and I are similar in a way…You lost your career, and I lost a person, but either way, we both planned for something completely different and had it taken from us. You grew from it, and I—well, I failed my lesson," I confessed and felt myself begin to tense up.

He must have sensed the change in my body because Luke pulled me closer and rubbed my arm, while he covered my hands that were in my lap with his free hand and squeezed.

"You haven't failed yet. You're still here. Many are the plans in a person's heart, but it is the Lord's purpose that prevails, Proverbs 19:21. While we may not have gotten what we had planned, God knew what was going to happen all along. There's a bigger picture, and until we willingly find and accept our purpose in God's master plan, sometimes He has to close doors, forcing us to make a change," Luke elucidated. For the first time, God's words and Christopher's death took on a different meaning.

"I have a hard time seeing God as anything more than a ruler who is harsh with His punishments," I confessed shamefully.

"Well, that's because you need to forget what you've been taught and open your Bible so you can read for yourself His love story that was written for you. Liz, whether you accept what Jesus has already done for you or not as the ultimate truth, it doesn't change the fact that it *has* happened. The only thing not accepting the truth does is it prevents you from being able to receive God's healing. It prevents you from the freedom that Jesus is waiting for you to claim." He shifted his body so that we were now facing one another and asked me to pray with him. Before I could answer, he took both of my hands into his and petitioned our heavenly Father on my behalf.

"Merciful and loving Savior, I come to You asking for Your healing for Elizabeth. Help her to see that in You, her burden is light, for You have already defeated the world. You already won this very battle for her. Help her embrace the truth that it's not too late. Thank You for knowing what's ultimately best for us and for bringing her into my life as part of Your perfect plan. Help us together bring glory to Your name, with the help of the Holy Spirit. Amen," he finished.

Then he pulled me tightly into his arms and held me for a moment before saying it was time for him to go. Right before he stepped out of the front door, he told me to look up Psalm 91:4 and added, "Let Him heal you, Liz." I stood at the door and watched him through my window until he was no longer in sight.

I climbed into bed and opened my Bible to the verse Luke shared with me and read: "*He will cover you with his feathers and under his wings you will find refuge.*" I fell asleep that night letting Psalm 91:4 be my ultimate prayer.

*****

For the first time in a long time, I was glad it was Friday. Apart from it being the last workday of the week, Fridays at Hillside were usually easy. And I needed easy, as my mind was lost, floating around aimlessly in the land of Luke.

After I woke up the children, I went into the kitchen and began making breakfast. I grabbed my phone, sending Lucas a text when I noticed that somehow, some way, yesterday, he and the children packed three separate lunches for the day. Each of the brown paper bags had our names on them and donned pictures drawn by the kids for decoration.

> *Good morning & TY. Because of you, I'm sitting & sipping my coffee instead of gulping it down. How did you find time to sneak this in?*

I sent the message and attached a picture of the bagged lunches.

> *You're welcome. The three of us got your back. Enjoy your coffee and have a great day.* 😘

Once again, I was needed in the office with Grace, and since Lucas and I had been texting all morning, I was more than okay with not having to teach a class. Grace caught me smiling a few times, and her face lit up.

"Okay, what gives? You've been on cloud nine over there for hours. Now spill," she chided, noticing the change in my behavior. Before I could answer her, the office phone rang. I quickly sent a text asking Luke what his plans were for the night once I finished with the call.

> *I have a baseball game. Will you come and cheer me on?*

Delighted by the thought of being able to witness Luke in yet another one of his comfort zones, I playfully goaded:

Be still my heart, say it isn't so…R U for real? 😮

I guess you're not into church baseball with a has-been ball-player-turned-preacher, trying to live out his glory days, huh? After then? When I'm all stinky and safe?

He replied, causing my heart to sink a little at the thought of him misunderstanding me and wanting nothing more than to assure him I was only joking.

JK, I'd love to go. As long as you don't mind a couple of tagalongs? & U=SAFE? Not a chance ❤

"Hey, Grace," I called over to my friend in a singsong voice after waiting for her to finish with her phone call.

"What's the deal with church baseball?" I asked, wanting as many details as she had to give. She explained how it used to just be a few of the local churches looking to have some fun over a friendly game of ball until about five years ago, when Lucas joined. And a few, well, they still have fun, but there are now more teams, and it is definitely more competitive.

"It's sort of a big deal around here. There's even a championship game at the end of the year. FCC won the first three years, going undefeated each season. And then one of Lucas's high school buddies from a church in Highland came up, giving 'em a run for their money. Ended up taking the trophy last year. It's all in good fun, but Lucas is on a mission to get that trophy back. He never was big on losing when it comes to baseball," Grace explained, and I didn't have a hard time believing that Luke didn't handle in things he's passionate about defeat well, not for a second.

"Pretty much college football in Texas then? Got it! Sounds like fun," I admitted out loud, while I tried to figure out if Riley and Chris would make it through nine innings of a ball game.

"I take it you'll be going to tonight's game?" Grace offered, more as a statement than an actual question. "There'll be lots of people there, kids too. It's always a good time. I'm glad you're going, and I'm sure Lucas will be too," she added with an approving grin that rivaled the way I was feeling inside.

*****

After work, I picked up my children from aftercare. I couldn't help but daydream about seeing Luke in a baseball uniform, being able to get a glimpse of what life was like for him when he was living his one-time dream. It was captivating for me, watching him passionately share his life in ministry. And I looked forward to seeing this other part of Lucas, which held a significant place in his heart as well.

Chris and Riley couldn't wait to go and watch Woo-cas play baseball. They barely afforded me the opportunity to get myself as ready as I wanted to before Luke was outside in the driveway, honking his horn. I went outside so I could get directions to the field when I noticed Luke taking the car seats from my car and putting them into his truck.

"I figured we could go together if that's alright with you," he called out while he fastened the seats securely in the back seat of his truck. My two little monsters were already at his side, waiting for him to help them get in.

"As if I could refuse," I answered, playfully giving him a hard time. And if there was any chance of me saying *no, it* was lost completely when he stood up in his uniform, came up beside me, and winked while sporting one of his heart-stopping Lucas smiles.

"You look amazing. This works for you," he said as he tugged playfully on my ponytail before leaning in his truck, turning back toward me, then placing a baseball cap on my head. "Perfect," he added. Then he pulled me in for a quick hug and placed a kiss on the top of the hat he just put on my head.

Thankful it was still bright enough on the drive over to the field that I needed my sunglasses, I took advantage of the opportunity to look in amazement at the incredibly sexy man sitting next to me. He sang along to the music that was playing in his truck, while he stroked my knee, occasionally tapping the inside of my leg with his hand along with the beat of the song. As I listened to him sing and witnessed the sheer certainty he possessed, I smiled to myself. *This man is always in his element*, I thought.

He must have caught one of my many smiles from the corner of his eye, because at one point, he turned to me, lifted his shades, winked, and smiled back just as we pulled into the parking lot. His teammates, along with their families, were already there and getting out of their vehicles while greeting one another. All ready for that night's game.

"Hey there, Lucas. You ready to win this one tonight?" Big Mike, as he was referred to, more to do with the fact that he was a senior than the size of him (even though he was a pretty solid man), also April's husband, greeted Lucas as he slapped him on his back and then proceeded to address me and the children.

"Good to see you, Elizabeth. I'm glad Lucas has yet another person to add to his cheering section. Maybe he will manage to pull off a long-overdue home run for ya," he teased. The two of them laughed. As Luke mumbled a reply to his teammate, he worked on getting Riley out of his truck and carried her along with his baseball gear. They waited in front of the truck for Chris and me, then the four of us walked along with the rest of the team, and I couldn't help but feel like we belonged there.

Once we got to the stands, Lucas sat Riley down on the third-row bleacher and knelt down to whisper something in Chris' ear. They both laughed after Chris nodded a big *yes* before joining his sister. To my surprise, Luke pulled me toward him and quickly pecked me right on my lips and then ran to join the rest of his team in the dugout. I stared after him, stunned by his kiss, licked my lips as I watched him run off in his tight pants, revealing his perfect backside, and I smiled.

A bunch of delighted smirks and inquiring minds were quick to ask for the details they knew were there. In that moment, Lucas declared us 'something' by offering a public display of affection in front of his family, friends, and what looked to be a good portion of FCC's congregation. The only thing I cared about was what my three-year-old children thought, so I bent down and asked Chris if he was okay?

"Yup! He asked if he could kiss you, Momma," he said, and I hugged him tightly, as Riley made her way over to her friend Marybeth, as if nothing happened. *Thank goodness they are only three!*

Choosing to sit a little lower in the stands so I could keep my eye on Riley and Chris while they played with their friends, I was warmly surprised by all the people who moved from where they were already sitting so they could come and join me. Grace and Lynn came down almost immediately. Both kissed me, and then the children, hello but moved back to their seats when the inquiring minds started to press for information about Luke's kiss. I was saved by the bell (so to speak) when Beth answered for me.

"Come on, are you really shocked? She's perfect for Luke, and those teeny tots of hers sweeten the deal. It wasn't a matter of *if.* It was a matter of *when,*" she rattled off nonchalantly, as if anyone who couldn't see how Luke and I made sense was utterly hopeless.

"I think it's great. Oh, hon, he is so, umm… good for you," April added, sitting down on the bleacher right in front of me and then leaning in and up to hug me as she nodded her approval.

Everything settled down once the game began, and I was thankful for the focus to shift its attention off of me. As soon as the first pitch was thrown, it was as if nothing happened at all, and I was perfectly content with that.

Luke played third base, and being here, watching him and cheering him on, was amazing. The fluency and precision his body executed during each play clearly showcased his gift for the game as well as it revealed the many hours and years of sweat, passion, and determination he poured into fine-tuning his skills through practice and hard work. It was like having a window into the past, showing me what life was like for Luke when he was younger. Or maybe even a glimpse of what the future would have been if he had played professional ball instead of making his love of Christ his career choice.

As focused as he was in the game in between plays, Lucas stole my heart (the way he always did) whenever he'd flashed me a smile or winked my way.

"Okay, Lucas, now you're just showing off," playful chiding came from who I presumed to be his friend from school, who now was pitching for the other team. When it was Luke's time up at bat, he hit the ball out of the park, but it ended up going out of bounds. Riley and Chris stood at the fence and cheered along with the rest of the crowd each time Luke went up to bat.

The bases were loaded into Luke's final up at bat, and they were down by two runs. The supporting chants from the people all around me had my nerves in a tight wad, as I, too, cheered for Luke. When the ball reached his zone, Luke swung with all he had and ended up getting a triple, sending in three runs for his team and ultimately winning the game. The excitement was intoxicating. And seeing Luke's eyes fix on me, as if I was the only person around as he rounded the bases before being stalled on third, left me smiling from the inside out. Not sure how it was even possible; he found a way to make my smile to grow even larger when the game ended after the next batter was out. Lucas came to the other side of the fence on his way to the dugout, scooped up Riley into his arms, and put Chris on his shoulders as he lined up with his teammates and shook hands with the opposing team for what was truly a good game. Together, the teams formed a circle and ended with a word of prayer, just as they had before the game began.

I couldn't help but become the aggressor when he reached me at the bleachers. I wrapped my arms around him and kissed him like he had so easily done to me each time before. In that moment, I allowed myself the freedom to not think but bask in the moment there with Luke until the giggles from my little ones snapped me back into reality with a smile. When I opened my eyes, the look on Luke's face stole from within me whatever words I had planned to say. This man, holding my children, was now a very important part of my life, and it felt fearfully fantastic!

Chapter 14

I was already in an exceptionally favorable mood after winning that night's game. But being kissed out of the blue by Elizabeth definitely brought things up a notch. I could barely believe that this stunning woman beside me was now somehow mine when just a short time ago, I hadn't pictured myself wanting to share my life with anyone. I was more than willing to dedicate my entire life, and all aspects of it, to Christ and Christ alone—and I had done just that. Yet in walked Elizabeth, and everything I ever thought I knew about my future was gone. Her returned kiss just confirmed that she was more than willing to give us a try and wasn't too intimidated by the kiss I gave her, publicly declaring my feelings before the game. As far as I was concerned, her kissing me back was the only thing I needed to fully free myself. No longer would I be holding anything back between the two of us while trusting in God's complete control throughout our entire relationship.

I was thankful for the offer my Aunt Grace supplied when she said she'd take Riley and Chris home so Liz and I could go out with the team. But I changed the plans for the night and said, "Ice cream first for everyone! On me," which scored me a bunch of squeals from all the happy children and some moderately unhappy groans from their parents, who were most likely concerned with the sugar rush they'd be dealing with after the ice cream.

"Thanks, Aunt Grace. Maybe we will take you up on that offer later, if Elizabeth agrees to come," I countered, to which my aunt happily nodded. We made our way to our vehicles, all in good spirits, and mine the best, as Elizabeth held my free hand and carried my bag as I carried her children.

"I told you, you weren't safe," Liz taunted after we strapped the kids into their car seats. In response, I brought her up against my truck and kissed her once again. Holding her still with my body while pressing her into the side of my truck, the two of us easily forgot that we had an audience.

"Bring it down a notch, Lucas. There are children all around," my mother's teasing snapped me back to reality as she scorned me with a grin, letting on that her statement was only half serious.

"Yes, ma'am," I answered and snuck one quick peck on Elizabeth's perfect lips before her face became reddened with blush.

"Even stinky," she whispered where only I could hear, then she climbed up into my truck as my friends all catcalled their approval. I smiled while I thanked God for giving me Elizabeth before I climbed into my truck to get some ice cream.

"I hope you aren't planning on a repeat from the other night, Lucas," Elizabeth tried to warn, but her face had a new ease to it, and her eyes seemed a little lighter.

"I wouldn't dare, sugar...You're sweet enough," I assured, offering a promise of my intentions, and I winked because I knew each time I did, she smiled.

* * * * *

When we arrived at the Twistee Freeze, an ice cream shop in the center of town, shaped like a giant ice cream cone itself with twinkling lights as sprinkles on the roof and all, the feeling of sheer contentment washed over me, as all my loved ones from my church family came together to celebrate. More than just a victory on the ball field but the love we had been gifted by sharing our lives with one another. Before the orders were placed, we joined hands and gave thanks to our heavenly Father for all of His blessings. I excused myself from Elizabeth and went to speak with the manager, letting the young woman know I would be taking care of everything, covering the cost for our group. On my way back, I was met with high fives from the little ones, more than satisfied with their ice cream treats. I easily joined in on the recaps and highlights from the game with my teammates and our devoted fans. I found myself seeking out a glimpse of Liz and the kids every so often and was comforted by the way she was accepted completely by each of my loved ones.

Riley and Chris were with Marybeth and Mikey, playing on the metal climbing apparatus that was set up for the children. At the table nearby, Liz was sitting between my parents. My mother's arm was wrapped around her shoulders, my sisters next to them on the left. Brian, Ashley, and Aunt Grace were seated on her right. While Liz was chatting effortlessly with my father before, they all erupted in rapturous laughter.

"What did I miss?" I asked, but it didn't even matter because the moment itself was perfect without the need for an explanation.

Pulling one of my moves out and throwing it my way, Elizabeth winked, flashing the most perfect grin on her face as she pulled her bottom lip between her teeth, while my dad teased, "Leave him hanging. Let him sweat a little," before winking at her and standing so I could take his seat.

After all were finished with our ice cream, and the conversations had naturally come to an end, I settled the tab as the rest of the group got ready to leave. Usually, the plan was to go to out for some drinks and socialize with the team (like we had done after each game the past five years). But that night, it didn't matter to me what I did as long as Elizabeth was by my side.

* * * * *

When I got to where Elizabeth was standing with my Aunt Grace beside my truck, the kids were already strapped into their car seats. Liz was waiting for me to confirm what our next plans were for the night and wanted to know if we needed Grace to watch Riley and Chris. I left the decision up to her, and she happily agreed to go out, taking my Aunt Grace up on her offer to watch the kids. We brought Riley and Chris home, and I was thankful I thought ahead to bring a change of clothes. Elizabeth led me to her bathroom and showed me where all the things were that I needed to shower. She breathed in a deep breath, turned away, and rejoined the party of three (Riley, Chris, and Grace) in the living room, while I got ready. Once I finished showering and getting dressed, I went out to the living room, surprised by how fast kids can fall asleep. Then Liz and I headed out to meet our friends at Benny's.

Everything was the same as far as postbaseball celebrating went. Except for the fact, I had the most beautiful girl in the world right there beside me, sharing in something that was special to me. The guys all teased one another while taking turns poorly singing karaoke, partially caused by their alcohol consumption, and the other part just *boys being boys*. I, myself, am not a drinker, never have been, apart from the occasional beer once in a while. But I never saw a problem with adults drinking responsibly, as long as they didn't get too carried away. At the bar, I ordered myself my favorite, a Blue Moon with an orange slice, for my first drink, and the rest of the night, I'd be sticking to good ole Pepsi on the rocks. After all my teammates and some of their wives and girlfriends had a turn playing rock star, I asked Elizabeth what she was going to sing. Before I finished getting my words out completely, she whipped her head my way, fiercely shaking it as fear literally consumed her, causing her body to become stiff as a board.

"No, no, no. I can't sing. I have the worst stage fright *ever*, not going to happen!" she confessed, as her body trembled, pleading silently with her stare not to push her on this. I rubbed her arms, assuring her it was okay, even though a part of me found it to be quite adorable that just the thought of singing terrified her. Kissing the top of her head, I wrapped my arms around her, holding her close as I began leading our bodies to move in time with the beat, hoping that if we danced, it would help cause enough of a distraction and calm her nerves. The rest of the night, Liz and I spent our time dancing, talking, and laughing, surrounded by our friends. All the events of the day led me to realize Elizabeth slipped so perfectly into all parts of my life effortlessly, causing me to smile.

It was a few minutes before midnight when Luke and I finally got home from Benny's. Once we pulled into my driveway, I was torn between saying goodbye (not wanting this perfect night to end) and going to bed so I could dream about all things *Luke*. I was pleasantly surprised when Luke not only walked me to my door but also came in to collect his things from my room and to say goodnight to his aunt and thanked her as well. After Grace assured me the kids were fine and hadn't woken up since they went down for the night, she hugged us both and left, closing the door behind her.

Unsure of what to do next, I went into the kitchen and offered Luke a drink. He declined, but he picked up my iPod from the counter and asked if I minded if he had a look. I nodded, offering my approval. After he swiped his finger over the many songs, he pressed play on the one I had been listening to last, and I was met with the most electrifying grin that lit up his already-ridiculously handsome face.

"I would have never placed you as a Bob Marley kind of girl," he uttered smoothly as he adjusted the volume and hit play. Gliding right up to me, smile still on his face, and then gracefully pulled me into his arms.

My heart began to race, and my nerves became a jumbled mess from our closeness; trying my best to play it cool, I questioned, "What did you think I'd have then?"

"Country for sure, Christian pop, maybe even rock, but not for a second, reggae." He then spun me around, brought me back into his embrace, leading me as we danced to "Turn Your Lights Down Low."

He sang the words right into my ear. Just before the song was about to end, he kissed me. Luke had the ability to take the world around me and make it all somehow just disappear. In that moment, there was no kitchen, no children, just me and this six-foot-four-inch rock-solid man with his arms around me, kissing me passionately, while he held the nape of my neck with his one hand and grasped my lower back pulling me against him with his other. I was disoriented when our kiss ended and felt myself pulling my lips inward with my tongue. My eyes were still unfocused, and my breath was barely there.

"Breathe, beautiful," he reminded me. Then he kissed me on the top of my head, thanked me for what he called the perfect night, and said goodbye, all while I was still lost and frozen in the center of my kitchen.

* * * * *

Things between Lucas and I seemed to fall right into place. We made time for one another often, and on the days when we couldn't get together, we spent our time either texting or talking on the phone.

About six weeks into our relationship, Luke ended up spending the entire day with Riley, Chris, and me. Once we finished putting the kids down for the night and were sitting together on the couch in my living room, he officially said the words *I love you*. Totally unsure why those words induced an unprepared panic to well up inside me, I went rigid.

"What happened? What just brought this on, Liz? It couldn't be the *love* word! You have to know that I love you," he pleaded, clearly afraid he did something wrong.

"I don't know. I guess, I just…I don't know," I tried explaining. But I couldn't even figure out what I was feeling myself, let alone trying to figure out how to put it into words to share it with him.

"Well, you need to forget whatever reasons you're trying to come up with, reasons why this isn't going to work, Liz. We are past that. The two of us—actually, all four of us—we work! I'm not going anywhere, and…I love you. Focus on the one reason it is going to work. Because God put us together, and stop…don't go there!" he pleaded, sensing that I just brought my brokenness over Christopher back into my mind after being able to keep his memory and losing him at bay since I decided to give Lucas and me a chance.

"I know what you're thinking. That's not fair. I can't give you the reason why that happened, but don't let it come between us again. Trust in this… trust in us, please!" he begged and kissed me as if all we were and ever had a chance of being depended fully on this kiss. Who knows, maybe he was right.

After Lucas left that night, I found myself, for the first time since we became official, lying in my bed, holding my pillow tightly, and crying myself to sleep. I was too afraid that if I brought my heartache and fear to God, He still wouldn't fix it, and this time, I'd end up losing Luke for no other reason than my own brokenness.

* * * * *

The next morning, I brought the kids to school but ended up calling out of work, taking a personal day, knowing fully that I wouldn't have been able to focus on my job with all that was weighing on my heart and mind.

I was feeling lost again.

I'd given all I knew how to give. Trying my best to let Lucas in, up until that night, things were going great. I think the fact that everything *was* going so well was exactly what stirred up my subconscious, demanding that I deal with the issues I had repressed for so long now. I drove over to FCC, not even sure what I was looking for. A part of me figured if I found Luke, then I'd see if he could help me, not wanting to further push him away. But another part of me hoped that he wouldn't be there at all.

When I got into the office, I felt this overwhelming feeling of paranoia and fear. I was relieved when Beth wasn't sitting behind her desk, and Luke's door was closed. Forcing my way over to Pastor Barry's open door, I knocked on the wall near the doorframe to get his attention. Noticing that I wasn't my typical self, he stood up from his chair behind his desk and directed me to take a seat, while he walked over and closed the door behind us.

"Elizabeth, what's wrong? Are you okay?" he asked and handed me a cup of water from the water cooler next to his door. Unsure of where I was going to begin, I took a small sip from the cup, placed it beside me on the small side table, and asked when Lucas was supposed to be in.

"I'm not trying to be sneaky…I'm not even sure what I am doing here. I just need help, Pastor Barry, and I don't think it's fair to Luke…if…" I paused, completely uncertain what I was trying to say.

"Okay. It's okay you came to me. Lucas wouldn't be upset by it, I assure you, and we don't have to tell him what we talk about," he assured, trying his best to set my mind at ease.

"I trust Lucas completely, and I don't want him to think otherwise. I just don't think he can help with this…A part of me, no matter how happy he makes me, just feels like this isn't real. The more time I spend with him, the more time he is with the kids… Pastor Barry…I can't lose him!" I said and cried with everything I had in me. Pastor Barry came over with the box of tissues from his desk, and after he handed them to me, he pulled me into his arms and hugged me as I let out years of pain.

"You know, Elizabeth, what you're feeling makes complete sense. You have never dealt with your loss," he offered as a way of rationalizing my fear.

"But, I have. I've moved away from all I ever knew. I have done everything I can to make sure my children have a good life when I didn't even ask for this life." I huffed as I wiped away my tears and took another sip from my cup of water.

"That's not dealing. That's the complete opposite. What you did was run, and I am glad you did because it led you here. But you are hurting, and until you can face that hurt head-on, no one, not even Lucas, is going to be able to fix things for you. I'm sure that having the proverbial rug that was your life plans ripped out from under you without warning was tough. I wouldn't be surprised at all if you have unresolved anger issues with not only the father of your children but God as well." Something in the way he said it caused the anger inside me to bubble up, threatening to blow if I gave it even a hint of thought. Luke had said similar things to me before about my anger, but right now, with Pastor Barry, it was different. As much as being around Luke set my every nerve to hypersensitive mode, he also had a calming effect somehow, especially when he spoke about God.

I tried to keep a lid on my anger, but when Pastor Barry went on about God loving me and never leaving me alone, I lost the ability to contain it any longer.

"Yeah, I know God never leaves us. He knows what's best…blah, blah, blah, but say what you will… He took Christopher from me and left me alone to raise the twins. I may have messed up and gotten pregnant, but I didn't ask to be a single mother. Now I have Luke, and just when I finally caved and allowed myself to see a future with him, God will take him away too!" I yelled, shocked by my rage and a bit fearful of what had been set in place now that I admitted to myself just how angry I was with God. For a moment, I wished I hadn't come. Something was happening inside of me, and unless I somehow faced it, I'd be the one who would end up pushing Lucas and everyone that I loved away this time. Not God.

So I listened as Pastor Barry continued, "That's true. You did lose Christopher, but you are not alone. I am sitting right here. Then there's Grace and Beth.

There's Deena and April. I can keep naming people, but I think you get the point. And then there is Lucas, right there beside you. Patiently waiting for you to let him in. Each one of us is willing to not only carry some of the weight for you, but we are even willing to help you unpack your bags so they won't have to be so heavy anymore. It sounds to me like you need to give God all of your anger so you can just see how *not* alone you are. You are surrounded by people who love you. Now you need to learn to love yourself by forgiving yourself already. Who cares that you made a mistake years ago? The past is the past, and nothing you do now will change it—God doesn't care. He isn't even thinking about that moment anymore, I assure you! And He doesn't because you know His Son, Jesus, already washed you clean the minute you asked for His forgiveness the first time years ago, and every day since, but you don't have to keep asking.

"Each day you carry this burden on your shoulders, God doesn't understand why. As far as the east is from the west, He has removed your transgressions. He forgot them! He carries no record, Elizabeth. The fact that you are not stepping away from the chains that no longer bind you is the same as saying all Jesus accomplished on the cross, all the sin He died for, yours, was too much for Him. Satan is the one that throws you and Christopher in your face. But you need to take that power away from him because he's a liar, and none of it's true! What God sees when He looks at you is His beautiful daughter, with whom He is completely in love with. He sees you trying your best and struggling, so He sent a family of people to help you. But instead of letting us help, you do all you can to push us away because you see imperfection and shame in yourself. But God sees perfection when He looks at you because of His Son," Pastor Wright passionately explained, no longer allowing me to run from the truth of the gospel of our Lord and Savior, Jesus Christ.

"Will you accept all that Christ has already done for you now, Elizabeth? Will you let Him finally heal you? Or are you going to keep on living your life as if your sin was too much for Him to conquer?" he asked.

As soon as I said yes, wanting more than anything to let my pain go and finally handing it over to the only One that could release me from it, Barry grabbed my hands and prayed, "Father, thank You! You just heard Your beautiful daughter finally offer her brokenness to You so You can heal her. Heal her, Lord. Take the pieces of her heart that were broken when she lost Christopher and help her cherish the love that was once there, forgetting the pain and letting go of the anger. Help her to truly see all the people You have given her so she doesn't have to feel so alone like she does at times. Help her let go of any guilt or fear Satan tries to throw her way so she can learn to love again. In Jesus's name I pray, amen."

* * * * *

Wiping the last tear from my cheek, I already felt as if my load was miraculously a little lighter. I thanked Barry for everything he shared with me before going home and opening my Bible. I fell asleep for an hour after spending much-needed time with the Lord, waking up close to lunchtime and desperately wanting to see Luke. He answered right away when I called and sounded relieved when he heard the tone in my voice.

"I'm fine, Luke, really. I went to talk to Pastor Barry this morning, and then I just spent time with God, and I feel—I don't know…but I feel different, if that makes any sense?" I declared, wishing he could feel what I was feeling for himself. I could hear the relief in Luke's voice when I told him about my morning. Apparently, he had been worried about me since he left the night before and wasn't sure what to do. He was torn between giving me space and forcing me to deal with my feelings. Thankfully, everything was going to be okay. More than okay, things between Luke and I now had a real chance. I asked him if he was free to have lunch, and he let me know he'd be right over.

I rushed into my bedroom, changed, and put on some makeup as fast I could before Luke arrived. As he pulled into the driveway, I ran out the door and jumped right into his truck before he could get out to get me.

"Hey there, beautiful," he greeted me, calling me beautiful as if it were my name. The relief when his eyes locked onto mine in his now-smoldering gaze sent a shiver down my spine.

I leaned over, grabbed both sides of his face in my hands, and declared my love for him.

"I love you, Lucas Andrew Walker, and I am sorry I have been so…frustratin'." Then I kissed him with everything I had in me, finally breaking free from the chains of my past that, until that moment, were holding me back. After our kiss ended, I sat back in my seat, buckled my seat belt, and stared at the man I knew I wanted to spend the rest of my life with.

Can I start this part with a *yeehaw*? Because seriously, that's about where I'm at right now. For real, though.

God chose *that* morning to answer my prayers for Elizabeth's heart to be healed from the past, and as I sat there listening to her share with me all that took place already, I gave Him thanks. As she opened up about how God was working in her life, she mentioned that a part of her struggled with the fact that she hadn't come to me with everything. Even though she was in the middle of a major life change, a part of her worried my feelings were hurt that she went to Barry. Truthfully, I assured her that even her going to my colleague was all part of God's plan. It became even clearer to me, as time with Elizabeth went on, that I wasn't the one meant to be used for that particular step in her life. I reminded her that in the past, the same message that had now been revealed to her had come up between us before, but she wasn't ready to receive it then. God knew all along when she would be ready. Just as God knew whom He was going to call on to be there for her as she gave her past over to Him completely, allowing Christ's forgiveness to fully break her chains. I was thrilled beyond words that she had finally gotten there.

I wasn't at all upset that it wasn't me. In truth, I knew wholeheartedly it wouldn't have worked if it came from me. I was incapable of breaking her with the tough love she needed to hear, and without it, she'd still be a prisoner, locked in chains that she already held the key to. However, I found it cute that she shared her unnecessary guilt about going to Pastor Wright with me. I already knew Liz was in his office when I showed up at church and heard her voice from behind his closed door. Once I realized she was upset, a part of me wanted to break down the door and fix whatever was causing the hurt for her, but I left, trying my best to give her privacy. I fell to my knees right outside the church's front door. And I prayed. I placed my face to the ground, praying for the situation taking place between our heavenly Father, my trusted colleague and friend, and the woman I loved. While in my prone position at my Father's feet, He allowed me to feel the presence of an army of saints as they surrounded us, and God's peace washed over me, filling my heart.

Liz and I ended up having lunch with one another, and once we finished, we decided to take a walk. We took our time, holding each other's hand as we leisurely strolled down the path in the park close to her house, enjoying our alone time before she had to pick up Chris and Riley from aftercare. When it was time for her to go, I, too, had to be on my way; I was needed at the church for a business meeting. I drove her home so she could get her car, completely content with the way things fell into place and hopeful for our future. We said goodbye in her driveway, planning not to see each other again until the next day.

"Call me later if you get the chance," she said as a bashful smile began lighting up her face.

"Always, beautiful. Talk to you soon," I answered, wanting to assure her that as long as it was within my will to do so, I'd always make time for her.

* * * * *

I'll have to assume the business meeting at the church went well, since people calmly spoke to one another around me. And everyone seemed somewhat pleased with whatever was decided. As far as knowing what took place, I couldn't tell you. My body was present, but my mind was off, appreciating that Liz was finally beginning to heal the only way that would work—God's way. I sat there next to Barry and thought about how Liz's face lit up as she shared with me the intimacy she experienced with God. Having experienced it for myself multiple times, I was elated that she, too, had her own personal encounter. And she willingly shared the intimate details that took place with me.

"I take it from your distraction at the meeting tonight, you've spoken with Elizabeth?" Barry asked as we cleaned up the conference room after the meeting.

"Yes, sorry about that. Please let me say *thank you* for your willingness to be His hands and feet, just as she needed. Barry, it's amazing seeing her appear so much lighter."

"No need to apologize. You didn't miss much here. What you missed you can read in the minutes. Thank God for Beth. As far as this morning, I'm just thankful she trusted me enough to come in. Praise

God for how He works! It's all part of His plan, my brother," he humbly conceded. The truth was right there in black and white, and it *was* all a part of God's perfect plan. But it was beyond exceptional that He was allowing me to be a part of it. There is nothing greater than being able to witness a person's life rise from the ashes because they finally have given themselves to Christ. Scratch that—the only thing greater is when that person is a person you love.

Barry and I spent the next hour discussing matters regarding the church, life in general, and my relationship with Elizabeth.

"How are things going between the two of you? It seems from the outside looking in that things are good, and the little ones took to you completely."

The two of us laughed at the thought, recalling one Sunday when Elizabeth and the twins came to a Saturday night service. It was a change for them, seeing as they usually attended on Sundays. Riley and Chris weren't altogether thrilled with the idea of not being able to go to their Sunday school class. So as Liz was trying to get them downstairs to sign them in to the nursery instead, the two broke away, running in opposite directions. Chris headed into the kitchen, hoping he'd find some goodies hidden in the cabinet, and Riley made it into the sanctuary, where she spotted me. Liz was mortified.

Her children were typically very well behaved, and that night was no different. Riley hadn't meant to act out. She just wanted to find me, and she had. Right before the service began, she came up, took the seat beside me, front and center, obviously lacking her mother's crippling stage fright. To be honest, even if the service had already started, I wouldn't have cared. The fact that she came to find me was touching, and those who were there to witness it that night thought so too. Riley pleaded with her mother to let her stay upstairs for the church service, insisting that she "Needed to wissen to Woo-cas do church." At Riley's insistence, the two of them sat in the front row, which, of course, caused me to smile throughout the entire sermon.

"Things are going great. I honestly feel as if I have known her all of my life. It's only been a few months, but, Barry…I'm ready. I am all in. Even though *I've* been all in since day one, I am really all in! I don't like when we have to part ways each night, and I can't stand missing things with the children when I am not there. I'm planning to ask her if she will allow me to keep the kids after their Head Start program one day. I want to ask them if they'd be okay with their mom and me getting married. Sure, it may seem too fast to some, but I don't want to waste any more time." As I confessed my future intentions regarding Liz, I knew I could count on Barry for support. And I took comfort knowing that he would continue to lift our relationship up in prayer.

"Don't let anyone tell you how to live your life, apart from God. The two of you have spent the majority of your lives planning and waiting for things that didn't end up happening at all. I don't see how waiting now will prove anything if you already know this is God's plan. I believe He put you both together, and no man, or opinion of man, matters," Barry agreed. Together we prayed for the wisdom to know when the time would be right for me to take the next step with Elizabeth.

* * * * *

After finishing up at the church, I was missing Liz and the twins so much that I decided to drop by unannounced after I left, hoping to catch them right at bedtime. When I pulled into the drive and turned off the engine of my truck, I could clearly see through the living room's open curtains. Lingering in my truck for a few moments, I was captivated by the scene unfolding between Liz and the kids, who were completely unaware of my presence.

Elizabeth was strumming on Riley's little pink ukulele as the three of them danced and twirled around, singing. I couldn't hear which song it was from inside my truck, but thankfully, when I got to the door of the house, it all became clear. I stood on the porch, not wanting the moment to end. I had never heard Elizabeth sing before, and she sounded perfect. The way she belted out the words to "Three Little Birds" (another Marley tune for my reggae girl), leading Riley and Chris into the chorus, was euphoric. I tried my best to be as quiet as I could as I snuck inside, but the three noticed my arrival, and sadly, Liz stopped dead in her tracks. Her face reddened from embarrassment, unsure if I had heard her, but the look in her eyes said she was still happy I had come.

Together, we prayed with the children and put them to bed. Once we were back in the living room, I wrapped my arms around her from behind, lifted her off the ground, and swung her in a circle as I gave her a little grief.

"You've been holding out on me, Ms. Strutton. You *can* sing!" Liz wiggled and giggled, trying her best to break free from my grip.

"I can't believe you heard me, Lucas! But I am glad you came. I missed you," she said, and I put her back on the ground, turned her to face me, and hugged her tightly, savoring the feel of her in my arms and the way she hugged me back.

"I hope you will sing for me again, and I missed you, too, beautiful. I didn't want to go to sleep without kissing you and the kids good night," I admitted, totally unashamed of my needs. Then I placed a kiss on the top of her head, just like I always did.

"What are we going to do about that, huh, Lucas? We're together so much that when we aren't, I spend all my time wishing we were," she confessed, going up on her tiptoes, trying to reach my lips for another kiss.

"Wonderful thing, isn't it?" I leaned down to give her a kiss before telling her goodbye for the night. I headed back home, where I could figure out just how I was going to ask her to spend the rest of her life with me.

* * * * *

Barry called me into his office later that week to discuss some concerns that had been brought to his attention by a few of the members from our church.

Taking the seat across from his desk, I listened while he uncomfortably shared complaints he received regarding my relationship with Elizabeth. He made it clear he didn't agree with their concerns but still had to share them with me regardless. I learned my actions made a handful of our older members uncomfortable. Recalling my declaration of remaining single at the time of my candidacy, they were now unhappy with the way "I couldn't seem to keep my hands off Elizabeth," causing them to feel as if I'd gone back on my promise and even questioned if my priorities were still in the right place.

"It's a small number of people, Lucas, but we can't just ignore it. A few unhappy people who feel as if they are being ignored can become tools for Satan to bring dissension into the church. I think it's best if we figure out how we should address the issue," Barry said. "Kind of offers proof—not that any was needed—that God has indeed blessed the two of you. Satan only rears his head when he is trying to prevent God's work."

I thought about what my friend/mentor had shared with me and tried putting myself into the shoes of our concerned parishioners before I offered my reply.

"It doesn't matter that my actions aren't going against God or even wrong for that matter. The issue is that my actions have offended people, regardless of my intentions. I'm not going to apologize for falling in love, Barry, and I know you aren't suggesting for me to. I would, however, like to arrange a meeting to address the ones willing to listen, offer my apologies for causing them to feel uncomfortable, and to reassure them that my priorities are still one and the same. Even though I now had Elizabeth by my side." I tried my best not to take these matters to heart, allowing Satan the foothold he so desperately wanted to have in me. Before the end of the evening, we had agreed to set something up in the morning. Barry sent out an email to the group of offended parishioners, offering to meet and further discuss their concerns.

I didn't get the chance to spend time with Liz and the kids that night like I hoped. Choosing instead, I spent much of my night in prayer, reading Scripture, and working on what I was going to say the next morning. When I went to sleep, I left my worries with God and trusted that no matter the outcome, His will would be done.

Chapter 17

I decided to make plans with my friends after Lucas called to let me know he needed to take care of some church-related issues, and he wouldn't be able to make it over after work like he planned to. As much as I enjoyed spending whatever time I had with Luke, sometimes it was nice to have some much-needed *girl time*. I found it refreshing being around people who understood the demands of motherhood and efficiently figured out how to work quality time into our playdates.

Accepting my invitation to get together, I spent the evening with Deena, April, and our four children. We met up at the local pizza place for dinner before heading over to my house, where our little ones happily entertained themselves while we mommas spent our time laughing and catching up on life with Lucas. My married friends were living vicariously through my whirlwind love affair with Luke.

As the three of us opened up about our relationships, I was reminded of just how much we didn't see of others, even our friends. The outward persona we allow people to see is just a tiny fraction of our innermost being. At times, I feel as if I'm just not enough, even when I am surrounded by people who genuinely care about me. All relationships have different sides to them that, other than the people involved, will never be revealed, and that's okay. But as I sat there, taking in all that my friends were willingly sharing, I felt a bit more *normal.* Sad as that may be. I clung to the advice that was being handed out. It was as if we were passing along our favorite recipes, the ones where time, love, mishaps, messes, and ample efforts from countless mistakes were poured in, transforming an otherwise standard dish into one of perfection.

"I think the most important thing is making sure that you never stop trying to impress one another. I really miss dating my husband. Mike and I seem to have no love life since Mikey was born, and it just stinks," April confessed.

"I agree. It isn't easy, but Jake and I try at least twice a month to have a date night, just so we don't become complacent, forgetting why we fell in love in the first place. April, let me keep Mikey overnight for you so you can go out with Big Mike this weekend. Seriously." Deena offered, clearly hoping her friend would at least think about it.

"I'm afraid, honestly. I just don't feel so hot anymore, you know? Never mind, neither of you would understand. You both look amazing, and I am all mom-bodied out over here," April conceded, clearly uncomfortable with the way she perceived herself.

"Oh, please, April, you are beautiful. I can't speak for Deena, but I have the same issues. A part of me is petrified of ever getting to a point where Lucas sees these stretch marks," I divulged, lifting my shirt enough to offer proof of my own insecurities as well. "I may look okay with clothes on, but not so much when I'm standing naked in all my motherly glory, especially when the lights are on."

"Both of you need to stop looking at yourselves as anything other than the beautiful mothers you are. I guess it helps that Jake makes sure I know that he loves me and my motherly badges of honor as well. I'm telling you, April, if you go out and spend some time with Mike alone, it will help you feel better about yourself. Not that I am saying we should need someone else to validate us, but it is what it is. Every woman wants to know the man in her life finds her attractive. We're only human, after all." Deena set in motion the plan of having Mikey spend the night later in the week so April and her husband could go out Saturday, then she turned her attention on me. "You are so stinking gorgeous. Lucas practically drools all over you, so stop being hard on yourself, Elizabeth."

"I can't believe he has never seen you naked. You two have been together awhile now, and Lucas can't keep his sex-deprived paws off of you. Obviously, Mike and I didn't wait until we were married before we did the deed. I couldn't have done it! I know I'm bad. Too late now! How in the world do you do it? Especially with Lucas?" April pried, nearly panting from the idea of squeezing some juicy details out of me.

"It isn't easy. Sometimes I don't know how he is so strong. I mean, don't get me wrong, I don't want to have sex until we are married, but you know…that doesn't mean it's not there in my mind sometimes. I'm glad we agree on the waiting thing and that he is so respectful, never pushing me or taking us someplace that makes it too tempting to back away from. But it's seriously frustrating sometimes when he stops kissing me, and then he just up and leaves. Later, after my hormones have time to calm down, I am thankful for his self-control, but definitely not in the moment. And that, my friends, is how Riley and Chris came to be." I chuckled, sharing the truths of life with my girlfriends, grateful that I finally had people I trusted and cared about that I could open up to.

The three of us continued, sharing with one another all the different things going on in our lives before calling it a night. When I went to bed, I was content with how things were going; and even though I was physically alone, and I missed Lucas, I still knew I was blessed with the life I had been given. Before I drifted off to sleep, I thanked God from the deepest part of my heart for all He had healed me from and all He gifted me.

Chapter 18

Barry set up the coffee urn and got everything ready to satisfy even the pickiest of coffee drinkers. For those who preferred something other than coffee, he put a new jug on top of the water cooler in the all-purpose room in the back of the church.

The people who came through the door didn't at all surprise me. And I was relieved. Figuring our differences in age and growing up at different times had more to do with how they felt than my relationship with Elizabeth itself. Once everyone was situated and settled in their seats, I stepped behind the small podium and offered up a silent prayer that God would lead me as I addressed His people who were seated before me.

"Good morning and welcome. I'd like to thank each of you for coming here and for sharing your concerns with Pastor Barry and me regarding my relationship with Elizabeth Strutton. While I am aware that my original stance of remaining single, as I had shared with each of you when you were considering my candidacy before prayerfully welcoming me to colead this church family, has indeed changed, my dedication to doing God's work and living my life as a representative of Faith Community Church hasn't change at all. As all of you here already know, I made the decision to put my faith before my personal life at a time when I thought that was what God was calling me to do. I was content with my decision, believing it to be the best for my life, as well as for those here in my church family. I never pictured anything else for myself until God brought Elizabeth and her children here to Faith Community and into my life. But we all know that even with the best intentions, we can set our plans as much as we'd like, but it is God who will direct each of our steps. I understand that many of you have concerns regarding my public displays of affection, and for that, I'm offering my sincere apology for offending you. I will not, however, apologize for falling in love with the woman God brought into my life. Even though I am not ashamed of any of the actions or ways I have chosen to show my love for her, I still feel that I should clear things up for any of you who are under the assumption that I'm living a sexually immoral life, which directly goes against the teachings found throughout the—" Abruptly stopping, I took the *speech* I worked on the night before, folded it in half, put it down, and stepped out from behind the podium before beginning again.

"I'm sorry, I can't continue reading that because that isn't who I am. I'm not the *read-your-speech* kind of guy. No offense at all to those of you here who may work that way. It just isn't me, and to continue that way feels dishonest. I vowed to God and myself to live by the will of God found in 1 Thessalonians 4:3–5, Colossians 3:5, 1 Peter 2:11, Galatians 5:19, and many more addressing our flesh and sexual immorality. More so, even when God placed me here to help lead His people on this journey, together with Christ, while on this earth. Before I met Elizabeth, I believed that I was being called to live a life of celibacy, and 2 Timothy 2:22, '*So flee youthful passions and pursue righteousness, faith, love, and peace, along with those who call on the Lord from a pure heart,*' was the scripture I clung to as my life goal and what I felt God was asking of me when He gave me a heart with a passion to serve.

"Once God placed Elizabeth in my life, I prayed and prayed. I spent hours on my knees, and in Scripture, making sure that it was not my flesh but indeed the will of God that I was acting upon. Then I went to my colleague and truest friend, Pastor Wright, and asked him to not only pray with me but to continue to lift the situation up to God in prayer, as we trusted Him to show me the way. I will assure you that although things between Elizabeth and me seem to be rather sudden and fast-paced, at no time during our relationship have Elizabeth and I done anything that would go against my faith and what I believe to be the ultimate truth, written in the Holy Scriptures. We have never spent the night with one another, and our physical intimacy has gone no further that what has been seen in public. I don't feel the need to hide my feelings for her when the two of us have placed our relationship in the hands of God and trust that what He has put together is for His greater good.

"God willing, soon we will commit our lives to one another before you, our church family, and our loved ones, as the teaching in Genesis 2:24 says, '*Therefore a man shall leave his father and mother and hold fast to his wife, and they shall become one flesh.*' That last part is a secret. I haven't popped the question yet, so please, keep that to yourselves until it becomes official. Rest assured, I do plan on asking soon," I announced with a grin.

"But back to the point. I ask that going further, you will all pray for me and my relationship, and if anything I do makes you feel uncomfortable, please trust that my door is always open, and I will be happy to pray with you and address any of your concerns. I can't help that I am overflowing with love for my godsent wife and can't always help myself from stealing a kiss. I hope you can tap into your love for one another and your own new beginnings, finding it in your hearts to forgive me and maybe even offer just a little leeway.

"May God bless each of you for your willingness to address the matters of your heart and for not harboring any ill will toward Elizabeth or myself. And most importantly, for not entertaining the hurtful act of gossiping, allowing Satan the chance to cause damage within our church family. I truly appreciate your time, your love, and your support. Thank you all for coming."

Once I finished, I made my way toward the back of the room, allowing people a chance to further discuss any manners that still may be weighing on their hearts, then I joined Barry by the table for some coffee. Barry nodded his approval and playfully gave me a little grief, asking if it was necessary for me to call him out on his written-out sermons. We both laughed, knowing that I meant no disrespect.

The outcome of the informal meeting was successful. My willingness to share my honest feelings, while also taking into consideration how each of them felt, provided us with a chance to see one another in a different light. Although we may still have slightly different views on things, God still is number 1. And once they were reassured that my dedication to my calling hadn't been skewed, I believe everyone felt more at ease.

* * * * *

Since the twins were currently attending the summer program at FCC, and I was one of their emergency contacts approved of signing them out, I decided to pick them up early to surprise Liz for lunch at Benny's, where she was currently working full-time during the summer. Surprised to see the three of us, Elizabeth happily seated us in her section and made sure she asked someone to watch over her tables, giving her the opportunity to join us. Knowing she'd approve, I let Liz know Chris and Riley were going to be spending the rest of the day with me instead of going back to the church.

Elizabeth easily agreed, completely unsuspecting of the grandiose plans I had for the three of us. Normally when I spent time with the kids during school hours, we'd go to the park, feed the chickens, pretty much whatever they wanted to do with their Woo-cas time, but today, I had other things set in motion.

After we finished eating lunch, and it was time for Liz to get back to work, the three of us each kissed her goodbye, letting her know we'd see her when she finished her shift.

With intentions of doing things properly, I drove over to my Aunt Grace's, where I planned to talk to my little buddies while we fed and played with the chickens, effectively killing two birds with one stone.

"So I have a question to ask you two. You know I love your momma, right?" I began, trying to gauge how it was going to go. Nodding their heads in unison, they waited for me to continue, while they tossed chicken feed on the ground.

"What do you think about me asking your momma to marry me? Would that be okay?" I threw out, knowing that if I took too long to get to the point, I would have lost them altogether.

"I guess so, Woo-cas," I got from a half-interested Riley, but Chris ended up answering with a question of his own.

"What does that mean?" he asked before looking up at me with the same-colored eyes as his mother, waiting for me to explain.

"Well, it means that if she says *yes*, we will all live together once we get married. Is it okay if I come and live with you and love you, Riley, and your momma forever, Chris?" That earned me a smile and a nod of his approval.

After playing in the barn and cleaning the chicken coop, I brought the children to the jewelry store with me to help me pick out a ring for their mother. Each one picked out which ring they thought she would like best. After narrowing it down to three different choices, I let the two pick which one we should buy. Thankfully, they agreed on the same one. On our way home, we stopped at the flower shop to pick up the 150 roses I ordered, one for each day Elizabeth had been in my life so far. We headed over to my parents' house, where my mother helped me prepare dinner, while my sisters entertained Riley and Chris, who helped set up all the flowers throughout my parents' living room.

I sent Liz a text telling her my parents invited us over for dinner and informed her that the kids and I were already there. Not long after I sent my text, she replied, letting me know she was on her way.

"I'm so excited, Lucas. Thank you so much for asking her here," my mother said as she hugged me. Just then, my Aunt Grace snuck in the back door.

My heart was pounding in my chest, more than ready to take this next step with the woman I loved, when Beth announced, "She's here!"

Chapter 19

I pulled into the driveway of Luke's parents' house, not able to deny the feeling of relief that I wasn't going to have to cook anything for dinner and looked forward to getting the opportunity to spend time with everyone. Ever since I met Lucas's family members, they have always treated my children and me as if we were a part of their family, and I found spending time with them to be refreshing. I opened the front door. Immediately I was met by Lucas, standing there, surrounded by *heaven only knows* how many red, pink, and yellow roses and a bunch of other people who I couldn't immediately identify behind him.

"Hello, beautiful," Lucas welcomed me, as my heart threatened to beat right out of my chest. I tried my best to smile back as I glanced around the room, wanting to better take in my surroundings.

"What's all this, Lucas?" I asked nervously as he grabbed my hands, donning one of his perfectly crooked dimpled smiles before he began.

"I love you, Liz, and lately I've been thinking a lot about how in the world I could possibly show you just how much. So I picked up these flowers, all 150 of them, one for each day you have been in my life. The yellow ones, I figured, could represent the friendship that started between us…Notice that there's only a few of those because…I just couldn't stop myself from falling for you from day one. But you are still my best friend. Next I chose pink because pink works its way up to red, and I wanted to represent the beginning of us when I tried my best to wait for you to finally open yourself up to the thought of letting me into your life. Then there's the red ones—oh, the red…" he said, and the devilish smile on his face caused my eyes to well up with the realization that in this moment, Lucas was going to propose. My hand covered my mouth as I waited for him to finish, tears spilling out as I stared at this outrageously beautiful man God placed before me.

"The red came the day you climbed up in my truck, took my face inside your hands, looked me dead in the eye, and said you loved me. And thank God there's more of those than any other color because the day you let me completely in was the greatest day of my life.

"As you know, I spent today with Chris and Riley, and together, after we talked about how much we all loved you, we decided that we love it most in the moments when we get to see you smile. I realized that I've been missing *way* too many of those moments each time we have to part. I asked your children a question today because I don't want to miss another smile." Lucas paused for a moment. Then he looked over toward Riley, who was standing next to Beth, holding a single white rose in her tiny little hand. And then to Chris, who was holding a velvet box in one hand and Jamie's hand with his other, and nodded. They both walked over to Lucas, who was now down on one knee. The three of them were before me, and I cried the happiest tears of my life, barely able to stand another second of suspense.

"Elizabeth, you have made me the happiest man on earth. You not only brought your love into my life, but you gave me a family of my own that I never dreamed I'd ever have. I don't want to go to a separate home anymore. I don't want to fall sleep without knowing you're right there, lying beside me, and I don't want to wake up another morning without you, Chris, and Riley by my side. So please, say you will spend all of your todays and the rest of your tomorrows with me as my wife?"

I stood there crying, unsure if I'd be able to find my voice if I tried. I nodded just as Riley said, "Momma, don't cry. If you say yes, Woo-cas can sweep over."

Thankful for the laughter, I finally found my voice and said yes.

Luke took me into his arms and kissed me while wiping away my tears. We both smiled at one another as we kissed each other's lips. He broke the kiss so he could slip the ring that Chris had been holding onto my finger. My children, enthralled by the events from their day, shared with me how they helped pick out my ring, a simple yet elegant design, one I couldn't have done better picking if I had chosen it myself.

My new engagement ring was platinum, with a round center stone surrounded by smaller round stones on each side, from the top of the band, ending just before the underside. After admiring the way it fit on my finger, I looked up at my now-fiancé and let him know how much I loved him and my perfect ring. Lucas brought my hand to his lips and kissed my knuckles right above my ring as my children tightly wrapped themselves around our legs, effectively completing our family's hug.

I excused myself to wash my face, hoping to rid myself of all the happy tears. Riley, clinging to my side, joined me in the bathroom.

"Momma, are you sad?" she asked while I splashed cold water on my face, confused by my tears of joy.

"Not at all, baby girl. It's just sometimes people cry when they are happy, and I am so very happy," I explained.

To which she then asked, "Is Woo-cas gonna be mine and Chrissy's daddy then?"

I hugged her tightly and whispered, "Yeah, I guess in a way, he will." And together we went to join our loved ones for dinner.

I learned that the flowers, Luke asking my children for permission to marry me, bringing them to help him pick out my ring, and the proposal itself weren't all he had up his sleeve. He also helped make everyone dinner. Lucas manned the grill, making some of the best barbecue I ever had. His mother helped him with all the sides: potato and macaroni salad, homemade baked beans, macaroni and cheese, and sweet rolls, all to go with the delicious pork ribs and chicken. Lucas knew everything that made me happy, right down to my comfort food, and I was going to spend the rest of my life with him. Unaware of the effect my thoughts had on my face, Luke snuck a kiss with a smirk, letting me know that the smile I wasn't even aware was there was the one he'd never get tired of seeing. Looking deep into my eyes, he assured me that not only could he not wait to spend the rest of his life with me, he also would be doing everything in his power to make sure my smile stayed on my face.

"You're perfect, Lucas. You lied to me in your response to my Dear John letter. You said that you weren't, but you really are," I said and kissed him on his cheek.

"As long as you think so, Liz, that's all that matters." He winked as he always had, and I knew I'd never get tired of watching him do that because it was totally Lucas.

* * * * *

Dinner was not only delicious and overly filling; it was the perfect glimpse of what life was going to be like for me after I married Luke. Not only was I going to be gaining a husband, a true life partner to face the good, the bad, and all things in between, not only were my children going to have a full-time father figure, but we also would officially become a part of this family, a family that has loved the three of us unconditionally from day one. When I made the decision to move here to Spring View, I found all the things I had hoped to find for my children. Plus, a million times more than I could have ever imagined.

Chapter 20

After dinner, Elizabeth and I joined my parents on the porch, while my siblings played with Liz's children in the backyard. Elizabeth explained how she had been seriously thinking about my offer of taking on a job as a full-time teacher at the church's new childcare center. After the success we had during the summer with the trial program, beginning in fall, we would have a full-time day care. She realized it was a good fit for her, especially now that we were going to be getting married. Even though at first she worried that people may assume that I only offered her the job because of who she was to me, the four of us assured her that her qualifications spoke volumes. I must say, I was pleasantly surprised to hear that she was up for it.

"It's kind of neat how we all just sort of fit together over at the church, each one of us being able to fill in where we are needed. It truly is a blessing," my mother offered, pleased with the idea of my future wife joining both our family and our church family.

*****

I was beyond ready to begin our married life together. With a few pleases and a whole lot of kisses, I was able to sell Elizabeth on the idea of having our wedding take place sooner rather than having a long engagement. We officially set our wedding date for September 20, leaving us only three months to plan everything. Having more help than we could have possibly hoped for would make things come together seamlessly.

Since my youngest sister, Jamie, had gotten married in the beginning of spring, she was willing to lend us all she had. And she was even thrilled to know that what she did have to offer was getting a second use. Her generosity helped take care of all the decorations for inside the church. Since neither Elizabeth nor I favored flashy, we agreed to have the reception in the large barn on my parents' property.

Elizabeth asked Aunt Grace to be her maid of honor. She asked both of my sisters and her two friends, April and Deena, to be her bridesmaids. This worked out well because Deena's and April's husbands were my choices for two of my groomsmen. The fact that Liz had become such good friends with two of my closest childhood friends' wives was beyond stellar. I couldn't imagine not being able to merge all parts of my life with hers, so the fact that we all fit was definitely another gift from God.

I was torn between asking my brother and my father to be my best man. I ended up choosing my father. Brian, sympathetic and understanding of my choice, was completely honored when I asked him to be a groomsman instead. It wasn't that Brian and I weren't close; it was more that my father and I had bonded over the past five years, especially after I moved into the guesthouse and began taking a genuine interest in helping him around the property.

My father is a very hardworking man. Quiet but very wise. He doesn't waste much of his time with words but rather proves who he is through his actions; all you had to do was pay attention. When Andrew Walker had something to say, it'd do you a great service to listen, because there'd surely be a little nugget of wisdom being dished out.

I remember clearly the night I told my father I was thinking about asking Elizabeth to marry me. When I approached him about it, the two of us were working in the barn stacking bales of hay. I mistakenly started off letting him know I wanted his advice. He looked at me through the brim of his straw cowboy hat and shook his head sternly.

Staring at me for a moment, as his mind went to whichever place it went whenever he was about to bestow some thought-provoking wisdom upon you, he said, "No. I'm not going to give you advice. Let's get something straight here, boy, you've never been one to listen to any advice I have given you since you were old enough to know better. How many years did I tell you to leave the left-handed curveballs alone? You didn't listen. Because, Lucas, when you set your mind on something, you go all in!

"And what'd I know anyway? You ended up learning how to hit that curveball right out of the park because you're stubborn as a mule. You don't need my advice about what you already know is right." Pausing for a minute so he could stand, he looked me dead in the eye before he continued.

"Now if you want me to give you my blessing? That, son, you've had from the second that little lady of yours had you whistling while you work.

She's good for you, Lucas. You're both good for each other." With a slap on my back, my father told me to get back to work. I did just that, but I felt myself standing a little taller and working a little harder for the man I loved and respected.

* * * * *

Most Friday nights, Elizabeth and the children were over at my parents' house having dinner. One night, wanting to see the progress my father, Brian, and I were making on the barn for our wedding reception, she and I walked over hand in hand so I could show her just how far things had come.

The building itself had good bones and only needed cosmetic repairs on the inside and, of course, a good cleaning. My father upgraded the electrical outlets and added a few new ones to the circuit breaker to better accommodate all the extra electricity we needed for the reception. Elizabeth wasn't all that picky when it came to her wishes regarding the details of our wedding. The one thing she knew she wanted, though, were stars inside the barn.

If I could, I'd rope her the moon and give her every star that shines in the night sky, but white string lights work wonders in making stars appear inside a barn, since my lasso wasn't long enough to grant her wish. My father and I wrapped every spot of the rafters that could be wrapped with those tiny lights for Elizabeth.

Brian and I moved all the animal feed, the hay bales, and farming equipment up into the loft. Whatever couldn't go upstairs, we moved into the stables with the animals, where it would be kept until after the wedding. Elizabeth was overjoyed by the idea of having our reception in the barn. As she took in what the three of us had already achieved in a few short weeks, she was impressed with how different it looked already. The kiss she gave me as her means of saying thanks made me want to work even harder.

* * * * *

One Saturday, after a long hard day working in the barn, Elizabeth curled next to me on the swing on my parents' back porch. Surrounded by family, we began talking; the conversation progressively led to where she and I were planning to live after our wedding.

"You guys are more than welcome to stay in the guesthouse where Lucas has been living, if you'd like," my mother suggested, knowing it would be large enough for the four of us, and she was completely on board with the idea of having us close by.

"Thank you, Momma. That is very kind of you both," I replied graciously, looking at each of my parents before I kissed Elizabeth's temple and continued, "I thought I'd let Beth have it. I think I am going to move in with Elizabeth and the kids in her place, at least until her lease is up, while we look for a place of our own. But I do appreciate your offer. The thought of being so close to you is a bit tempting, I must admit," I finished, humbled by the offer my parents had made.

"It's about time," Beth teased, offering a jab at me for living in the house for as long as I had and more than ready to get a little privacy of her own.

"Hey, Lucas fixed that place up sweet, Beth. You should thank him for making it beyond move-in ready," Brian threw in for good measure as he took his almost-sleeping child from his wife's arms, giving her a chance to relax.

"Give me my nephew, Brian. Tell Daddy you want your Uncle Lukey, right, Daniel?" I taunted my brother, happily taking the four-month-old child from his grasp, giving the newer parents a break. Holding my nephew in my arms was always moments I cherished, even while he slept peacefully. Children grow up too fast, and before long, they want no part of being held.

Watching me interact with children would sometimes cause Elizabeth to feel sorry for me because she knew I would never be able to have any biological children of my own. What she didn't understand is that she gave me children with her ready-made family. I love Riley and Chris as if they were my flesh and blood, so I truly don't have any regrets. I knew that I was beyond blessed to have been given all I had, especially when I was told children weren't going to be in the cards for me. Now because of Elizabeth, I was filling in the shoes of the father that her children, sadly, never gotten the chance to meet.

After Brian took my soundly sleeping nephew from my arms, he, Ashley, and baby Daniel got ready to head back to their home for the night. Sitting with my parents, I mentioned the twins' up-and-coming fourth birthday.

"Liz, we need to throw them a big birthday party. After all, you only turn four once, right?" I pressed excitedly, as I stroked Elizabeth's hair while she lay across my lap on my parents' porch swing. Before she could refuse, my mother piped in, just as thrilled with the idea as I was.

"I love it. Have it here. They love the chickens and all the farm animals. We can make it farm themed with a petting zoo. Oh, Elizabeth, you just have to do this for them!"

"I like the idea, but it's just too much! I can't possibly afford what the two of you have in mind. Perhaps if we scale it down a bit? They're turning four. I'm sure they'd be more than happy with feeding the chickens and having ice cream with Marybeth and Mikey. And before you go and play hero, Lucas, remember we still haven't paid for everything for the wedding," Elizabeth warned as she looked at me. Putting even more emphasis into her glare, she made it clear that she wouldn't be allowing me to help financially with the party for the twins.

"Nonsense, those are my grandchildren now. I say spoil them. We have some animals here. I know a guy who rents ponies for parties. And you know, Chuck over at the church has all sorts of party equipment. He'll certainly work something out with us. We can get a bounce house, cotton candy machine, snow cones, the works. Nothing is too good for my little helpers," my father, of all people, chimed in. Then he threw a wink Liz's way, knowing that she'd never challenge him.

Realizing it was hopeless to go against the Walker clan once my dad got on board, Elizabeth agreed with a sigh and a slight roll of her eyes, causing me to chuckle. I leaned down, kissed her pouty lips, and was more than content with the fact that I won.

* * * * *

It was close to the usual time for Liz and the kids to head off for the night. Before she went to get Riley and Chris from inside, my mother insisted that Elizabeth let them stay over at Mi-Mi Lynn's and Pa- Pa Drew's for the night. My mom then suggested that Elizabeth and I go out on a date. Excited by the thought of getting alone time with my girl, I pleaded with my eyes for her to agree. Thankfully, she did, asking me if I minded if she went home so she could get ready first. I agreed, letting her know I'd pick her up an hour later.

My stomach flip-flopped out of control the entire drive home. I was looking forward to spending alone time with Lucas and wanted to look my best for him. I washed up in the bathroom and threw on a sundress that I always wore with my tan cowboy boots. After pulling a small section of my hair into a clip, I curled it in big loose curls before tossing my tan cowboy hat on to see if it worked. Liking the way it looked, I took it off so I could put on some mascara and eye shadow and placed my hat back on my head before putting on some of my nude lip gloss. I spritzed myself with a little bit of my vanilla-scented body spray and then quickly brushed my teeth. Just as I finished rinsing off my toothbrush, my doorbell rang, letting me know that my hour was over, and my time was up.

Opening my front door, I found Lucas standing on my porch with a bouquet of fresh flowers in his hand. Taking the flowers from him, I gave him a quick kiss and thanked him for being so thoughtful.

"You are such a gift, Lucas. You always seem to surprise me with just how thoughtful you are. How in the world did I get so lucky?" I said as I cut the ends off the flowers and placed them in a vase and then filled it with fresh water.

"God knows what He is doing, beautiful, and my life has been triple blessed since He brought me, you, and the kids together," Lucas replied. Then he took me into his arms, and he kissed my lips softly, silently letting me know with his kiss how much he loved me.

We went to a country bar in town called the Stone Pony, where we met with a few of our friends. Apart from going to Benny's after the baseball games, Luke and I never really went out on dates alone. Given the opportunity his parents offered, we planned on taking full advantage of the night we were given. No worries in sight.

After we spent a few hours dancing and having a great time with our friends, Lucas and I headed home. Usually, he would walk me to my door, but that night, he stayed in his truck instead. He didn't say why, but I figured it was because my house was empty. Knowing Lucas as I did, he would have tried to avoid putting us into a situation where we'd be tempted beyond the point we could resist. Keeping control was hard enough when the kids were there. Alone? Why risk it? We struggled just to say good night and separate all the nights Luke came to do devotions and helped put Chris and Riley to bed. The closer we get to our wedding day, it became all the more difficult. And knowing that I had been down that road before, I was thankful that Lucas could exercise so much restraint.

Nowhere near ready to say good night as we sat in my driveway, I remained seated in Luke's truck, holding his hand while we talked with one another.

"How do you do it, Lucas? How do you always break away when you kiss me and leave so easily?" I whispered, slightly embarrassed by my question that revealed my weakness to him.

"It's the hardest thing I ever have to do. I love you and want nothing more than to stay. I hate leaving you, Liz! I want to be with you in all ways, and it takes all that I have in me at times to walk out your door. I could never do it alone, though, and I thank

God He gives me the strength to leave you when I want nothing more than to stay," Lucas confessed hoarsely, the pain of his restraint saturating his voice, as he swiped his finger over his phone to show me the app he had installed that counted down the days until we no longer had to part. Chuckling, I showed him the same one I had on my phone labeled *Days Until Luke IS Mine*. Together we laughed, delighted by the fact we were both thinking of the same thing.

"Liz, I am already yours, have been since day one. But I know what you mean. Oh, what a day it will be! Now I must apologize, because I have to let you go without walking you to the door like I want to...because I know I won't be able to leave if I do. And I promised I wouldn't do that," he said as he leaned across his center console and tenderly kissed me good night.

"I wouldn't have been able to say no either, so thank you, Lucas. I love you. See you tomorrow," I said as I climbed out of his truck and closed the door.

"I love you, too, beautiful. Sweet dreams, Liz," Lucas returned through the open window, starting the engine and turning on his headlights. He waited in my driveway until I was safely inside my house before he pulled away.

*****

Lucas began planning Riley and Chris's party almost immediately. He called Chuck from church and figured it was a clear sign and a blessing when the date he had in mind for the over-the-top shindig was available. I had to agree with his divine-intervention line of thinking, seeing as it was just around the corner from their birthday, and the normally booked Chuck was free. Chuck happily agreed and offered to provide whatever Lucas needed to pull off the farm-themed party.

Pastor Barry's wife, Mary, offered to do face painting with Jamie and Ashley. Big Mike, Jake, Brian, and Lucas agreed to fill way too many balloons, not only to decorate the backyard of the farm but to give to the children as well. Lucas convinced some of the teenage congregants from FCC to dress up as clowns as well. I have to admit, he pulled it off without breaking the bank. Even though I was assured by Andrew and Lynn from the get-go not to worry about the money, I was still impressed. From the beginning, the over-the-top birthday party they planned seemed to be too much. However, it ended up being a true compilation of family and friends coming together to help one another out, all for the sake of having a good time with their loved ones while celebrating my children turning four.

Planning two parties in less than three months may have been a lot, but Lucas had no problem helping whenever I needed or asked for it. He used whatever connections he had available when the situation demanded, making the task at hand one that was more rewarding than grueling. Seamlessly, Lucas switched topics from birthday-party planning to wedding invites after we got the children off to bed. We were sitting on the couch. Lucas, along with the help of his mother, had already gotten his list together and was asking me who I planned to invite to our wedding.

"I guess it's customary I send one to my parents, and maybe a few others. You know, I'm not convinced that any of the people I invite will come," I conveyed, unsure how I even felt about it.

"You couldn't possibly think your own parents wouldn't come for real, do you?" he asked, searching my face with hope for a sign that I was being overly dramatic, to which I simply shook my head and shrugged.

"You've known me how long? In all this time, tell me how many times I've been on the phone, received visitors, or even just had someone reach out to me? Apart from the occasional correspondence with Christopher's parents, that is?" I flatly pointed out.

"Babe, my life was different before you and all your family. I never knew what it meant to have all of…well, everything I have now, thanks to you. Christopher, his brother, Joshua, and their parents were the closest thing I had to *family*, and they don't even come close to all I have now that I have you."

"I'm so sorry, Liz. I can't imagine how hard that must have been. There's got to be hope, though, right? Listen, the conference I was telling you about, the one in Odessa, Barry asked if I could go in his place since Mary hasn't been feeling well. I thought that maybe you and the kids could come along with me, visit your hometown so I can see where you're from, what made you, you, and well, I was hoping to get your parents' blessing too. What d'ya say?" The undying passion that burns so strongly inside Luke when he sets his mind on something was just too hard for me to resist.

"Just so you know, Odessa is pretty far away from Keybridge, but I suppose it's much closer than

Spring View is. Fair warning, you aren't missing much. However, it would be nice to let Riley and Chris see their grandparents. I wouldn't mind showing you off either, but only if you promise to kiss me like you do while we're here," I half-heartedly agreed, demonstrating the exact kiss I was expecting, trying to forget about the idea of going back home.

"Kissing you has never been a problem for me, beautiful. The fact that I can't seem to keep myself from doing it almost became a problem, if you remember. Not too long ago either," Lucas assured me before kissing me again, easily making us both forget about Texas for just a little while.

* * * * *

My nerves had my stomach in a knot the day of our trip to Texas. I never looked so forward to spending time in a hotel in Odessa before. And I was relieved that we were going to be staying there for a few days at the conference before having to face my hometown. More than once, I tried to convince myself that this was going to be a pleasant trip, even though I was far from convinced it was true.

Once we landed in Texas and collected our things from the baggage claim area, Lucas, Chris,

Riley, and I picked up our rental car. We stopped for a quick bite to eat on our way to the hotel we would be staying in for the next two days. The room that was booked was a single with one bed for Barry and Mary, since they were the ones who initially booked it. Fortunately for us, there were vacancies. The hotel concierge switched us to two rooms that were next door to one another without any issue. Each of us took a child for the night, switching children the next night, trying to be as fair as possible.

The three-hour car ride to Stickville, USA, a.k.a. my hometown, a.k.a. Keybridge, was an entirely different story. Luke somehow managed to keep declining my offer of turning around and going someplace, anyplace else, to make this a vacation worth having. I think I might have been able to get him to change his mind if we hadn't already arrived at my childhood home.

Dust flew up all around our rental car as we drove down the gravel driveway. As much as I wanted to feel excitement, I just couldn't stir any up. Neither of my parents came out to greet us, even though we were only five minutes earlier than my estimated time. Only my mother was there to answer the door when we rang the bell, letting her know we were there. Before inviting us to have a seat, my mother hugged each of us, stiff as a board, as if we were practically strangers. She went into the kitchen and brought out a pitcher of iced water and peanut butter cookies. I did my best to be polite and forced a smile onto my face. Thankfully, Luke tried engaging my mother in a conversation, and to my surprise, I think he even got her to relax a little. If I had something to compare it to, I believe I may have even seen her offer him a genuine smile.

My father made his point, loud and clear, by choosing to keep us waiting for over an hour before gracing us with his presence. The look on his face when Lucas stood, and my father had to tilt his head back slightly to look him in the eye was worth the drive over on its own. Daddy dearest ended up taking Luke on a tour of the house, barely giving any attention to the fact that his grandchildren and I, whom he hadn't seen for over a year, were currently sitting in his house, in his living room, on his couch. Completely fed up, I decided to take Chris and Riley outside for some fresh air.

Taking in a deep breath, I tried my best to remind myself that this was no longer my life anymore, and just as I began to repeat it, hoping to believe it, a much-friendlier voice called out a welcome. Christopher's mother ran over from her house next door toward the three of us. Once she finished hugging her grandbabies, surprised by how much a year had changed them, Mrs. Morris gave me a hug. Still holding me tightly, she let me know how great I looked and told me how happy she was that we had come for a visit.

The four of us walked over to the house next door—my second home, so to speak—and sat together on the back porch, while Chris and Riley played with Lucky, their dog.

It didn't require any special skill or mindset to appreciate the fine home that Mr. Strutton was walking me through, as he proudly pointed out each of the rooms. The structure itself was sound, and the additions and improvements he made throughout the years afforded him a nice piece of real estate. It was a bit more challenging for me to bite my tongue when he spoke of Elizabeth, dishing out little jabs here and there. I did my best to make small talk with the man, but no matter what I offered up, Charles just wouldn't bite.

Coming from the only family and home life I have known, and now seeing something so completely different, caused my heart to ache painfully in my chest for Elizabeth. As we continued to make our way through the last part of the house, I wanted nothing more than to be with her and the kids. Getting the tiniest glimpse at what her childhood must have been like, I needed to go and wrap my arms around them, hoping to further prevent anything like that from ever happening again.

I sent up a silent prayer for God to completely take over, knowing I needed Him to help calm the anger that was rapidly growing inside. I listened to Liz's father talk about her as if she was nothing more than a burden he'd been cursed to carry. Almost immediately, during the tour of the house, I realized that Mr. Strutton had mastered the art of deception. Picking and choosing the scripture he saw fit as a weapon for his bigoted mindset, to which I repeatedly tried to remind him of mercy and grace. When the man spoke of his daughter, he was cold, lacking all emotion, as if she were no more than a stranger off the streets. After listening to the man carry on, I believed Elizabeth would have been shown more compassion if she had been a stranger. When the tour finally came to an end, bringing us both outside on the porch, I felt a smile work its way onto my face when I heard the vivacious laughter coming from Chris and Riley, who were playing next door.

"I want to thank you, Lucas, as a man of God, for your willingness to take on my daughter's mistakes. I'm sure that wasn't an easy decision for you, especially being a man of God. But thankfully, you have provided her a chance of redemption. I pray that God will bless you and accept your marriage."

My body became rigid. I whipped my head around, making sure this man was looking directly in my eyes, as I did my best to blow out a prayerfully calming breath. "With all due respect, sir, those children are not a mistake—they are gifts from God. My decision to marry your daughter was one of the easiest ones I ever had to make. I love her for all that you can't even see she is. My decision to marry her has nothing to do with offering her redemption. She was given that freely the day she accepted Jesus into her heart.

"I came here in hope of receiving your blessing, but I'm afraid that's no longer necessary, because God gave me Elizabeth and those children, and God is the only One who needs to bestow a blessing upon us. It'd do you a great service to read and pray upon 2 Corinthians 5:17, '*Therefore, if any man be in Christ, he is a new creature: old things are passed away; behold, all things have become new.*' And try to remember 1 Peter 4:8, '*Above all else, love each other deeply, because love covers over a multitude of sins.*' Now if you'll excuse me, I'm going to go join my family. Thank you for taking your time to meet with me. Good day, sir." I managed to walk away, while thanking God my words came out as respectful as they had. On the inside, I wanted to scream at the top of my lungs.

During my fit of rage, I hadn't realized there was a man standing off to the side on his own property yet close enough that he may have heard the interactions between Mr. Strutton and myself. I nodded toward the man whom I assumed was Christopher's father. I worked on taking deep calming breaths before reaching my hand out to introduce myself.

"Sorry about that. I'm Lucas Walker. I'm guessing you're Mr. Morris? Pleased to meet you, sir." After walking away from Liz's childhood home, I began feeling a bit of relief wash over me as my body and mind finally started to relax.

Christopher's father took my hand firmly into his before pulling me into a typical guy hug—one arm over the shoulder with a firm pat on the back thing that I'm pretty sure all men do.

"The name's Robert, Lucas, and there's no need to apologize for standing up for my Lizzie like that, something I think Julie and I should have done long ago." And with his words, I now felt as if this trip may have the potential to turn around. But all I wanted in that moment was to walk over to Elizabeth and hold her in my arms.

"Well, Robert, as I said, I *am* pleased to meet you, but if you don't mind, I need to go see Liz for a minute," I said as my eyes locked onto her in a stare. Thankfully, Robert laughed his approval, assuring he'd be right behind me.

* * * * *

I took Liz into my arms and kissed her too many times to count, while letting her know how sorry I was. Doing my best to assure her just how much I loved her in between each kiss, the two of us stood holding one another for a few minutes, while the children played, blissfully unaware of anything other than playing with the dog, just as it should be. This time when I looked into Elizabeth's eyes, I saw all the strength she had inside her and all the brokenness she had healed from. All thanks to our loving Savior! And I couldn't help but kiss her again. With a bashful smile, she let me know she wanted to introduce me to Riley and Chris's Me-Maw and Paw-Paw.

Before the introductions were made, Robert pulled Elizabeth into his arms and hugged her the way her father should have.

"Lizzie, I am so sorry, sweetheart. Please forgive me! Your daddy doesn't speak for us at all. We love you and those children, and we are so sorry that we haven't been here for you," he spoke with the honest rawness of a man who felt the heaviness caused by the pangs of genuine regret.

"Lucas, this is my wife, Julie, and we'd like to have you spend the night here with us. We have plenty of room, and I won't take no for an answer. In fact, I insist on it," Robert informed as Julie welcomed me with a hug and kiss before taking Elizabeth in her arms, holding her tightly as the two of them began to cry.

"Lizzie, there is no excuse why I haven't been more than a letter or phone call here and there, but I need to tell you this. It was just too hard for me, seeing you so dead inside. I missed you all so much, but I hoped if I let you go, you'd learn to be happy. You'd learn to finally let Christopher go. I prayed every night you'd find your Lucas, and thank God you have. You look so happy, and you're the best momma my grandbabies could ever have. I don't want to miss any more time, you hear?" The two nodded and smiled through their tears, as Robert and I fought to hold back tears of our own.

Once things settled down a bit, Mr. Moris walked with me back over to Elizabeth's parents' driveway so I could move the rental car over to his since our plans had changed. We were staying with them for the night. Julie met me when I stepped inside with our bags from the trunk and led me to our separate rooms. She put the kids together in a guest room downstairs so they'd be with their momma before taking me upstairs to what clearly, at one time, was her son's room. Now a guest room, it still displayed some of his trophies and a few framed pictures revealing memories of a life that was taken much too soon.

"I hope you don't mind. This was Christopher's room. I have another room if you'd be more comfortable, but it's smaller, and as Robert and JR say, it's girlie." Shaking my head, I did my best to assure her I was more than fine with where she placed me. After I put my bag on the foot of the bed, I picked up a photo of their Lizzie and Christopher and smiled. The two had their arms around one another's shoulders and were making silly faces at the person behind the camera.

"I'm glad she found you, Lucas. She sure is something, that Lizzie, and it warms my heart to see her looking so good and happy again. Thank you!" Julie said, as she smiled at the picture I held in my hand.

"It's an honor to have been gifted her. I'm sorry it had to be at your son's expense, though. But I assure you, I love her and your grandchildren with all I have in me. I thank God every day for bringing them into my life," I expressed unequivocally, knowing that the situation wasn't the easiest. Yet there we were, both more than willing to embrace it, allowing God to heal and grow new beginnings for all of us.

Julie and I were over the heavy and onto lighter topics as we walked down the stairs and were met with the extraordinary sound of laughter coming from the kitchen. Robert, Liz, and the kids were in the middle of making a mess. Flour was smudged all over their faces, as the four of them decided to bake cookies. Julie and I smiled at the sight. Making her way over to the group, Julie headed off to the left of the center island and began making dinner, while I decided to join in the fun of baking cookies.

It was quite the sight, seeing my prim and proper Elizabeth messy with a smile on her beautiful face, and I was reminded of our beginning, the night

I put ice cream on her nose. As the memories flooded my mind, I grinned, a big ole cheesy grin, knowing how blessed I truly was.

After dinner was finished, and dessert was cleaned up, Elizabeth took the kids in for a bath. Even though I knew she'd refuse, I offered my assistance. With the decision being made for me, I was determined to make the best of the situation. I took the opportunity the bath time had offered to get to know the Morrises, and we sat together in their den off to the side of the kitchen, each of us drinking a cup of coffee.

Happily, I answered the questions the Morrises had for me. The ones I assumed would have been asked by Liz's father and thanked God that she at least had these two wonderful people who were more than willing to step up to the plate since her father had failed her. The conversation naturally led to the topic of God (you'd be surprised how often that happens when people find out you're a preacher), and much like with Liz when I first met her, they, too, had been misinformed about what it means to be saved.

"I don't mean to be rude, I think you're alright, son, but as of late, I think God should be left on Sundays only. I won't tell you who I'm voting for if you keep your preaching inside your church. Fair enough?" Robert offered as a warning. Not willing to let it go without assuring them that Jesus heals, He doesn't condemn, I was inwardly thankful when Julie apologized for her husband's remark and asked if she could ask me something. I encouraged her to ask her question after nodding respectfully to her husband.

"What good is Jesus if we still have to break our backs when we mess up? I listened on Sunday mornings when I used to go to church, and each sermon talked about healin', forgiveness, and mercy, but then when my child and the love of his life shared a beautiful moment with one another, and were even blessed with my precious grandbabies, there was nothing they could do to be forgiven by a man of God? I'm sorry, but I don't see God like that at all! I believe Christopher is in heaven. And I think that God was the One that showed Christopher how to look out for his family, making sure Lizzie and his kids wouldn't be alone when he found Spring View. Convincing Lizzie to move there before he died. I just know, I feel it in my heart, that Christopher wanted Lizzie to find you, and if I am wrong, then I have no interest in getting to know the God you speak of. My God is loving, not cruel," Julie huffed, and I can't possibly express how relieved I was that in her heart, the door was open. With God taking the lead, I shared with her the true gospel of Christ.

"You are so right. Your son is in heaven, for sure. Now this may seem a little harsh. The way I see it, please trust that I say this with all due respect for your lost loved one. I do believe God has a plan for everything. Every good, every bad, and all the things in between." I paused for a moment when Elizabeth curled in beside me on the love seat, Chris went to sit in between his grandparents, and Riley climbed up on my lap. Before I could continue with our conversation, the front door opened. This caused Liz to spring up, squealing as she ran and jumped into the arms of whom I assumed was Christopher's brother, Joshua.

"Joshy…oh my word, I am so happy to see you!" Elizabeth declared, hanging onto the closest thing she had to a brother and any real semblance of family she ever knew.

"Take it easy, baby girl…I'm wounded," Joshua announced to which she gasped, unaware, and apologized for attacking him.

"It's okay, and I am just about completely healed," he offered as he placed his hand on his right shoulder. "Never mind that, old news. You, on the other hand, look fantastic, Lizzie! Now where are my niece and nephew? And where is *he*?" Joshua half-heartedly teased, clearly excited to see the little ones while acting the part of the older brother. He readied himself to pick me apart. What a relief it was too. This is what Liz deserved more than anything, someone from her past to come to her defense and look out for her and her children.

I stood, firmly shook Joshua's hand as Elizabeth sidled up beside me once again, beaming from within. She reintroduced her children to their uncle, who was at a loss for words with the realization of how much time had passed since he had seen his family. Before Joshua took a seat on the couch with the children, I thanked him for his willingness to serve our country and was surprised when he confessed what motivated him to join the Army in the first place.

"Honestly, I'm not a hero or anything. I only joined to stop myself from making one of two huge mistakes. I was worse for the wear after my brother died. I started drinking. It got out of hand as I watched Lizzie dying inside. I couldn't take it. If I would have stayed around town, I would have either been a good-for-nothing drunk, or I would have forced myself to marry Lizzie. That would have ruined both of our lives. She is like a sister to me. Seeing her so broken when she was the brightest light around when

Christopher was alive, I just couldn't…" He shook his head slowly while he changed his focus to the children beside him and smiled. Once he regained his composure, he looked at me and continued, "Thanks for putting that smile back on her face. You're alright in my book, and as long as it stays there, we'll be good," Joshua admitted, and Elizabeth quickly wiped away a tear before she excused herself.

* * * * *

Elizabeth hadn't seen Joshua since the twins were four months old. Much like his mother, he believed that if he forced Liz to step out on her own, she'd learn to live again. But selfishly, he admitted that being around them was just too hard for him. Regrettably, his decision, as much as I was glad that in the end it all turned out okay, caused all of them to miss too much time with one another. I wanted nothing more than for all of them to be an active part in our lives from there on out.

After we had gotten the kids in bed for the night, Joshua explained to Elizabeth and me that he was shot in his shoulder while serving time overseas. He counted himself lucky that he hadn't lost a limb or, worse, his own life, like so many other soldiers had. He also confided in us that while he was in the desert, he read his Bible all the time and truly gave himself to the Lord.

"I guess for some it takes a tragedy. In my case, I had lots of time, so I started looking for Him. Then I was shot and spent my coherent time praying. I ended up meeting the real Jesus in Afghanistan and knew I could never go back. He is my Lord and Savior evermore. No matter what brings you there, getting there is all that matters."

Offering a genuine smile, I understood the life-or-death change all too well myself.

"I couldn't agree more. I found Christ on my deathbed as well. You're right—it doesn't matter what it takes as long as you get there."

"Now there's a preacher that I just might spend my Sundays listening to," Joshua teased. In that moment, I knew that we were going to get along just fine due to our shared brushes with death and our love for Elizabeth, Chris, and Riley.

Sitting there while we all laughed and reminisced, I was assured that pushing Liz to take this trip was indeed the right thing to do. I adored being able to witness another side of her that I had never seen before. She was silly and carefree, and her laugh came so effortlessly while she sat with her true family.

It simply warmed my heart. Watching her interact with Joshua, being able to witness an almost child-like relationship between the two of them, offered me an impression of what the good parts of her child-hood were like, at least as far as the Morrises were concerned.

"Guess y'all have to relocate to North Cakalacky, huh? While I'll admit Lucas *is* quite the preacher, that commute will surely put a whooping on ya," Liz joked. Clearly hoping that one day, they might give the idea of moving closer some genuine thought.

* * * * *

"I know that things were especially hard for you today, but I am still glad we came. I love seeing this side of you, Liz. You are so fun and carefree here," I shared my observation with her when the two of us were given a moment alone, right before going to bed.

"I am glad we came too. My parents, I expected nothing less from, but it was good to reconnect with the Morrises. Thanks for pushing me on this." She kissed me with full intentions of allowing me to feel that gratitude through the touch of her lips. Message received.

Just before we parted ways at the foot of the staircase, I asked Elizabeth to pray with me. We joined hands and thanked God for the way He works and the way He was bringing healing to this family after so much hurt and lost time.

* * * * *

"I wanted to ask if there'd be any way possible for you to make it out to North Carolina for the twins' birthday party? I know it's short notice, and I apologize for that, but truthfully, we just threw things all together at the last minute," I told the Morris family the next morning as we sat together, sharing breakfast. The look in Elizabeth's eyes was hopeful, but I noticed the slightest hint of disappointment hidden behind them as she more than likely calculated the odds of how slight the chance would be, seeing it was only two weeks away.

"Oh, we'd love to. I'm just not sure if we could get there on such short notice. I promise you this, if we can't make it, we will surely come for a visit before the wedding. I mean it, Lizzie, from here on out, things are going to be different. You can count on us," Julie promised as we finished our food.

Joshua set his parents up on video chat. That on top of the agreed twice-a-week phone calls, letters, and planned visits, they could all *see* one another as if they lived closer. Without even trying to hide the sadness brought forth by the realization it was time for us to go, Elizabeth thanked her *brother*, Josh, for all his help and didn't stand a chance of fighting back the tears that began to fall down her cheeks as she hugged him goodbye.

"None of that, baby girl. You'll see, things are going to be different now. I'm going to bother you so much you'll wish you never came out to visit," he said as he wiped the tears that were steadily falling down her face. My heart broke as I witnessed the raw emotions being shared between the two of them. But I believed that this wasn't really a goodbye as much as it would be a new beginning for all of them.

"Never. Not gonna happen. You know, there's a base in North Carolina, and I think you should transfer. That way we can get Mom and Dad to move there too. I don't want to miss any more time with y'all. I love you, Joshy, always have! Even when you were being a pain in my rear," Elizabeth teased. I wanted nothing more in that moment than to be able to freeze time for her so she wouldn't miss out on anything more.

Through smiles and tears, we all said our good-byes with a promise that things would be different from there on out.

*****

Riley and Chris slept through most of the car ride to the airport. I was thankful that we booked our return tickets out of Amarillo for our trip home, which made our car ride closer to an hour instead of the four hours it took to get there. Liz, for most of the drive, sat in silence as she stared out the car window, looking out at all the flat browns and earth tones of the landscape that used to be her home. I knew this trip had been hard for her emotionally, but I was still certain we made the right decision by coming.

"Whatcha thinking, beautiful?" I asked, breaking the silence as I kissed Elizabeth's hand that I held in mine while I drove.

"Well, it's…bittersweet is all. I am looking forward to going home and getting back to my life, but I'm going to miss them." Once again, a tear slid from the corner of her eye as we drove farther and farther from her hometown and the Morrises, her true family.

"I bet. I'm so glad I got to meet them. I believe them, Liz, it's going to be different now, you'll see. Hey, Robert even put my number in his contacts on his phone, so that means something, right?" I wished with all I had in me for the ability to set Elizabeth's mind at ease as I squeezed her hand tightly.

"Yeah…I'm glad you got to meet them too." She rested her head against the window, where it stayed, looking out as a lonely tear would fall every once in a while. The rest of the ride to the airport was in peaceful silence.

* * * * *

We returned home from Texas and immediately fell back into our daily routines. Liz was working full-time at Benny's, occasionally picking up a few extra shifts when she was needed. As promised, the Morrises, all three of them, kept true to their word. They reached out to Liz and the children, just like they said they would. And I was grateful they even made an effort to keep in touch with me. Getting to know each of them apart from Elizabeth was eye-opening. Without a doubt, they most definitely are good people with great hearts and kind souls, making the most they could of the life they had been given. That much I gathered just from meeting them and spending the night at their home. But getting to speak with them, having them seek me out for advice, and likewise, looking to them for advice as well was truly wonderful. I was hopeful that the doors weren't closed as far as Mr. Morris getting to know God. And I found that as much as Robert tried his best to put God on a shelf, and I tried my best to let him be the one to bring the subject up, the more he would find a way to bring God into each of our conversations. I made sure I answered each of his questions to the best of my abilities, trying not to offend him as I took things back to the basics. More often than not, it's easier to minister to a new believer than it is to help one who has been brainwashed his entire life with untruths and legalism without being taught the message of grace.

Chapter 23

The busyness of working full-time at Benny's and planning the wedding with Lucas made time fly. Many nights after work, I'd go to the Walkers to help as much as the guys would allow and treasured how much closer Lucas's mother, Beth, Jamie, and I had grown from spending so much time with one another.

"So tell me about this Joshua? Is he single?" Beth asked quizzically, pressing me for details about my God-given brother.

"Joshy's great. I'm pretty sure he's single. He's been overseas for quite some time and has only been home for the past three months since his injury." I pulled up photos on my phone that Lucas had taken of Josh and me on our trip to Texas and one in his army uniform and handed Beth my phone.

"Oh wow! He's easy on the eyes, that's for sure. How is he doing by the way? Will he be cleared to serve again, or will he be medically discharged?"

"Not sure yet. I guess it could go either way. He is trying to arrange for his medical evaluation to take place here since the appointment is scheduled so close to the wedding. I think a part of him wants to be discharged, but another part clings to the comradery his platoon offers. He has a hard time dealing with the fact that he's no longer with his men, and being here, Stateside, messes with his brain. He feels like he's abandoned them in a sense. It's got to be tough on him, but I selfishly want him to be discharged and move here, of course."

"I can only imagine. It's so strange to me. I think I'd be praying that I'd get released, hum… Guess that's why I'd make a terrible soldier. Lucky for our country I never enlisted," Beth unapologetically admitted, and we all easily chuckled our agreement.

* * * * *

For some reason, my shift at Benny's was extra grueling one night. Customers seemed to be unsatisfied with just about everything. No fault of mine, of course, but they were displeased nonetheless. I chalked it up to the full moon and was pleased once my shift was finally over. As much as I was looking forward to relaxing after my long tiresome day, that wasn't in the cards for me. It was the day before the twins' birthday party, and I was expected at the Walkers to help get everything ready.

When I pulled into the driveway, I was pleasantly surprised by the amount of people there to help. Lucas's entire family, and most our friends, were already busy setting up for the party, and it looked as if there wasn't too much left for me to do. I greeted everyone with a smile and thankfully found the strength to jump right in and get to work on the few things that still needed to get done.

Lucas greeted me with a kiss and asked if I could help him hang the stringed flags across the property. He wanted the flags to serve as markers, distinctively setting apart designated spots for each of the different areas. The two of us playfully worked together as all of our other helpers kept themselves busy with their own tasks.

"Hey, no fair, Lucas. You have a foot advantage over me," I teased at how easily he made everything seem.

Lucas winked, offering me one of his sexy smiles, causing my heart to turn to mush.

"Eh, you're doing great, Liz. Keep up the good work," he playfully teased. But when he was close enough that only I could hear him, he whispered, "And I love watching you stretch and contort in all sorts of crazy positions, trying to keep up."

Feeling my cheeks blush from his flirty confession, I snuck in a quick kiss, truly amazed by just how much Lucas got under my skin.

When everything was finished, the group of us enjoyed hot dogs and hamburgers on the grill. I was in the kitchen with Grace and Lynn, getting drinks ready for dinner, when the doorbell rang. Lynn nodded over in my direction, silently pleading with me to answer it.

Completely unaware of who could possibly be coming over since pretty much everyone we knew was already here, I opened the door and was overjoyed when I found myself face-to-face with the Morrises, Joshua included! Not even trying to stifle my emotions, I squealed my excitement as I hugged each of them and welcomed them in.

"I can't believe you made it. I'm so happy you're all here! Chris and Riley are going to be thrilled to see you guys," I declared, hugging them all again.

"We wouldn't miss it for the world, Lizzie. When we realized we could make it out, Lucas thought it would be a good idea to surprise you. I almost slipped a few times, especially when I had to pretend otherwise," Julie confessed. I was once again taken aback by just how thoughtful Luke was.

Hearing the commotion and wanting to greet the Morrises, Lucas walked in the back door. Before he was able to officially welcome my family, I threw my arms around his neck and kissed him.

"Thank you, babe. I love you so much for *all* of this. I can't believe you sometimes…Thanks!" I relayed, completely caught up by my soon-to-be husband's thoughtfulness. I kissed him without any reservation or thought as to who may be watching. Lucas gladly accepted the means by which I had chosen to offer him my *thanks* and unabashedly kissed me back.

Lucas welcomed his future in-laws with hugs and asked how their trip was. He took their bags and placed them off to the side.

"The flight was pretty decent. I won't complain," Robert answered, to which Joshua, Julie, and I all laughed in unison.

"That's a first, you not complaining, ha! Thank the good Lord for a miracle," Julie supplied, allowing the rest of the group to join in with laughter.

"Well, I could always offer some advice on things, I'm sure, but seeing as I never flew a plane before, I figured I'd keep it to myself this time," Robert responded, clearly pretending to be wounded by his loved one's jab.

"Look at that, an old dog can learn new tricks. Or is that more of a…you've finally figured that all things, be them true or not, don't have to be spoken, even if you are a *jack-of-all-trades*, Pop?" Joshua teased.

Robert pretended to think it over for a moment before adding, "Shoot, I'll tell you what, what I have to say always matters, and if you were smart enough to listen to the advice I give, you'd be sure to do things the right way the first time. You should know that by now, son." With that final thought, the laughter came to an end, as Riley and Chris excitedly greeted their grandparents and uncle, happily pulling them outside so they could show the new comers the decorations in the backyard and giving them all a chance to get something to eat.

The simple dinner and relaxing chitchat was more than welcoming to all the helping hands. The

Morrises easily slipped right in, just as my children and I had. Once all our helpers were done eating and socializing, they said their goodbyes and headed off for the night. Andrew, Robert, and Lucas took the Morrises' luggage over to the guesthouse, where Lucas lived.

"We figured that you and Robert would be comfortable staying with Elizabeth and the kids. This way, we could just move Lucas into his old room. Joshua, you are more than welcome to join your parents out in the guesthouse, or you can stay with us here in the main house. The choice is yours, and either way, you're welcome."

"Thank you, ma'am. I'm sure either would be more than accommodating," Joshua offered politely, showing off his good nature and true Texas charm, all the while making the United States Army proud.

Lynn and Julie went into the kitchen, comfortably talking with one another as they set up the large carafe and began making coffee for the remaining group. Taking a moment to truly appreciate the way my past life was seamlessly meshing with my new one, ultimately providing me with a present life I never dreamed would be possible, I gave thanks to God.

"Whatcha thinking about all serious? Your wheels are turning, and I think I can see a bit of smoke coming out of that pretty little head of yours," Joshua teased, perfectly fitting into the big-brother role as he had my entire life.

"I'm just so glad I get to have all of you still in my life. For a while, I thought I lost you when I lost him, you know? But…so not going there. This is a happy moment, and I am very much so. I can't believe you're here. Thanks, Joshy, I love you!" I blew out a calming breath after I finished, doing my best to fight back the tears. Happy or not, I did not want to cry.

Joshua took me in his arms, understanding what I meant. We were moving past the pains from our yesterdays and were more than ready to begin making new memories in the present. Simply, he let me know that he loved me too. And we hugged a little longer before the guys got back from dropping the luggage off at the guesthouse.

"It's a nice spread you've got here, Andrew. If you wouldn't mind, I'd like to have a look around in the day. I've got a few hundred acres myself, but it's nothing compared to the valleys and scenery your place has to offer. So green, too, it's beautiful! Out in the part of Texas we're from, you can see for miles.

Makes fieldwork easy if not monotonous, but it is what it is. You running for profit or strictly pleasure?" Robert asked, as he pulled his grandson up on his lap.

"Thank you. I'd be happy to show you around after the party tomorrow or Sunday if you'd like," Andrew cordially offered, thankful for the compliment. He turned his attention briefly to the ladies, who approached bringing coffee and dessert. He thanked them both before he continued to answer Robert's questions regarding his land.

"Our land is more for pleasure, I'd say, and I don't have nearly the acreage you do. This here is just a tad over fifty acres, but we still manage to get a little bartering done with some of the other smaller parcels, friends of ours. I no longer have the amount of chickens I once had, so selling isn't a valid option anymore, although it did help bring in some extra money when the kids were growing up, though. Sold all but two of my cows, just too much work. We've got a goat that thinks she's a dog and a couple of horses. I just enjoy the beauty of it and living out my cowboy dreams without having to stake the livelihood of my finances on it," Andrew explained while revealing his contentment in the way he chose to make use of his land.

"You keep Lizzie away from your horses, don't ya? She knows how to ride, but she always seems to rile them up after she takes them out. Every time she rode my boy Christopher's horse, he wanted nothing to do with my son for the next couple of days," Robert relayed with a smile as he looked lovingly toward me and winked.

"Oh, come on, Pop. You know its 'cause she's a softy. She always let Duke stop and eat whenever he darn well pleased. Used to get Chris all in a bunch too. She's a sucker," Joshua chided, revealing the not-so-clever secrets of my horse whispering.

"Hey, he was always hungry, and I aim to please," I huffed out my simple explanation, not caring in the slightest that I was wrong in my ways of dealing with the horse or, more accurately, not dealing with the horse.

Everyone on the porch happily laughed at my expense, while I sat there just soaking it all in, basking in all the love from each of my God-gifted family members.

"Guess I should be thankful I no longer have my own horse, huh?" Lucas teased after he pulled me into his arms as we readied ourselves to say good night.

With nothing more to offer in my defense, I simply smiled up at him, going up on my tiptoes for the kiss I couldn't wait for him to give me. He kissed me softly until Joshua coughed out an interruption, willing me to hurry so we could walk to the guesthouse, where he and I were going to spend the night with his parents and my children.

* * * * *

Early the next morning, I woke to the sound of delivery trucks and voices that were already busy setting up the last part of the party. My children were dressed and ready to head over to the main house for breakfast, as I wiped the sleep from my eyes and began making a pot of coffee. Joshua moaned out his protest, from the barstool at the counter of Lucas's kitchen, at the *way-too-awake* crowd outside. I offered him a cup of coffee, completely agreeing with his moans and relating to his level of *not quite ready* to begin the day.

"We'll take the kids over for breakfast. You two get a move on, would ya?" Julie scolded, as Joshua and I both laughed.

"You really fit in around here, Lizzie. I'm glad you found Lucas. He's a good guy," Joshua made known his approval while sipping his coffee, both of us dreading the idea of having to function after such a late night.

"Now I just need to convince you all to stay, and life will be perfect. Come on, we've gotta get over there. Breakfast waits for no one. I promise, you can shower first when we get back before the party. And if you hurry, you might be able to squeeze in a nap." I winked, and the two of us headed over to meet the others for breakfast.

Joshua and I greeted everyone and began dishing food onto our plates before we took our seats at the table. Once I had all of my favorites on my plate, I took a seat next to Lucas and snatched a piece of bacon off his plate, even though I already had a few slices on my own.

"Hey now, you snatched my bacon before even giving me a good-morning kiss. I can't help but feel used," Lucas teased, but I knew it was all in good fun.

"Sorry, babe. Good morning. I love your bacon…I mean, I love you," I played right back, stealing a quick kiss before beginning to work on my food. "Did your daddy get to eat yet? He's outside busy working with Chuck, setting up the bounce house. I'll feel terrible if he hasn't eaten," I asked Luke in between bites of my food.

"Not terrible enough to quit eatin', huh?" Joshua laughed before Lucas assured me that his father was fine, and like usual, he insisted on taking care of things.

Lucas and Robert went out to join Andrew, making sure that everything was set up accordingly and that Chuck was compensated for the use of the bounce house, while the rest of us finished up breakfast.

* * * * *

Taking full advantage of the break the Morrises provided, I ended up spending a bit longer than usual in the shower and getting myself ready for the party. When I finally finished, I headed over to find Lucas, who was busy playing with my children, getting them pumped up about their birthday party.

"Don't you look all purdy?" Joshua teased, overexaggerating his southern drawl intentionally.

Lucas froze after doing a double take, as he looked me over with obvious approval. The way his eyes gleamed as he took in the sight of me made me feel as if I was absolutely stunning. Wanting to keep up with the farm theme, I chose a red-and-white gingham dress with my cowboy boots and hat. I pulled my hair half up and left the other half down, set in loose-barrel curls, placed on both sides of my shoulders, giving the illusion I was wearing pigtails. I took care not to overdo my makeup, and what I did apply was subtle, choosing to highlight my eyes with just the right amount of color.

"I'd say you do. You look amazing!" Lucas complimented as he pulled me in for a kiss, making sure I knew he definitely believed it to be true.

"Thank you, gorgeous! I had to try and get up to your level at least. Glad you approve," I countered, as I now admired Lucas in his tight blue jeans, navy fitted T-shirt under a gray-black-navy-and-white flannel and his black cowboy boots. His hair was deliberately tousled just the way I liked it, and his beard was barely there, just enough to tickle my face when we kissed.

"With you by my side, I always look good, beautiful." With overexaggerated gagging sounds, Lucas's friends interrupted our too-sweet moment, wanting nothing more than for us to dial it down a notch.

"We get it, you're both gorgeous. Now isn't this supposed to be a kids' party?" Big Mike finally called out and happily brought his son to Riley and Chris, who were busy playing in the bounce house.

The party went off without even the smallest of a glitch. The children, as well as all the parents, thoroughly enjoyed themselves. Julie and I took a seat on the porch, enjoying the sight of Lucas with my birthday boy and girl.

"He loves them as if they are his own. It warms my heart," Julie said with a smile as she waved to Riley, who was taking her turn on a pony ride.

"He does. He truly does, and they took to him from day one as well," I shared, as I too looked on fondly while my children enjoyed themselves.

* * * * *

Things were once again calm and peaceful. The birthday party was a complete success. Riley, Chris, and many of the adults were officially spent for the night, if not physically, mentally for sure. Andrew took Robert on a tour of his property before the sun set, and Julie, Lynn, Beth, Lucas, and I sat together on the porch, enjoying the late-afternoon air.

"Momma, Jules, how long are you here for?" I questioned, breaking the quiet calm of the tiredness I was feeling, as I snuggled up against Lucas.

"We're here for the week. Have you found a dress yet, Lizzie?" Julie asked.

"I actually haven't. I'd love for you to come along, since you know me and my aversion to frills or anything too over-the-top girlie, for that matter.

Please say you'll come," I pressed Julie, looking forward to sharing a special mother-like moment with her. Lynn had already gladly agreed to come along, and I was grateful for her willingness to do so. But I wanted the one person who knew me best to be there with me as well.

"Of course I will. I'm looking forward to it. Thanks for including me, but you sure are cutting things close. Guess that works in all areas when you leave yourself only three months to plan a wedding. You never were big on making a fuss over the details, were you, hon?"

"It's one of the things I love most about Liz. She is just so easy to please. She never worries about the little things, and she always finds a way to go with the flow," Lucas mentioned as he kissed my temple and pulled me closer into his side.

"I lucked out with the greatest wedding planners. Everyone really has helped out a lot. Things are coming together fairly easy. Lucas is going to be wearing a tan tux with a cream-colored tie. We just didn't think formal black tie was the vibe we wanted. Our love story is more country, laid back. The guys aren't going to be wearing jackets at all—vests and brown ties only. And to coordinate, the girls all found dresses in the earth-toned color theme we wanted. I can't wait to see it all come together." I was thrilled by the ease with which our wedding was coming together.

"She even insisted on cowboy boots, which I am thrilled about. Gotta love Elizabeth's mellow personality," Beth added.

* * * * *

The girls from my bridal party and Lynn met up with Julie and me at the dress shop in the center of town, with high hopes of helping me find a dress for my rapidly approaching wedding. The store was a bit overwhelming with all the toile, beads, and puffy princess dresses, but that didn't stop my friends from joking around and teasing me a little, all in good fun of course. Somehow they even managed to get me to try on some of the dresses we all knew I'd never agree on, insisting that it was a bride's rite of passage, a must.

"What *are* you looking for?" Sarah Mae, the sales coordinator, asked, trying the best she could to cater to my needs.

"Well, I want feminine but not frilly. Nothing *poofy* at all," I explained as I searched for a dress in the tiny section that had less-formal styles hanging on the rack.

"Lizzie, what about this one?" Julie exclaimed, holding up *the* perfect dress. Upon further inspection, I found that it was indeed just what I was looking for. It was a high-low dress, the front landing just below the knee and the back dropping down longer, giving the tiniest suggestion of a train without reaching the ground. The color of the dress was off-white, a true antique color, with a beautiful lace overlay fully attached to the satin material underneath. The lace alone came up over the shoulders, revealing a modest yet stunning V-neckline from the underlay. Once I put the dress on, I knew it was just what I had in mind. It was perfect! When I walked out to where my friends and family were waiting, their gasps of approval only helped seal the deal.

"Oh, Lizzie, it's perfect! Let me guess, the boots are staying too?" Julie laughed as she patted a tear that fell from her eye.

"The boots are a must! I'll find a different dress if the boots don't work. Do you think they do, though, or should I cave, for the ceremony at least?" I was beginning to second-guess my desire to wear my favorite boots, even though I thought they made the whole thing me and knew I was going to wear them anyway.

"We're all bootin' it with ya girl, so the boots are a must!" Deena proclaimed, firmly offering her approval of the dress.

"You don't even need alterations. You look stunning right off the rack. Lucas is going to be floored when he sees you. You two may never make it through your vows. I'll make sure I tell Barry to make 'um quick," Ashley offered, nodding her head with a playful grin on her face. "Do you Lucas, do you Elizabeth—I do, I do, sorta thing."

Just before we were about to pay, Lynn showed me a veil that she thought would be a perfect match with the dress. Even though I hadn't planned on buying one, I loved the delicate simplicity of it and tried it on for good measure. My mind was now made up: the veil she had found changed everything, and I decided it more than perfectly tied the whole thing together. Thankful that Lynn was willing and able to make this day special for the two of us as well, I hugged my future mother-in-law tightly before she snatched the veil from my hand, insisting she would take care of it for me. Dress shopping was more than just successful; it was a true bonding experience, where each of us not only laughed and had fun, we all truly enjoyed ourselves as well.

With my dress tucked neatly in my trunk, we decided to let the men fend for themselves, choosing to continue our outing by having lunch at the country diner, Aunt Mel's Place.

"I can't believe how things are just coming together so perfectly, Elizabeth. I'm so happy for you and Lucas," April mentioned as we each looked over our menus.

"It's been such a relief, that's for sure. Lucas really has been a great help, as are each of you. I'm not sure I'd be this far into planning if it weren't for you guys. Thank you, truly!" I humbly confessed as we all took turns placing our orders.

Lucas tried his best to get some sort of hint out of me when we got home, but all I let him know was that dress shopping had been successful, and no matter how much he begged, he'd have to wait until our wedding to see my dress. I was so thankful when his mother told him to *leave it alone*, effectively bringing his playful prying to a halt.

*****

After the Monday group meeting at the church, I stayed behind, wanting to ask Brian and Ashley about an idea I had for the wedding in hopes of surprising Lucas. My nerves already threatened to cripple me before I even got the words out. With a forced shake of my head and a slow and steady breath, I tried my best to calm myself and approached the two before I chickened out.

"I have a huge favor to ask the two of you, and I am talking huge!" I began. With just the thought of what was going to come next, my stomach threatened to heave.

"What's up?" Brian asked as he began putting away the sheet music and clearing off the stage.

"I want to sing a song for Lucas at our wedding, but I have extreme stage fright. I was sort of hoping that if I could somehow work through it with you guys, maybe, just maybe, I could pull it off."

"Awe, I love this idea! How sweet, Elizabeth. Lucas will be in his glory. I'm game," Ashley immediately offered whatever assistance I was hoping to find.

"Do you have anything in mind, and what are we working with here? Lucas says you can sing, but as far as his opinion where you're concerned, he is a bit guilty of donning the rose-colored glasses, I'm afraid.

Not that I don't love ya!" my future brother-in-law teased with a grin.

"I'm no Ashley, that's for sure, but I do love to sing. I just can't do it when I know people are listening, that's all. I have a song in mind, and if you're willing, then I'd appreciate whatever help you can provide." My hands noticeably trembled as I handed both of them the sheet music I ordered online.

Brian looked over the music and smiled. "Way different than what we are used to playing here, but I'm game. Let's see what you've got!"

"Wait! I can't just sing it! Can you and Ashley sing it, and I'll sing along for the first—oh, I don't know, sixty million times?" I shot off nervously. My heart was pounding frantically in my chest, so loud it was deafening in my ears, as I felt a blush fully begin to cover my face.

"Sure, we'll give it a go. You join in when you're comfortable," Ashley agreed and began counting off so her husband knew when to begin.

The first attempt ended with Brian and Ashley singing the entire song, learning the correct beat, while I barely whispered along to the tune. No matter how hard I tried, my nerves just wouldn't settle. As much as I wanted to surprise Lucas, I feared that this hurdle was too high for me to jump, even with help.

"I have an idea. Brian, you sit. Make it more relaxed and not so, I don't know…not so stagelike. I am going to sit next to you, Elizabeth, and you sit right here, but face the other way. Pretend you're alone. Close your eyes if it's easier for you." Ashley put two chairs together facing opposite directions, hoping to give me the illusion that I was, in fact, alone.

The two began again, and this time, Ashley's plan worked, allowing me the freedom to belt out the words in certain parts of the song, as long as I kept my eyes closed, I was able to envision myself sitting in my car. By the halfway point, I was fully into the music. I didn't even realize Ashley had stopped singing, and it was just me and Brain.

"Okay…very good! You can, in fact, sing. We just have to work on figuring out how to make you feel as if you are all alone. My suggestion is we do this as often as you're willing to. If you can get used to Ash and me, we can try adding some of the others and see how that works. I have faith in ya. We've got what, a few weeks till showtime?" Brian relayed, his optimism giving me just enough courage to commit to my final goal.

"I think we should meet after group each week, and since I think frequency will play a big part in getting you to relax, we should figure out other times when we can get together, at least in the beginning. Once you can stand up and do it, we can stick to Mondays. What do you think, ladies?" Brian asked as he strummed his guitar with the melody of my chosen song. Ashley and I both agreed with a nod.

Planning the wedding, doing my pastoral job at the church, and helping Elizabeth out with Riley and Chris whenever I could really took up the majority of my time. It's easy to fall into a routine without realizing that the things you truly love to do are getting pushed off with an easy excuse of after this or later. Not willing to forgo any more quality time with Elizabeth, I decided to surprise her on a Wednesday night after the kids were in bed.

Jumping into my truck, I headed over to the supermarket, picked up some cookies, some red nail polish, and a small bouquet of flowers before making my way over to her house. I sent her a text letting her know I was there, not wanting to wake up the kids by ringing the bell or knocking on the door.

She opened the door in her PJs and robe, her hair pulled up and held in place by a clip, looking as beautiful as ever. I handed her the flowers after kissing her. “Hello.”

“What’s all this, Lucas?” she asked with a skeptical look.

“I miss you. I want to sit and chat like we used to, and I decided that I would paint your toes as we shared cookies. I want to talk about nothing and everything all at once,” I said, pouring us each a glass of milk before we made our way over to the couch.

Liz laughed as she bit her bottom lip when she realized I actually bought nail polish and was literally going to paint her toenails. Nodding her head while keeping the smile on her face, she turned sideways, placing her feet on my lap. Taking her right foot, I began rubbing it, not wanting to rush any part of the time we had together. Liz rested her head on the back of the couch and closed her eyes while softly moaning her approval and appreciation of the much-needed massage I was freely giving.

“So tell me about what’s been going on? For some reason, during the wedding planning and life itself, I feel like we just don’t make time to talk like we used to,” I admitted, truly hoping to rectify this unintentional situation we had found ourselves in.

While I took turns rubbing both of her feet, we spent the first hour catching each other up on the little things that may not have seemed important, but when you love one another, those little things matter. As we continued to talk, I got busy with the red nail polish. She laughed, probably doubting my skills, while nodding her approval just before I began.

"What? You don't think I can do this, do ya? I can assure you that I stand a better chance of not painting your whole toe if you'd quit wiggling," I warned with a wink. I turned my body slightly so that I could pin her leg under my armpit, hoping to keep her foot still.

"Yes, sir. Have at 'um," she obliged kindly before adding, "I don't think I could ever say it enough. You truly are perfect, Lucas. Still not sure how I ever get so lucky?"

Concentrating on keeping the red on just her toenails (it's much harder than it looks, especially that little one), I thought to myself, I was the lucky one, knowing I was blessed beyond measure to have her in my life.

* * * * *

Elizabeth put me in charge of all things flowers since apparently I did "such a wonderful job with the wedding proposal," in her own words. Aside from asking for her input while designing the bouquets for her and the girls in the bridal party, I picked out and ordered the flowers for the barn and the fresh flower arrangements for the church. Elizabeth, more than graciously, loved what I came up with. Truth be told, as low maintenance as Liz is, she would have been thrilled if I picked dandelions, wrapped them in Scotch tape, and threw them around haphazardly! So as much as I was pleased that she offered her seal of approval, I sought help from both of my sisters whenever I felt it was needed.

When we got the chance after the kids were in bed at night, Liz and I worked on decorating large mason jars with "Luke & Liz" and our wedding date on the front. We used a paint that looked like glass etching when it dried, filled each jar with candy to use as wedding favors for each person who would be attending our wedding. We placed them all together in the middle of each table to function as centerpieces as well.

My father, brother, and I had completely transformed the barn into more than a perfect place for our reception. We hung wide off-white satin sashes between the rafters, giving the illusion of a tent ceiling, with white lights strewn in the same manner in between. Each of the barn's rafters was completely wrapped in white lights, offering more than enough illumination while providing a romantic ambience.

Once we got the bigger jobs out of the way, I spent most of my free time sanding and shellacking the wooden barn floor. Needing for it to not only shine, I also wanted it to reflect all the lights that would be twinkling from above.

When the barn was close to being finished, I pleaded with Elizabeth to stay away. I was working on a surprise for her that I didn't want her to see until our reception. The last time she went inside the barn was the day that she asked my father if he could hang an antiqued metal chandelier that she found at a yard sale, in the center of the room. The fixture she had found sparked an idea that I shared with my father which caused us both to find as many antique wooden picture frames as we could. We collected close to thirty frames and sprayed each of them white and then distressed them so they wouldn't lose their antique feel.

Julie and I spoke often as the two of us worked with one another, taking care of the photos I wanted to put inside the frames. Directly behind the table where Liz and I, along with Chris and Riley, were going to be seated, my father and I hung all the frames with a clear fishing line to help serve as a backdrop behind where she and I would be seated while we ate. Wanting to find a way to include Christopher, Elizabeth's first love and father of her children on our special day, I placed, front and center, a photo Julie had sent of her son in one of the sixteen-by-twenty frames. On both sides, I also added a few of him and Liz together in the smaller frames. My father looked on approvingly once it was all up. Both of us were completely satisfied with the way it had turned out.

"I think you've done the right thing, honoring Christopher like this, Luke. But I don't think you should wait until the reception to show Liz. This is going to be something that gets to her, you know? Heck, I never met the guy, and it gets me right here," he said, while rubbing his chest before continuing on. "I think you should bring her in alone, maybe after the rehearsal dinner or something. But I don't think it should be on your wedding day. Here, let's ask your mother. She'll know what's best," he said, as my mother stepped in between the two of us, taking in, for the first time, our finished work. She didn't need to offer her opinion because the look on her face and the tears in her eyes confirmed what my father had suggested. Stretching up onto her tiptoes, my mother pulled me into her approving embrace, and she whispered just how proud of me she was.

* * * * *

The weekend before our wedding, the guys and I got together for an unofficial bachelor party. Being a pastor, strippers weren't something that interested me in the slightest, so the traditional would-be male bonding over too much alcohol paired with liquor-induced impaired behavior was completely lost on me. Don't get me wrong, I have no issue with the male-bonding part and looked forward to spending an entire weekend away with my family and friends.

I said goodbye to Liz the night before I left, wishing for her to enjoy her weekend alone with her friends. Julie and my mother planned to take turns watching the kids, affording Liz bonding time as well.

"You behave yourself, Lucas," she playfully warned, knowing without a doubt, she had nothing to worry about. "And don't hurt yourself, you hear?" That warning I took to heart, seeing as my weekend was one that was going to be filled with adventure. We kissed goodbye, and I smiled when I realized that was the last weekend that Liz and I would be spending apart. In a week, she was going to be my wife. Mrs. Elizabeth Walker—God, how I loved the sound of that.

* * * * *

"So, Lucas, you sure you're ready for all this?" Jake asked as Mike and my brother answered for me, both nodding their heads in unison.

"Of course he is. And why shouldn't he join with all of us who forwent our bachelor years for the sake of love? All men deserve to suffer together. All for one, and one for all!" Mike cheered, as we all playfully toasted, knowing that despite his words, all the men there were truly happy.

The first day of our weekend celebration, Jake, Mike, Brian, and my brother-in-law, Mark, went up in the mountains. We planned on spending the day fishing and white water rafting. My father was to forgo the adventurous part and planned to meet up with us for dinner at the pub on the outskirts of town. After dinner, we would be headed out to the Panthers versus Saints game. Barry, a few others from church, along with Robert, who was scheduled to arrive in the afternoon from Texas, would be meeting us at the game. Thanks to my sister Beth's best friend, Leighton, her father, the offensive football coach for the Carolina Panthers, gifted us boxed seats to the game as a prewedding gift. As much as baseball is my sport of choice, I'm a guy, and football holds second place in my heart. At least as far as sports are concerned, that is.

Once we got to the stadium and were situated in our private room where we welcomed one another, the group of us made small talk and snacked on the food that was set up for us as we waited for the game to begin. It didn't take long for the testosterone to pour out as we cheered on our favorite team (at least for the night anyway). At halftime, with the Panthers up by a field goal, we all toasted the reason we were there. Robert willingly spoke up for the group, as he not only thanked everyone for inviting him. He then acknowledged God in prayer and wished nothing but the best for his "daughter" and me as we began our married lives together next week.

It was late Saturday night when we finally got home from the game. I was thankful that the Panthers just barely pulled off their win, but still a win nonetheless. I also was relieved that I didn't have to worry about having to prepare a message for my church family. I officially was on vacation for the next four weeks for the wedding and, of course, our honeymoon.

Just as I laid my head down on the couch in my parents' living room, Mike decided to offer me some *friendly* advice on what I assumed was his version of the birds and the bees. I couldn't help but laugh. He tried his best to fill in all the gaps, but I cut him off completely when he got to the anatomy part, not willing to find out just how far he was going to go. I assured him I knew the mechanics of it all and begged him to spare me all his sordid details.

This was truly what having a fulfilled life was all about. Having people around you that you could count on and trust. Knowing that they had your back even when they took joy in cracking jokes at your expense. I was blessed. I allowed myself to take in all that was taking place around me and found myself hoping that Elizabeth was enjoying her time with her loved ones as well.

* * * * *

The guys and I spent our Sunday at the golf course. I'm not even sure how we managed to make it there at 6:00 a.m. for our 6:30 a.m. tee time! Nearly all, in complete agreement, mumbled our objections to the brain that decided an early tee time was wise after having such a late night. Since it was my father, he just quipped matter-of-factly, "Suck it up, gentlemen." And we did just that.

While Lucas was busy spending his weekend being a manly man with the guys, I happily spent mine fully adhering to the definition of girlie girl. Beth, Lynn, Grace, Deena, April, Jamie, Ashley, and I all spent time at the spa, while Julie and Mary insisted on watching the kids. As much as I wanted my mother, for all intents and purposes, to be with me on our day of pampering, Julie made arrangements for just the two of us to spend the Friday before the wedding getting our nails done after having breakfast together.

"I can't believe the two of you are going to a horse ranch in Hawaii for your honeymoon. I mean, I know it's the ideal destination, but seriously? Do you really think that you'll want to be working? On your honeymoon?" April teased, hoping I'd see the foolishness in Luke's and my decision to do what we truly enjoy instead of just relaxing on the tropical island with one another. Sure, just being with one another would have been wonderful, but Lucas and I didn't have a traditional dating relationship. I came with children, and even though we would be married, we looked forward to getting away and doing things as a couple, not as parents.

"We aren't going to be working the whole time. That's only the last four days," I corrected.

To which she added, "I still don't think ten days will be enough time for you to get to know one another in the biblical sense, of course, if you get my drift. But, hey, have fun with that."

Knowing that her teasing was meant in good fun, I happily provided, "We have ten days and the rest of our lives for that." Knowing in my heart that all the time I have on earth with Lucas would never be enough.

* * * * *

The Wednesday before our wedding, the Walkers, Morrises, along with Luke, my children, and I met one another for dinner at one of the standard chain restaurants located in the center of town. After dinner, Lucas, apparently intent on figuring out the reason behind my crippling stage fright, decided to take the opportunity to ask Joshua what the deal was, if there even was one.

"What's the deal? I know she can sing. How do I get her to do it?"

Joshua shook his head as he carefully sipped his drink before providing, "It's not going to happen. Not without her throwing up, shaking uncontrollably, crying, or if you're really lucky, all three. You won't. But there is a trick to catching her. I'm surprised you haven't already figured it out," he conceded. His *brotherly* advice offered Lucas a little cheat sheet to some of the secret ways around me that he learned while we were growing up together.

"As smart as she is, she has yet to realize that just because she can't hear herself singing when her earbuds are in, the rest of the world can still hear her. You won't catch an entire song or anything, but she always slips up and belts out a few verses here and there." He laughed as Julie added to the discussion from the table next to us.

"And she can't help but sing when she is driving. Lizzie, I never understood what your holdup is. Your voice is absolutely beautiful."

No doubt my face was now completely reddened, trusting it was all in friendly spirit. Even so, I still felt 100 percent embarrassed by my issues. Especially when I realized *all eyes were on me*. Hello, stage fright! Shooting Lucas a look, praying he'd change the subject, and quickly for that matter, I was more than happy when he kissed my lips and apologized for unintentionally putting me on the spot.

* * * * *

After work Thursday night, I drove over to my future in-laws. I hoped to ask Lynn if I could borrow the dress that she wore to church a few Sundays back. I had wanted to ask her since the day I saw her wear it. But once my children's birthday party was over, and with all the busyness of planning the wedding, I never got the chance. Once I got there and asked her permission to borrow it, she warmly pulled me into her loving arms, happier than I ever expected her to be. After leading me into her bedroom, I stood by the foot of her bed while she retrieved the dress from her closet. Once I put the dress on, I noticed a tear in her eye as she looked to be overly enthralled with the idea of me wanting to wear something of hers to the rehearsal dinner. With a thoughtful smile appearing on her face, she ducked back into her closet, returning with a container of straight pins.

"You look beautiful as ever, Elizabeth, but I just can't agree to this frumpy old lady's length for tomorrow's rehearsal." She took the bottom of the dress that ended a little longer than midcalf and began to pin it up so it would stop mid knee. "And as always, those boots of yours really make it something else," she offered her approval of my tan cowboy boots.

"Actually, I am going to wear nude pumps tomorrow, really throwing everyone off," I informed with a wink. We both laughed while she finished the last stich in the hem.

* * * * *

Everyone arrived at the church in time for the rehearsal. Pastor Wright greeted us and began informing each person where he/she needed to be and what he/she should all be doing during the ceremony. The men all took their place in the front of the church, while Beth and Jamie held Chris and Riley by their hands as they made their way to the back of the church, out into the foyer.

Before I joined my girls and children, I walked over to where Robert, Julie, and Lynn were sitting in the pews in the front, and with a shaky voice, I addressed the man who had always been like a father to me.

"Mr. Morris...Dad?" I began, as he looked up, waiting to see what I wanted.

"Do you think that maybe, well...I have no one to give me away, and well, I was hoping that you would be willing..." And tears fell steadily down my face. Thankfully, he stood before I could even finish asking him the question, pulled me into his arms, and nodded.

"Oh, Lizzie, sweetheart, I'd be honored to give you away. Thank you...Thank you for asking me." He kissed me on my forehead as he, too, cried mixed emotions. I knew while he held me in his arms that he was furious that my own flesh and blood turned his back on me. But in that moment, he was also overwhelmed that I thought enough of him to ask him to do me the honor; offering me a true father-daughter moment with the man who truly was my *dad*.

There wasn't a dry eye in the room when he took my hand, placed it into the crook of his arm, and together, we walked to the back of the church, where we waited with my bridal party for our cue to walk down the aisle.

* * * * *

The rehearsal itself was smooth sailing. Everyone learned what was needed and expected of us, and since a wedding ceremony wasn't exactly rocket science, we finished up at the church in no time at all. Each one of our family members and our friends met up at Benny's, where we booked the private room in the back of the restaurant for our party. The group of us spent the night talking among ourselves, as we filled up on delicious food that no one from our party had to prepare.

We knew the very next night at our wedding, we'd be dancing and having a wonderful time celebrating Lucas and my commitment to one another. But we didn't let it stop us. We all made sure to live it up in that moment, truly enjoying being in each other's company. A few people decided on singing karaoke, while the rest of us danced, completely savoring the opportunity we had spending time with our loved ones.

* * * * *

More time had passed than I had realized before I was brought back to the realization of how late it was getting. Lynn announced that we should all start heading out "so we could each get a good night's rest before our big day." Walking over to me, her future daughter-in-law, she hugged me tightly and let me know how much she loved me and couldn't wait to see me walk down the aisle the next day. Arrangements were made in advanced for Chris, Riley, baby Daniel, Marybeth, and Mikey to spend the night at the Walker ranch with Lucas's parents and the Morrises, who had been staying with them. The men, minus Lucas's father, were staying over at Deena and Jake's house. To make things easier for us ladies, we were spending the night at Grace's.

Right before we were ready to leave, Lucas appeared. With of all the commotion of getting ready to go, no one noticed that he slipped away until he returned. Lucas knelt down in front of Riley and opened a red velvet box, revealing a golden locket. Removing the necklace from its holder, he presented it to my little girl, who looked up at him with a grin. Lucas opened the locket, revealing three hearts. Each one held its own picture.

"I wanted to give you something to represent your whole family, seeing as tomorrow, I won't only be marrying your momma. But I will also be promising to spend the rest of my life with you and Chris too. Your father's picture is right here, thanks to your Me-Maw Julie, so you can have a piece of him right by your heart, where he will live forever. You and your brother are in the middle, because the bond that you two have with one another is one that will only grow stronger each day. And right here on this side is a picture of your momma and me. Each one of us loves you more than you'll ever know, Princess. Thank you so much for picking me to be your daddy. I am the luckiest man in the whole wide world." He then took her into his arms and kissed her on her cheek.

I felt Joshua's arm wrap around my shoulder as the tears just poured from my eyes. Every person around us cried, as we all witnessed such a tender moment between a *new* daddy and his little girl.

After he finished with Riley, Lucas turned to Chris and presented him with a box that held a golden compass. Engraved on the front were the words "Should you ever find yourself lost," and when Lucas opened it, the inside cover had a small picture of Christopher and one of Lucas as well, etched into the gold, with the words, "I promise I'll do my best to help you find your way." Looking up to the only father my children had ever known, Chris wrapped his little arms around Lucas's neck and told him he loved him.

I cried so hard Joshua had to completely hold me up as I witnessed the raw beauty of my life standing before me. Julie and Robert came to join me at my side with Joshua. All three holding me in their arms as I stood there, emotionally overwhelmed, taking in the sight of my future husband, the man I was head over heels in love with, and my children. The four of us were coming together as a family, all thanks to Christopher finding Spring View for me. And of course, God's perfect plan that offered us a chance of finally finding home.

I kissed my children and said good night to everyone, as Lucas took my hand in his and walked me over to my car.

"This is the last time I have to kiss you good night and leave you, Liz. Can you believe it? I can't wait to see you tomorrow, and I can't wait until you are officially Mrs. Lucas Walker," he said with a sly grin in the sultriest voice I have ever heard.

"I love you, Luke! And I can't wait till you're officially my husband." I threw my arms around his neck and kissed him with all I had in me.

"Knock it off, you two. You aren't married yet. Save something for tomorrow, will ya?" Brian reprimanded as he pulled his older brother's arm to further make his point.

Biting my lip, I smiled at Lucas, the butterflies in my stomach flying wild.

"Good night, beautiful. I'll see you tomorrow at the church. Eleven o'clock on the dot. I waited nearly thirty years for you, Liz. Don't keep me waiting," Lucas ordered with a wink.

"I wouldn't dream of it. Nothing in the world can stop me, you'll see. Good night, Luke."

* * * * *

I woke on my wedding day, filled with anticipation and utter joy. I don't remember falling asleep but was relieved that I had at some point, allowing me the ability to feel recharged and more than ready to marry Lucas. Sipping on my cup of coffee, I decided to send my soon-to-be husband a quick text.

> *Good morning, Luke. My countdown clock says you're officially mine in 4 hrs., 54 mins. and 4 seconds. Just checking to make sure you won't be standing me up…*

My friends teased me, accusing me of "cheating" by having contact with Lucas before the actual wedding. Not caring in the slightest, I smiled as I read his response.

> *Good morning indeed, beautiful. The best in fact (heart eyes emoji), & I have already told you, I've always been yours–today is just a formality, making you officially my wife. See you in 4 hours, 50 minutes, and 26 seconds. I'll be the one waiting for you at the altar, in case you forget.* ⛪

The girls had already shown me the dresses they had picked to wear weeks ago, but seeing everyone finally all dressed and ready to go left me with unexpected tears of joy in my eyes.

"Thank you, all. You all look so incredibly gorgeous! I can't believe how much you pulled off me, all the things I like, and who Lucas and I are so perfectly. I don't think I could ever fully relay just how grateful I am."

"Oh, sweetheart, it's our pleasure. I am so glad you are marrying my nephew. Although, I must say, you had me worried there for a while, making me wait eight months to agree to meet him. Even then, it wasn't easy. But I knew, I just knew all along that you two would be perfect together. Now let's get this party moving. To the church!" Grace affirmed, and I made quick work at blotting my eyes before getting into the waiting limousine outside.

* * * * *

Mr. Morris, my dad, sat beside me with the twins, in the limousine, on the ride to the church. I tightly grasped the hand of my God-given father as I carefully listened as he spoke.

"Lizzie, I couldn't be more happy for you and my grandbabies. It's not often that we are blessed to find true love in our lives, and here you've been offered it twice now. If I trust anything in my heart, it's that today, my boy is looking down on the three of you from heaven. I believe he is truly happy that you found someone who will love you just as much as he did. After tonight, I know Christopher will be able to rest in complete peace."

I looked at the man beside me, the man who has loved me over and beyond all the trials and heartache we endured. I thanked God for giving me the father

I always longed for. During the short drive over to the church, I let the three people with me know just how much I loved each of them. I loved them with all of my heart.

As the limo pulled up to the church, the once-somber moment between us rapidly morphed into one of excitement as we met the girls from my bridal party. One of the photographers was on hand, ready to capture a picture of us as I exited the car for the very last time as Elizabeth Marie Strutton.

"Let's get this show on the road!" my father happily announced as he took my hand firmly and placed it in the crook of his arm.

The Wedding

I've spent more than enough time at the front of the church, standing with the groom, as a groomsman, and as the officiate. I have to say, being the groom is like nothing I have ever experienced in my life. Check back with me when I see Liz in roughly six minutes, because that moment is going to have this one paling by comparison. And as this day goes on, one moment after the next will keep replacing the one before it as the greatest moment in my life. There I was, about to become a husband and a father! As the church music began to play, I knew I was more than ready for this part of my life to begin.

Taking one last loving look at all of our loved ones sitting in the pews, there to witness and offer their love and support for Elizabeth and me on our wedding day, I smiled. Not at anyone in particular but all of them at once. Just before the doors leading into the sanctuary were opened, my father clapped me on my shoulder, tightening his grip firmly and said, "Thank you, Lucas. I couldn't be more honored to stand here beside you today. Do what you must to fully *take in* your bride as she makes her way up here to you, but whatever you do, son, stay put. You hear?"

My father, my best man, offered with an upturned brow as I chuckled, understanding that he must have known exactly what I was feeling inside. I was certain in that moment that if I should fail and try to run toward my soon-to-be wife, before she was officially handed over to me, he'd be right there putting a stop to it, allowing her the moment she so desperately deserved to have.

Ashley was the first to start the procession of the bridal party. She wore a tan ruffled dress with small white polka dots and a smile that only deepened when she met with her husband. Because our church had two separate aisles, my groomsmen walked down the one farthest from the door, where the ladies they were paired with walked down the aisle closest to the foyer. At the end of their separate aisles, the two came together and walked, arm in arm, the short distance to the front, where Elizabeth and I would be taking our vows.

Jamie had on a knee-length light-brown dress and a smile that not only offered her contentment but also let me know how happy she was for me. Her eyes lit up when she briefly joined together with her husband at the front of the church, where the two kissed one another respectfully before taking their position in the front, behind me.

Next was Beth. She had on a deeper tan-and cream-colored dress that flowed slightly behind her as she walked at a steady pace. She was met by Joshua, my soon-to-be brother-in-law. Deena followed my two sisters, wearing a longer pale-yellow gown. Next to make her way down was April, who, in keeping with the theme, also wore a dress that stuck to the neutral tones Liz and I chose as a reminder of her Texas home. And like the two pairs had before them, she joined her husband, Mike, after walking down their separate paths. Each of the three married couples chose to kiss one another when they first joined together from their separate aisles.

My Aunt Grace was the last of the ladies to make her way down the aisle, and she looked as if she was ready to explode from all the love she had for both Elizabeth and me. With Liz's blessing and persistence, my aunt wore the dress she wore for her own wedding reception, feeling it was the perfect way to not only remember but to honor her late husband, Gary.

I laughed out loud with the rest of the church as Chris, in his light-brown tuxedo, made his way down the aisle carrying a chalkboard sign that said, "Get ready, Daddy Woo-cas," while Riley, in her little beige ruffled dress, hair set in curls with flowers strewn throughout, carried her own sign that read, "Here comes your bride!" Feeling my heart clench in my chest after reading, for the first time, my name, along with the word *daddy*, I was hit all at once with the enormity of what was now my life. As the twins took their seats beside my mother and Julie, I forced out a calming breath, knowing I was about to lay eyes on my bride. Cognitively, I forced myself to smile, counted to three, and waited for the wedding march to begin, announcing that Liz was finally headed my way. I fixed my eyes on the double doors, the only things standing in between me and seeing the woman I was going to be spending the rest of my life with.

The doors opened, revealing an absolutely stunning Elizabeth. She had her eyes fixed on Robert, who was whispering something near her ear, causing her face to light up as they made their way to the top of the aisle.

I can tell you a million times, and I know I already have, but it still won't, and never will, do justice to how incredible Elizabeth looked in that moment, in all her wedding glory. She was the picture of pure beauty. Her eyes locked on mine, and the lip-biting grin that easily spread on her face simply took my breath away. She wore a dress that personified her completely. Simple yet radiantly beautiful, and the way it fit her body made it seem as if the dress was made with only her in the designer's mind. Her cowboy boots, that she wore almost always, now had a blue ribbon wrapped around the pulls. The familiarity her favorite boots offered her added a little extra bounce to her stride as she made her way to where I was standing, waiting for her. I did everything in my power *not to run to her*!

I winked at her once she and Robert made it to the front of the church, just as Barry asked, "Who gives this woman before us in holy matrimony?"

Robert deservingly answered, "Her mother and I do," before kissing her softly on her cheek, placing her hand in mine while hugging me firmly with his free arm.

"Liz, you look incredibly perfect. God, I love you!" I blurted out, not being able to help myself. The entire church erupted in joyous laughter with the confession I made while forgetting that my mic was hot, allowing them to hear the words I had meant for her only.

Not missing a beat, Liz had me shaking my head when she covered her mic and whispered, "As long as you think so, gorgeous." And she winked.

More than ready to get on with the formalities, I firmly placed Elizabeth's hand in my arm as we turned together to face Barry, who greeted us both with an approving smile.

"Good afternoon, and welcome. As you are all well aware, we have come together today to celebrate the whirlwind romance that is Lucas and Elizabeth. I've been a believer most of my life, and I have to say that when God makes clear His purpose, it's hard not to stand in awe as His amazing plans unfold. I had the fortunate opportunity to witness Elizabeth and Lucas growing together from the very beginning. After their meeting in the parking lot, Lucas admitted that after just barely five minutes of knowing his Liz, life for him would never be the same." At his words, I squeezed my Liz's hand and smiled, as my friend took us all on a trip down memory lane.

"Lucas and I prayed with one another daily about their relationship. Even though I knew from our very first meeting, just as he had, that Elizabeth was definitely Lucas's gift from God. I listened each time he shared how he was feeling and just how much this beautiful young lady had effectively gotten under his skin. Over the next few weeks, she worked herself straight into his heart. But as I stand here before all of you, I'm telling you, God as my witness, he already loved her the moment he laid eyes on her. He just needed a little time to admit it to himself. Somehow, I don't think that's really a secret, though.

"Anyway, I had the privilege of getting to know Elizabeth as well. And with her permission, I can say that she and I have shared some very intimate moments with our heavenly Father. With God taking the lead, Elizabeth was able to heal from years of past hurts, all the while she entrusted me with the heaviness she once carried alone.

"As a man of God, I have seen couples come together countless times before, but I have never witnessed two people being brought so clearly together by the hand of God Himself, as I have had the pleasure of seeing firsthand by being a part of my two friends standing here before all of you today.

"I see the look of impatience hidden behind the smile in Lucas's eyes as he stands here at my mercy, waiting for me to get on with it already. Don't worry, Lucas, no offense taken. I know that you've waited twenty-eight years for this, so let's begin, shall we?"

Taking my bottom lip between my teeth, I smiled, totally unashamed at my impatience and was relieved when I heard the sound of laughter coming beside me from my now-blushing bride.

"Please, if you will, turn and face one another. Now join your hands together as you profess your love to one another, before God, your heavenly Father, your Creator, and all of your loved ones, who are here to witness your commitment as you take your marital vows." Elizabeth and I faced one another, and I felt, as she trembled in my hands, her stage fright set in.

"It's okay, beautiful. Look at me. It's just you, me, and Barry. Don't worry about anyone else. I've got you!" I said, willing her to focus on me alone, not caring at all that the whole church once again could hear me.

After she blew out a strong and steady breath, she nodded her head slightly and locked her eyes on me. Barry continued, "I already know the answer,

Lucas, but I still have to ask. Do you take Elizabeth to be your lawfully wedded wife, forsaking all others?"

Nodding with absolute certainty, I said, "I do!"

"Do you, Elizabeth, take Lucas to be your lawfully wedded husband, also forsaking all others?"

I bit my lip, and I smiled as she, too, said, "I do."

Barry asked for the rings, and after my father handed them both over to him, he began again, "Lucas, I'm pretty sure you've got this part down. So please, when you're ready, profess your love and offer your promise to your bride as you place the ring, chosen as a symbol of your undying love, on her finger."

With a nod of my head, I looked deep into Liz's eyes, making certain she knew beyond the shadow of a doubt, I meant every single word I was about to speak.

"I take you, Elizabeth, to be my wife from this day forward, to join with you and share all that is to come. I promise to be faithful to you every single day of my life." As I placed the ring on my wife's finger, I proudly finished, "Please accept this ring as a token of my love. This is my promise to you—I will respect, trust, help, honor, and care for you in sickness and in health. I will share all of my life with you. When needed, I will forgive you, as we have been so graciously forgiven. I will do all that I can to better understand you, the world we live in, and the journey we are embarking on together from this moment on. I promise all of this before all of our loved ones and with God as my witness, for as long as we both shall live." Taking my hand and lifting it to her face, I wiped the tear that escaped her eye just as it began to roll down her cheek.

"Okay, well done, Lucas. See, I told you he had it down. Now for you, Elizabeth," Barry slowly offered the words I had spoken to Elizabeth for her to repeat, and with each word, I knew I was one step closer to being her husband.

Just as my outrageously beautiful wife uttered the word *life*, I pulled her into my arms and kissed her before Barry had the chance to pronounce us husband and wife. As we kissed, he playfully teased, "By all means, Lucas, you may kiss your bride. Not as if you were waiting for my approval, apparently." And all of our loved ones clapped and cheered around us, while I continued to kiss my wife.

* * * * *

Riley and Chris joined Elizabeth and me as we faced the crowded room together, for the first time, as Mr. and Mrs. Lucas Walker and family. Chris took Elizabeth's hand, and I lifted Riley up and carried her down the aisle, holding in my other hand, with all I had in me, the hand of my wife.

"Mommy, can we ride in the wim-mo again with you?" little Chris asked. I have to admit, as cute as it was, and as much as I'd give him anything, his limo ride was going to have to wait until later. I wanted to sneak a quick ride in private with his mother, my Liz, my bride!

"Later, little man. You and Riley are going to ride with me and Aunt Grace for now, okay? Daddy Luke wants to tell Mommy just how pretty she is, okay, bud?" Beth swooped in to the rescue, saving Liz and me from having to be the official bad guys.

Thank God for Beth!

As I sat with my arm around Liz, I confessed, "I don't think there are enough adequate words in the English language to describe how fantastic you look or how incredible I feel. I love you, Liz, with all that I am. You are so beautiful." As a smile began to work its way onto her face in realization of the truth of my words, I stole a kiss. And I continued to kiss her for the ten-minute drive to my parents' barn.

Chapter 27

I mustered up all the energy I could to break away from Lucas's kiss as we pulled up to our reception at his parents' barn. Somehow, I ended up finding the strength when he reminded me that after we celebrated with our family and friends, we'd never have to part, ever again.

With a steady hand, Lucas helped me from the limousine; I took a moment to rest on a wooden bench outside the barn. I knew what was waiting behind the barn doors and wanted to prepare myself for what was coming with just a few quiet moments with my husband, my strength.

Thankfully, Lucas had taken me inside the barn the Tuesday before our wedding, showing me the special way he had chosen to honor Christopher. As I took in all the pictures of not only Lucas and me but also a photo of Christopher, front and center, I fell to my knees and wept.

Deciding that I needed a moment, I sat down on a bench halfway between his parents' house and the barn. Closing my eyes, I took a few calming breaths before Lucas sat down beside me. I opened them once I felt my more-than-understanding husband lay his head on my lap. Lucas reached up, offering me a copper coin while saying, "A penny for your thoughts." God surely knew what He was doing when He gave me Lucas. In that moment, I was comforted by the realization that no matter what life threw at me, I no longer would have to face it alone.

"I just wanted to slow things down a bit. I needed a moment to absorb some of your strength before we head into the masses. Thank you, Luke, for always knowing what I need. Even when I am not so certain myself sometimes. I love you, forever and always!"

Leaning down, I placed a kiss on Lucas's lips, while he was still resting his head on my lap. We sat together in that position, taking a minute to recharge. When I was ready, Lucas stood up, offered me his hand, and promised, "As long as I am alive, you will never have to face things alone, as long as you'll have me, of course. Now if you are indeed ready, I hope you will allow me the honor of showing off my beautiful bride?" Bowing before me, he looked up, and when the smile I offered assured him of my readiness, he lifted my hand to his lips, kissed my knuckles softly, and winked.

Just before we walked into the barn, where we'd be introduced as Mr. and Mrs. Lucas Walker and share our first dance with one another, my rock of a husband whispered into my ear, "I've got you. You can do this, Liz. Together, with our heavenly Father, we can do all things." In that moment, I knew he was offering me a genuine promise to be there for me always. And with my borrowed strength from Lucas, we walked into the barn after the emcee announced our arrival.

Some might say that the song we picked for our first dance is a bit cliché, and I suppose, being a very popular song, it may very well be. But I didn't care, especially when Lucas fell to his knees before me and belted out the beginning lyrics to "At Last" by Etta James.

Holding my left hand in his as he covered his heart with his right, Lucas effectively found a way to make the surrounding commotion seemingly disappear as he sang to me, "*Aaaat laaaast*, my *loooove* has come *alooong*. My lonely *daaaays* are over, and *liiife* is like a *sooong*." Offering me a sexy smile, he rose, firmly pulled me into his embrace, and we danced as husband and wife. The whistles and the clapping barely registered in my mind, as I allowed Lucas to lead as we swayed together to the tune. He sang the words to me, stopping every once in a while to twirl me around and steal a few kisses.

Our first dance as a married couple finished, and it was time for the father-daughter dance. Robert proudly made his way onto the dance floor, bowed at his waist, and took my hand in his as I curtsied. The band began to play "Here for You" by Neil Young, and the two of us, with smiles on our faces, fell easily into step to the more upbeat rhythm of the song, perfectly keeping in time with the classic rock melody.

"You know, I am here for you, right, Lizzie?" he said. Not waiting for my response, he kissed me on my cheek, and I held him as tightly as I could, buried my face in his shoulder, and cried from a mix of happiness and pain. The certainty behind his words and the realization that even though life hadn't turned out the way we had planned so many years ago, it was indeed still good. Having him here, holding me in his arms, I knew I was loved. And I knew that I loved my dad.

"Come on, I'll walk you over toward Grace. She'll help you get washed up. That's enough crying, you hear?" he firmly stated as the song came to an end, but I knew it was because he was close to losing his own battle of breaking down with me.

"I love you, Dad!" I said, as I squeezed him tightly. I fell into Grace's arms so she could lead me to a place where I could regain my composure and fix my makeup without an audience.

I splashed a little cold water on my face and laughed at my reflection in the mirror.

"I don't think I can take much more of this emotional roller coaster, Grace," I admitted to my friend. "I mean, I know that everyone cries at weddings, but *sheesh*, enough already!" I was thankful the bathroom we used was in the main house, affording us a little more time to get things under control than if we would have used the closer ones.

"Today has been perfect, Elizabeth. I know it's been tough, but it's authentic and real. You can't take that for granted or wish it away. The hardest parts are over. Now let's get you back to that handsome groom of yours and celebrate your love," Grace exclaimed, while she helped me reapply my makeup.

Not wanting to give away the surprise I had planned for the end of the night, I simply whispered,

"How right yet incredibly wrong you are, dear friend. The night is hardly over."

With an uncertain look on her face, Grace and I made our way back to the reception, where all of our loved ones were waiting.

* * * * *

"How'd I know we'd bump into you, Lucas?" Grace teased her nephew, who met us halfway between the main house and the barn. "No more tears, Lucas. So keep your sweetness to a minimum, will ya?" she playfully warned before hugging me quickly, leaving Lucas and me alone.

"Don't talk…Just kiss me, please!" I pleaded and thanked God that in that moment, he did what he was told without any hesitation.

Dinner was served, and I was relieved by the distraction that was offered by the commotion of the staff bringing the plates to our guests. Just before we were ready to eat, Barry offered a heartfelt prayer, giving thanks for all that was taking place and for the food we were about to eat. Inwardly, I let out a sigh that I didn't lose it, grateful that his words were perfect with just the right amount of happy.

"Not bad, huh?" Lucas blurted out after taking his first bite of his filet mignon. I nodded in agreement.

* * * * *

After dinner, Andrew stood from his seat. Preparing to make a toast, he clanked his fork against his glass to get everyone's attention. Looking nervously over at Luke, I let him know I wasn't sure if I could handle anymore. Pulling me into his side with his arm across my shoulders, I leaned into him and prayed that God would give me the strength to *not* break down again.

"All of you already know that I am a man of few words, so keeping true to my character, I'll try to keep this short and sweet," my father-in-law began and winked at me, causing me to smile.

"Elizabeth, I couldn't have picked a better woman to love my son if I had picked you out myself. Thank you for everything you mean to my boy and for everything you mean to this family and me. Lucas, I couldn't possibly be happier than I am for you right now. I sit here and thank the good Lord for making up for all the hills you had to climb in your life by bringing Elizabeth and the kids to you.

He has made up for the struggles you had to face and has given you a family of your own. I'm so glad that I get to share in this life with you all.

"I don't need to offer either of you any advice because I know you'll do right by one another. But the one thing I have to say to the two of you is, above all things, love one another. When all is said and done, love is what gets us through to the other side. Never forget how you feel right now, and do whatever you need to do to feel that love each day of your lives. Love is a choice. So always make it a point to choose and feel it.

"One other thing. I'd like to officially welcome the Morrises into our family. Thank you for doing right by not only Elizabeth but my son as well. As a father who nearly lost a child, I completely understand how conflicting it must be to offer your blessing today, knowing that what Luke and Liz have found in each other came at the loss of your son Christopher. Okay, that about does it. I promised my daughter-in-law I wouldn't make her cry. God bless and much love to you both!" Tears only threatened to fall but were surely put away as I took in Mr. Walker and his beaming smile. He winked right at me when I returned a grin of my own. I threw my head back, laughing out loud while thinking, *Like father, like son.*

Chapter 28

I offered my utmost thanks to God, as I absorbed all the love and support that was freely being offered to Liz and me. Elizabeth stood beside me for most of the night, and I couldn't have been more proud to have her there. Occasionally, the demands of our guest and their desires to talk to each of us would separate us momentarily. Each time I found my wife through the crowds of people, my chest puffed up, and I stood a little taller while grinning from ear to ear.

Our guests were all momentarily asked to clear the dance floor so that my mother and I could share our own private moment with one another. Searching through the masses, I spotted my mother seated by my father and walked over to their table. I asked her if I could have this dance. Her eyes, saturated with love, gleamed up at me as she stood with her hand in mine, and we made our way to the dance floor. Spending a good amount of time over the past few weeks, listening to song after song, wanting to find something that would make this moment one we'd remember always, I toyed with the idea of picking one of her favorites, but I felt that the one we would dance to needed to come from me. After narrowing it down to a few, I comfortably decided on "Take Your Momma" by Scissor Sisters. Above all else, I wanted to have fun with my mother, offering a lighter, more relaxed, and laid-back moment instead of the more traditional mother-son dances. After all this day had to offer already, I was convinced I made the right choice when my mother's face lit up, and she laughed while playfully smacking my arm. Lynn Walker revealed to each person watching just how much life and energy she had hidden inside her. Moving to the faster pace of the song, my mother beamed her approval, overfilled with joy as we danced.

* * * * *

Elizabeth and I made our way back onto the dance floor. This time, we each had a child in our arms. We began swinging and swaying, keeping up with the fast-moving beat of the music, allowing Riley and Chris to spin us silly. Making sure to be fair, we switched up our little partners every now and again. When the tempo slowed, we each lifted a child, holding him and her close, while we rocked to the beat of the music. Elizabeth held our son, and I held our daughter, and as a family, we basked in the newness that Elizabeth and my union had given us.

After rocking out to a few songs, Chris and Riley let us know they were tired of dancing. So their mother and I led them back to the table, where they had coloring books to keep them and their friends busy.

We talked with our friends at the children's table, all of us appreciating the bond our children shared with one another. Then Liz and I walked together outside for a brief reprieve from the loud music and side conversations. Elizabeth informed me that she needed a few moments in the ladies' room. I pleaded with her to not keep me waiting too long. As regal as ever, Liz slightly bowed her head to the side, rapidly blinked her eyes as she smiled, playing back, "As you wish, my love," before turning on her boot heels and confidently striding away with Deena and April.

Making my way back inside, I took a seat at the rented bar just beyond the double doors to the left of the threshold. I joined up with Barry, who was sitting next to his wife. Jake and Mike took two of the stools near mine and who also, like myself, were waiting for our wives. The three of my friends each took that opportunity to offer their congratulations once again and quickly shifted into the simplicity of everyday chitchat without hesitation. I knew by the look on Jake's face that our women had returned, so I stood up from my barstool, pulled out the one beside me, and waited while Liz took a seat.

The group of us made small talk before Barry and I began talking about things a little more on the serious side. Though we didn't want to spend time talking about work, we needed to make sure that everything was squared away while Liz and I were away on our honeymoon. I felt Elizabeth's hand slip from mine as Barry continued to hold my attention at the bar. I didn't give much thought to her leaving my side, assuming she went over to check on the children or was whisked away by one of the many people who had yet to have their own private moment with her. My ears perked up as I took a sip from my glass (offering my thanks to our loved ones who were around me). My attention was lost on my friends entirely when I heard the shaky voice of my wife over the sound system up on stage. She was standing where the band had been throughout our reception. I locked in on her, unsure what she had planned, and noticed the original band was now off to the side. My brother and our band from church were the ones beside my gorgeous wife, who was returning my stare hard. Complete and utterly beautiful, Liz stood there as she took a few breaths. Nervously, she started to strum Riley's little ukulele, the one I had witnessed her playing when I caught her singing "Three Little Birds" with her children.

Once my eyes truly focused on hers, every single person in that room around me faded, as I prepared myself for whatever surprise she had up her sleeve. I listened, not fully convinced that what I wanted most in my heart was actually going to happen. I stood up in front of the barstool, all my attention on the love of my life. My heart pounded as I waited to see if she was going to face one of her biggest fears right there, in front of our loved ones, just for me. She addressed the crowd for a moment, trying her best to steady her breathing and, ultimately, her nerves. Closing her eyes tightly, she took one more deep breath as Brian and the rest of our church band began playing what I recognized right away as "Turn Your Lights Down

Low" by Bob Marley. My absolute favorite song since the night we danced to it together in her living room, where I sang the words into her ear. As I began to walk with purpose toward my incredibly brave wife, I handed my father (who was seated at his table) my glass of champagne just as she began to sing. I wanted to be there right beside her, not across the room from her. I needed to hold her in my arms, right where she belonged.

Once she realized I was on my way, her nerves began to transform her stage fright into certainty as she sang for me as if we were completely alone. Witnessing her leave behind any trace of whatever fear she once had, I was in complete awe. She was amazing! I couldn't have been more proud of her, and was 100 percent madly in love with this woman. And I wanted to make sure that the whole world knew it. In one giant step, I leaped on to the stage, directly in front of my wife, as she sang out the chorus.

"I wanna give you some *love*, I wanna give you some good, good loving." I pulled her into my arms and began to sing right along with her before taking the microphone from the stand in front of Brian. I handed Ashley the ukulele so there was nothing between my wife and I. The smile on Elizabeth's face as she nodded her approval for me to sing the second verse of the song was all the encouragement I needed. I, too, sang for the woman of my dreams. I'd do anything to keep that smile she gave me on her face forever.

Elizabeth and I continued singing the rest of the song, taking turns, and then coming together as we continued to look into each other's eyes. If I hadn't been totally surprised by this whole thing, I would have sworn we practiced it a million times. We worked so perfectly together, swaying to the beat while we shared a deeply intimate moment in front of all of our loved ones. When the interlude offered a slight break from singing, I took the opportunity to tell her how much this meant to me.

Pulling her closer, tightening my grip, I pressed my lips to her ear and whispered, "I am so completely in love with you, Mrs. Walker. You are absolutely amazing. I can't wait to spend the rest of my life loving you and getting your good, good lovin'." Not realizing everyone could hear me due to the microphones, once again, and not caring in the slightest, I kissed my wife, and the entire room cheered their approval.

Elizabeth, with a fierce hunger, kissed me back and, as if *on cue,* broke away to sing her response. There wasn't a doubt in her mind as she belted out the rest of the song, making sure I knew she meant every word she was singing to me.

"I love you. I love you. I love you, and I want you to know right now..." I dropped to my knees in front of my wife, for the second time tonight, never wanting this moment to end. As tears slipped from my eyes, together we finished the song between kisses. Holding her hand, I prayed with all I had in me. I thanked God for the gift He gave me in Elizabeth, Riley, and Chris. And I begged no one in particular, but everyone nevertheless, that someone had caught this on video so I could relive it every day of my life. Once the vocals of the song had finished, Liz bent down, kneeling with me, and we kissed again.

Once the sound of my brother's voice broke over the cheers and whistles coming from our family and friends, the two of us were brought back to the moment of hundreds of eyes upon us.

"Well, hey now, Elizabeth and I practiced that song for weeks, and it never ended like that, I assure you, everyone. I'm sure that I am speaking for every person in this room when I say I love you both, and I am so honored to have been a part of your truly wonderful day. Being able to witness God's love and purpose come together in both of your lives—oops, pardon me, the four of you. My niece and nephew are just as big of a part of this special day. But truly, it has been a blessing in itself, and I couldn't be any happier for you all. Anyway, what I'm trying to say is go, go get started on your wedding night because you're dangerously pushing the envelope here, and I don't think I need to remind you, there are children in the room—two of them are yours—hint, hint," Brian teased before finishing up with, "But really, all joking aside, go start the rest of your lives right now! And in the wise words of our dear ole dad, always remember to love and cherish one another, be patient and kind, especially when it's the hardest to do just that. And keep on putting God first, and this will only be the beginning of your happily ever after. God bless you both."

Elizabeth squeezed my hand as a tear slipped from her eye. We both hugged Brian together, then the rest of the group, thanking them each for everything, especially their love and support.

I wiped away a second tear that slipped down Liz's cheek before I lifted my wife into my arms and carried her away. The hoots and hollers began again as the two of us left our wedding reception, knowing that we were now, and will forever be, one.

About the Author

Cindy is an avid reader who felt truly blessed when God took her passion for fictional romance and gifted her with her own stories to share. After becoming homebound due to chronic illnesses, she found an escape through her new world that ended up bringing her even closer to God.

A wife, mother of four daughters, and working for a local nonprofit, Fostering Hope Florida, Cindy finally felt led to share the stories of how God moves in the lives of her beloved characters from Spring View.

Cindy enjoys sunshine, sunsets at the beach, music, and lots of coffee. She feels especially close to her Creator each time she takes in His beautiful masterpieces all around her.